T0356347

YORK'S RIDE

York's Ride

A Novel of Old California

MICHAEL DENNIS CASSITY

UNIVERSITY OF NEVADA PRESS | *Reno & Las Vegas*

University of Nevada Press | Reno, Nevada 89557 USA
www.unpress.nevada.edu
Copyright © 2025 by University of Nevada Press
All rights reserved

Manufactured in the United States of America

FIRST PRINTING

Cover images: Christine_Kohler / marlenka (iStock)
Cover design/composite illustration: Diane McIntosh

Library of Congress Cataloging-in-Publication Data available upon request.

ISBN 978-1-64779-183-4
ISBN 978-1-64779-184-1
LCCN: 2024032131

The paper used in this book meets the requirements of American National
Standard for Information Sciences—Permanence of Paper for Printed Library
Materials, ANSI/NISO Z39.48-1992 (R2002).

For Margaret Dalrymple
1939 to 2022

Alas, poor Yorick! I knew him, Horatio

Hamlet, ACT V, SC. I

LORD, *make me to know mine end, and the measure of my days, what it is; that I may know how frail I am.*

PSALM 39:4

CONTENTS

YORK'S RIDE

PROLOGUE

Looking Back

The heart of the country held no fascination for me anymore. I was born there in the sticks and bush of middle Missouri in 1902. But when Ma died I was drawn to the West, lured by the stories she told me about my uncle. I could spend all day telling you the stories Ma told me. They were good stories, but I'll save them for another time. Let me tell you about York's ride.

A boy, the master of the strongest horse I ever saw, wanted to ride his horse in "The Race of the Century." In a way he got his wish. York Toby was a Maidu from the tribe that has lived here in northeastern California for thousands of years. The horse was wild, from the Smoke Creek Desert of Nevada, bred by a mustang stallion and a French draft mare, a Percheron.

Back then Blind Charlie told York and me stories about the way the Maidu see the world, about the mountains, the animals, and the way it all began. I learned about Rattlesnake and Raccoon . . . and the Rolling Skull that devoured itself. Blind Charlie came upon his name because his dark eyes were always directed away from his listeners' faces, deeply rooted in wrinkles above his ruddy cheeks. More comfortable in his native Maidu tongue, his English was nevertheless poetic, lyrical—and one very quickly learned to appreciate his expressive but unique vocabulary, which he blended with Maidu terms. The result was a magical mixture, an extraordinary blend of sounds and images. He once heard the Sophocles's story of the blind prophet Tiresias, who predicted the story of Oedipus, and he never minded the "blind" label after that. "That Sofooklees, he be good storyteller, truly."

Blind Charlie was half Maidu and half Atsugewi, but he grew up in Maidu country, in Indian Valley in a tribal family called the Tosi-Koyo and the Ta-Si-Dum. York just happened. He never knew his mother or father.

York and I were born about the same time in different circumstances, 2,000 miles apart, two cultures, and yet we were thrown together for the same reason: we were without mother or father. I was born healthy. He was born afflicted. I was born in warmth, he in coldness. I was to enjoy a long life. York would have a short life. As a boy I would be visited by voices and images of the father I never knew. York's life would be filled with the voice and presence of Blind Charlie, his tribal father. What we shared were the stories. From the first we both learned to live with the tale, to draw from it, and to add to it.

Most of this tale is from me alone, as my memory serves me. Parts of this story belong to Blind Charlie . . . and his burro. It was the solitary figure of Blind Charlie, I remember, who as the day was ending on crisp fall or winter days—the Indians rarely told such stories in the summer—who sat opposite us and shared unforgettable tales in his quiet, peaceful voice. His burro, Hercules, was an uncommon animal, and when Blind Charlie was not with us, he was usually with Hercules, his only companion on hikes through the mountains. Hercules had been a gift from a longtime friend of his, Benjamin Kurtz, a Jew from New York, who mined for gold in the mountains surrounding the valley before he died in 1910. Hercules was the only burro I ever saw sit on his haunches—like a dog, I mean. He first learned that trick, I think, when he resisted being pulled by Benjamin up the steep slopes to one of his diggings.

I reflect back across three-quarters of a century, and I cannot separate Blind Charlie's stories from my early years with Uncle Martin and The Commander, from my mother's death and the stories she told me of my father, and from Pa's voice—my guide and conscience. York's ride, the story of Meshuga, the Great War, and the memories I have of fishing and hiking along Indian Creek with John Thornton are all woven into the same tapestry.

Chapter One

MISSOURI

"Stay away! Don't . . . !"

Black and huge, the horse reared over me as I lay pressed back against the clumps of grass along the bank. His mouth was red and foaming, the lips flexed back mockingly over his teeth. Paralyzed, I saw his front hoofs, sharp dancing shadows high against the sun and overhanging branches. The horse was lathered, fiery, covering me with the pungent odor of sweat and horsehide. The two front hoofs were falling now, with the animal's intent to kill, full of hate and malice toward my face. I was incapable of yelling, barely choking as the dark shape closed in rapidly. The eyes . . . those red eyes drilled me . . . drilled me . . .

I covered my face instinctively, rose quickly, panting.

"That horse again, John Thornton!" I shouted. But it was silent and John Thornton was sleeping on a covering of leaves next to the creek. He opened one eye and closed it slowly. My fly rod was still beside me in the shade where I had left it before dozing. I was hot and sweaty and angry at myself for slipping off to nap. Guilty, I knew I could have been home helping Ma.

I thought about the black horse again. Where had it come from? I was shivering now. Why the black horse? Ma said a big black horse had kicked me in the mouth when I was only three. I still had the scar on my upper lip where it had healed in a broken, uneven blemish. But I barely remembered it. Ma just told me about it. But . . . it was . . . the black horse of my dreams . . . was always the same horse.

It was hot and humid on that summer day of 1914. I had gone fly-fishing with John Thornton and spent the entire morning casting a Quill Gordon along Brush Creek in several of my favorite pools.

Watching my heavily waxed floating line as it drifted, cast after cast, I lost track of the time. I didn't return until after lunch, and I expected Ma to give me the devil for being late. She was in bed sick with a fever and was awful hot. Doctor Brandt had visited the day before and said she needed rest. He gave her some medicine, but I could tell he was worried. He said he wouldn't be back for two days because influenza was sweeping the whole county that summer. Ma was a strong person in many ways, but I could tell she was tired when she told me that morning to go on out and have a good day fishing.

"Jim-darlin', bring some fish back for us this time, and be careful," she had said, smiling weakly. She never told me to do anything without telling me to be careful. She sometimes called me "Jim-darlin'" and I had grown up thinking that it was part of my name. Of course, she was the only person who ever called me that.

I was kicking stones along the dirt path between the old cemetery and home when Pa broke in. Pa's voice was stronger than ever, but as gentle as I always imagined him to be. I could see him now as he was talking, and I stopped for a minute. The old cemetery swept down in a grassy slope from the base of the Baptist church's white clapboard siding to the creek about 200 feet away. It was a lonely place cut out of the dense woods. The rutted gravel road was overhung with large elms in the summer. I looked at the granite and marble stones standing on the overgrown grass and weeds as I had a hundred times before. Pa's stone was over there next to the gravel drive that circled in front of the double doors.

Pa's stone was flat on the ground, nothing fancy. I left the path and walked over to Pa's gravesite. Ma's stone was next to his, but it was unfinished, waiting there for Ma to die. There was no one around, and the only noise was the buzzing flies around my damp neck and ears and the occasional chatter of the cicada, two creatures that seemed not to mind the heat. I looked down at Pa. Whenever I heard Pa, he was always on a horse. Sometimes a black horse, sometimes a white one, like the pictures Ma had at home on the piano and the bedroom walls.

You oughta hurry on home now, Jim. You've been out too long.

"I been asleep, Pa!" I said. "I fell asleep down under my favorite sycamore along the creek!"

I looked around as though that great devil of a horse was nearby. He could have smashed my face, killed me for sure. It was so real that I had looked around, frightened, expecting thundering hoofs any second. But only flies buzzed around my head. Even the birds were muted by the heat.

As I came running into the house with my two good-sized perch, I was drawn up almost immediately with a sense of dread, not because I expected to be scolded for being late, but because I knew something was wrong.

"Ma, I'm home . . . caught two nice perch!" I yelled, and my words hung there for a moment in the stillness and then seemed to drop lifelessly from the air as if I could see them spilling across the sheets of music strewn carelessly across our coffee table.

I cannot explain why I knew things weren't right. I just knew, and I was fighting back a growing fear. The walls seemed to close in now, their grayness pressing.

"Ma? Ma?" I was afraid to go into her room.

I was angry at myself for staying out so long. And I was afraid, the kind of cold fear that wraps your heart and stomach in a prickly chill. I stood there shaking, my bamboo fly rod still balanced in my fingers, afraid to move. The silence of the parlor was shouting at me, louder than a room full of people, to move. To John Thornton everything was normal, and he came bounding in from the open door to the porch and raced for her bedroom, pushing back her partially open door. John Thornton had the terrible habit, for an 80-pound black Lab, of leaping up into the middle of the bed. I would catch the devil for that, too, but she didn't make a sound as John Thornton jumped and bounced on the bed.

"Ma?" I said weakly.

She had died, I believe peacefully, in her sleep. John Thornton and I sat by her bedside for I don't know how long. I was still shaking and I was crying, but I remember mostly just shaking. Her eyes were partly open and she had fallen on her side off her propped-up pillows.

It was gray and quiet in her room, and the white lace curtains were fluttering inward at the open window. It's strange how a person can remember images like that even after all these years. Then I wadded up John Thornton's two ears in my fists, and with tears now streaming down my cheeks, I brought my head down to his and commanded him to stay. Barefooted, I ran all the way into Huntsville to fetch Doctor Brandt. He wasn't there, of course. He was too busy in that hectic summer to hang around his clinic. Many people besides Ma had died. Mrs. Dovey, his tall, skinny attendant, who doubled as our teacher during school, told me to go on home and she would be out later to take care of things. I had always thought of her as a fearful bag of bones, but now I appreciated her control in the midst of my confusion and hurt. Doctor Brandt wouldn't be back until late.

That was over seventy-five years ago now, and it's unearthly to me that I can remember that day more clearly than all the days that followed. My mother was a real beauty. She was striking with her coal-black hair, black eyes, and long dark eyelashes. Even though she always struck me as small and frail, there was strength in her bearing and weight in her voice. There were several men who wanted to marry her after my father died of complications with peritonitis. His appendix had burst when I was only two. I was too young to remember many of these suitors. Even as I grew older I can recall only two with any clarity: a shy and self-conscious farmer named Harry who had a place several miles down the dirt road from Darksville and another disappointed caller from somewhere near Kansas City named Carl. What I remember mostly about them is they were uncomfortable with me. They didn't know how to talk to me, saying things like, "What a big boy you are." I wasn't big and they knew it. I only saw them a couple of times, and then no one came calling for Ma again. She told me she was happy enough taking care of me and the 300-acre farm we owned in Randolph County, about 2 miles outside Huntsville. She said that my father, Tim, was a great man and that he was the only man she ever wanted. She didn't mind being alone, she said, and besides she had me. It always embarrassed me when she said that, but I remember I was proud that Pa was Pa, even though I never knew Tim McLaverty or was able to call him Pa. Ma read books and played the piano and found peace within herself. She didn't have to go outside her own little world to find contentment. I think the men who came visiting her in hopes of marrying discovered that she was smarter than they wanted her to be. They couldn't stand that, so they left.

Everything I knew about my father I learned from several old copper-colored photographs on top of Ma's upright piano and the hundreds of stories Ma told me about him. I can remember never wanting to interrupt her when she got on to telling me stories about Pa. Some little incident would remind her of him and she would begin. Her expression would take on a different look—she was retreating momentarily into another world—and because she was good at telling stories I never tired of hearing about Tim McLaverty.

My father was an amateur middle-weight boxer who had never been defeated. His opponents had come from as far away as St. Louis and Kansas City, and he had traveled to Chicago to compete in one tournament. His reputation had spread as a one-round knockout artist. The professional managers came repeatedly to sign him up for better things, but he had refused. Altogether, Ma said, he had fought over forty fights, all but four ending in knockouts. And then, he had quit. No explanation, Ma said. He just got tired of boxing, she thought.

Once he had fought a much heavier opponent, a huge man named Blood Burns. Ma had an old poster on the kitchen wall, a colorful red and blue cardboard advertisement. I had seen it a thousand times, but I never asked her about it. Sometimes the most obvious clues scream for a question while we go in search of other leads. Ma never talked about the poster either.

Pa was also an outstanding handler and trainer of horses. Ma said when anyone had a particularly troublesome horse, they would call in Pa.

"There wasn't a horse he couldn't break," she told me. "Once a powerful stallion was brought to him from somewhere out in Utah. This horse, and I saw him, had run wild for a few years on the open range out there in that godforsaken land. No one could control him with that mustang blood of his. Somehow the horse was given over to a man in St. Louis who knew your pa. Your pa was asked to see what he could do. You weren't born yet, Jim-darlin', and we had a place just outside Jefferson City. Tim broke and trained that wild animal in just three weeks. And I tell you, that horse was mean. Tim wouldn't let me anywhere near him."

"What happened to the horse?" I had asked.

"Lord, Jim-darlin', I don't know. He won some races, I think, and then he ended up in Iowa someplace as a stud. We moved here shortly afterward, so your pa didn't keep up with it. I think your father's heart was mostly with horses and fly-fishing. I was a distant third on the list." Ma smiled because she knew it wasn't the truth.

"What color was the horse?"

"Black, Jim-darlin', as black as the coal in the bin."

I didn't tell her about my black horse. That was my terrible secret. Whenever Ma told me these things I hoped that somehow I would make Pa proud of me. Maybe it was the voice and image of Pa that began enlarging dreams of my father by the strength of my imagination. I wasn't always certain, as the years went by, that the voices and images were products of my imagination. I once told Ma that sometimes I thought Pa was so near he could talk to me. She didn't think anything about it. She just said that yes, maybe he was. One thing was clear: I knew enough about Pa from Ma's stories to know I fell far short of Timothy McLaverty. I had a lot of growing up to do and some pretty big shoes to fill.

One of the photographs on the piano was in a small wooden frame, a picture of a dark, bearded cowboy on a white horse. Ma didn't know much about the man in the picture except that it was one of my father's brothers, Martin, who had gone out West in the nineties to mine for gold. Ma said that she hadn't heard from him after Pa died. She didn't know what he was doing now. Last she heard was that he had a place and was running some cows somewhere up in the mountains of northern California. Maybe he was dead. That always bothered me. Ma always thought people were dead if you hadn't heard from them after several years. Her expression for it was that "they just dropped off the face of the earth." I wondered how someone dropped off the face of the earth. I knew the world I lived in around Randolph County was very small—I saw all the maps at school. The big world both scared me and attracted me even then. But "falling off the face of the earth," even though I knew what my mother meant by it, set in motion frightful images of unknown distant places. I didn't want that to happen to me. On the occasions I looked at my uncle's picture my imagination was always sent soaring. And like any boy who read and reread *King Solomon's Mines* or *Treasure Island* or *The Call of the Wild*, I was always dreaming of faraway places and adventure, anyway. The photograph was almost an icon I worshipped in these times of daydreaming. Uncle Martin and my pa had come from their native Ireland when they were both young boys, leaving their parents and brothers and sisters. As Ma told it, the hardship of living in Ireland in the 1870s had forced many Irish to seek a new life in America. Tim and Martin went to live with an uncle William in upstate New York. I remember little, if anything, of my father's other brothers.

Ma was buried two days later in the old cemetery next to Pa after a funeral service at the Baptist church in Huntsville. I wouldn't hear Ma's sweet voice again call me "Jim-darlin'" again, but I would continue to hear Pa's.

Ma didn't have any relatives at all in Randolph County. My maternal grandfather was an English merchant captain and had worked the trade routes between Portsmouth and the Orient. When I was very young Ma and I used to see him every year or so, but then the visits began to shorten and his absences lengthen. Ma was always upset when he came because he spent most days and nights in a drunken stupor. Grandma Martha had died giving birth to Aunt Celine in Baltimore after the family had emigrated from England to the United States. After that, Grandpa had taken to drinking and had returned to Dorset. The girls had stayed with Grandpa's sister, Aunt Jessie, in Atlanta. Grandpa, I guess, led an adventurous life as a sea captain again, but Ma and I learned years before that he had disappeared ashore at Buenos Aires. We never learned anything more. Of course, Ma said he had dropped off the face of the earth. Her two sisters both lived in Atlanta, and she hadn't seen them, so far as I knew, all the years she had me. I only knew them as Aunt Leah and Aunt Celine—the "two aunts who live down Lanta," I called them. I can remember not thinking very much about these broken attachments when Ma was around. She was my world.

But when she died I realized that I had no roots. Ma had always talked about roots, but I never understood until I was really alone.

I had no understanding of what it meant to be alone. Ma's death did not move me to depression or even sadness. I was carried along numbly by neighbors and friends who believed I was more affected by Ma's untimely death than I really was. I was sometimes angered by their sympathy. I wanted to be away from them. In the coming days I would feel that loss and I would hurt inside. But something in my constitution helped me to weather the emotional storms with a calm I didn't know I possessed.

The church was full of Ma's friends, some from as far away as Moberly and College Mound. Aunt Leah and Aunt Celine sent cards, and that was our last contact. Neighbors made a commotion over my future. I was too young and couldn't live on the farm alone, obviously. I moved in with Doctor Brandt until my "affairs," as he called them, could be arranged.

"Jim, do you know anything about your aunts in Atlanta?" asked Doctor Brandt, who was trying to find strands of family I knew little about.

"Nope," I said, not at all interested in Aunt Leah or Aunt Celine, but I told him about my uncle who lived in California, not expecting much.

Then three weeks later Doctor Brandt learned more about Pa's brother who lived in California. I was surprised, for I knew that this must be my uncle Martin, the cowboy in the photograph come back after dropping off the face of the earth. Doctor Brandt must have come across some leads by sifting through all of Ma's papers and letters. My mother had seldom uttered a word about Martin McLaverty except "he must be dead," and now it was a mystery to me how Doctor Brandt had managed to locate him. A few weeks later, then, when Uncle Martin expressed an interest in taking me in permanently, I was afraid. I knew nothing of Martin McLaverty and California—I knew only the dreams and the adventures I had manufactured in my imagination. Nevertheless, the decision was out of my hands. Doctor Brandt made arrangements for my travel west by rail.

I spent time at Ma's grave and told her where I was going. I told Pa, too, but it didn't seem the same because I never talked to him. He always talked to me and I had to listen. I thanked him for Ma and my fly-fishing gear. When you never knew your father it's hard to believe he is listening under a cold slab of granite. I preferred Pa's visits in my imagination. But, somehow I think Ma was listening under the mound of chrysanthemums and lilies. John Thornton lay mournfully nearby, jowls to the grass, uninterested in my words thrown out confidently under the humidity of a gray afternoon lightning cloudburst.

Ma's stone monument was simple. It read "Charlotte McLaverty, May 16, 1881–June 29, 1914," freshly cut words into an old stone that had been next to Pa's since he was buried here over ten years ago. It was exactly like Pa's now, which I had seen many times, but never thought it to be more than just cold granite. I looked at my father's marker: "Tim McLaverty, September 8, 1875–March 15, 1904." I lifted myself from the damp grass and walked away.

John Thornton and I said goodbye to the farm, its small white frame house, the bleached, peeling outbuildings, and the gigantic hay barn where I used to jump from the loft and land waist-deep in the crib of oats. I tossed rocks into the pond, scaring frogs and sending black bass darting in the shallows. John Thornton bounded into the water in his futile efforts to catch anything. There were catfish in there big enough to name, but I spent most of my time presenting a dry fly or popper to 4- and 5-pound bass who fed on the surface in the early evening. We said farewell to Huntsville and Randolph County, to Doctor Brandt, Mrs. Dovey, to my school friends, and others I had known in those gentle, rolling green farmlands and the thick forests of elm and beech and ash I had roamed. Ole Bill and Carley Jake, the farmers over the hill, continued to tend our cornfields and stash away crops in the barn. Doctor Brandt said he would take care of the house, a quiet, lonely place with no neighbors.

The only possessions I really cared about were Ma's photographs and Pa's fly-fishing gear. I packed up the two scratched and tarnished Hardy reels, the three H.L. Leonard Tonkin cane rods, and leather pouches filled with flies and streamers; stuffed the pictures off the piano in my bags along with a few clothes and several of Ma's precious books; and took two of my H. Rider Haggard novels off my bedroom shelves and my old dog-eared copy of Jack London's *The Call of the Wild*. I had named my Lab John Thornton, an awkward name for my dog, but I admired the kind Yukon adventurer who had befriended Buck—from my favorite book. I rolled up the Blood Burns fight poster from the kitchen wall and carefully wrapped that in my bags, too. I left everything else to the care of Doctor Brandt and Uncle Martin. John Thornton and I would travel light.

I was twelve. It would be over forty years before I returned to visit Ma's gravesite.

Chapter Two

OUT WEST

The train jerked to a stop. I was hurled forward in my seat, hitting my head on a rack next to the window. The man traveling next to me, who spent every waking hour reading a book, helped me up and saw that my forehead was bleeding. He pulled a handkerchief from his pocket and called the conductor. But the conductor was busy outside now with the cattle surrounding the train. I could hear men yelling through my open window, and dust now streamed into the coach. Windows slammed shut and people were coughing. The man went back to his book.

A cowboy, his faced covered with a bandanna, hustled the cattle away from the train. Our eyes met for moment, and then he turned and herded the cows away. Before long the train slowly pulled away.

My train would arrive in Sacramento by the end of July. Aside from this one incident with cattle blocking the tracks, mostly everyone was talking about what was going on in Europe as the train passed through the plains of Kansas and on into the Rockies after I switched over to the Denver & Rio Grande. The archduke of this land and the kaiser of that land and threats from the Russian front broke out of the haze of cigar smoke that hung over the salon car the whole day and night. I understood there was going to be a big war over there. The three days on the train I spent mostly dozing or looking out of the windows at an endless land of tan and gray, rarely green like the Missouri I had left. Only the Rockies and the Sierra Nevada broke the monotony. These mountains were high and majestic beyond anything I could have dreamed about. And I had a nice cut and bruise to remind me of cow country.

The Nevada desert was white and dry and salty. My mouth got

dry just looking at it. I wondered how anyone could draw breath in those barren spaces, and I remembered again my mother's falling off the face of the earth. Nevada must be the face of the earth, and if there were a place you went to before you fell off, then this must be it. But at the same time, I was drawn to it. The loneliness of it beckoned in some mysterious way I could never account for.

The train was clicking along across one of those huge white dry lake beds. I was drifting and was about to slip off to another nap during the last afternoon of the trip when I noticed a dark streak miles away across the desert floor. I watched it for several minutes trying to make out what it was. A stretch of haze, dust probably, settled long behind the moving dark line. I watched the line move with the train and I imagined that it was drawing closer to the train as we moved west. But it did not; it only seemed so in my eyes.

"Ghost Horse," said the quiet passenger to my left. He, too, had followed my gaze across the desert floor to the north. I looked at my companion. He was wearing the same clothes since Kansas City. I thought he must surely be uncomfortable with his tie and dark coat on. The wind blowing through the open window was hot air from the moving train, and it didn't cool us down much.

"I'll lay you odds that is Ghost Horse and his herd," he continued.

I had no idea what he was talking about. What were "odds"? Who was Ghost Horse? I cannot remember the man's name now, but I remember that he spent most of the trip out from Denver reading Thomas Hardy's *Far from the Madding Crowd*, and I knew that I had that very title packed in my bags. Ma often had read Hardy, for her mother had been born and raised, like Hardy, in Dorset. But I was mostly ignorant about Thomas Hardy and was afraid to bring up the subject with the stranger next to me. Ma had read passages to me from Hardy, but I had preferred to read H. Rider Haggard, Jack London, or James Oliver Curwood. By the time I was ten I had read the Allan Quatermain series at least twice, and I liked *The Call of the Wild* better than any book. Curwood's *The Gold Hunters* and *The Danger Trail* had brought me to crave the North. The strange thing was . . . that here I was really alone, without father or mother, yet I still felt I had friends—the friends I had made in my books, friends I would always have.

"Who's Ghost Horse?" I asked, recalling the black horse of my dreams. My pulse quickened.

"He's a legend out here," the man replied. "He's a wild stallion running free out there, and no one can catch him," he said, ". . . no one."

There was a long bit of silence when we said nothing. I captured images of Tim McLaverty and the bay stallion in St. Louis.

"How do you know that's him?" I asked, staring out at the black streak. I could not see horses at all, only a moving streak followed by a long, thin cloud of Nevada desert dust.

"That's Ghost Horse, all right. I wonder why the herd is ranging so far south. They mostly travel up around the Smoke Creek Desert farther north."

I continued watching until the dark streak finally disappeared. The sun was still high but a change had come over the barren mountains to the north. Already they had become bluer, a darker, more forbidding place, and Ghost Horse and his herd of wild horses dissolved into them.

The stranger said nothing more and went back to his volume of Hardy. I could not stop thinking about the stallion roaming free and wild. I dreamed about Ghost Horse and that stream of trailing dust all night long.

I watched as the sun reflected off the American River and the flat dry farmland as we neared the city. I was surprised by the golden stretches of grass and the thousands of bent and scraggly gray-black oaks. It was mid-morning when we pulled into the station. John Thornton was tethered in an enclosure of sawdust and hay in the baggage car at the rear of the train. Sacramento was a sleepy agricultural center in the summer of 1914 trying to call itself a city.

Uncle Martin met me on the platform as the conductor led John Thornton down to me from the baggage car. John Thornton, his tongue hanging out the side of his mouth as always, was lunging and pulling him all over the dock. Tired of his containment, John Thornton nearly knocked me down when the conductor let him go. John Thornton outweighed me, I guess.

I was on my back with John Thornton all over my face when I realized that Uncle Martin must be here on the platform somewhere.

I don't remember what I expected back then. About Uncle Martin, I mean. I can only imagine that I counted on a real cowboy like the cowboy in the photograph on Ma's piano with his dark beard and stained felt hat. But that picture had been taken some twenty years earlier down in Arizona someplace. In truth, Martin McLaverty was short and stocky, and in every other way was the very opposite of what I pictured a cowboy to be. I don't know why I imagined him tall. Pa wasn't tall, Ma said.

If Uncle Martin was a disappointment, at least he was very visible. While others at the station blended anonymously into waiting arms, Uncle Martin stood up on a large baggage cart looking for me. I pushed John Thornton off my chest and sat up. Uncle Martin was just a dark suit and hat, not the cowboy I knew from the old photograph. I watched as he jumped down and came forward. I should say he stalked forward, for that is the way I would describe his stride. He strutted, head forward, arms swinging wildly in a cadence designed to waste little time. A man of great energy and determination, I must have thought.

"Jim?" he said, smiling thinly. I nodded and he shook my hand and grabbed me by my shoulders, wrapping his large meaty hands around my puny frame. John Thornton stood between us.

"Uncle Martin?" I asked meekly. I suddenly felt almost ill because I felt betrayed, let down. But Uncle Martin wasn't at fault.

"I'm your Uncle Martin, Jim, and I'm glad you're here," he said so quickly I could hardly understand all the words, and he smiled again, his lips pressed tightly together and stretched across his face. The conductor came up to John Thornton then and grabbed the leather leash. But Uncle Martin took hold of his tether and the conductor moved on. I reached down and tugged on John Thornton's ears.

"Fine-looking animal," he blurted.

"Good boy," I said to John Thornton, and I looked up at my uncle. I remembered what Ma had said and knew now that he had not fallen off the face of the earth.

Uncle Martin struck me as a man who found curling his mouth into a smile a physical hardship. I would learn later that his tough life had so hardened him that he seldom laughed. This always put a distance between us, for Ma was one who laughed often. Martin was one of Pa's older brothers, and I guessed him to be much older than Pa would have been, probably at least fifty. He was bald with just a fringe of gray hair around the base of his white felt hat and over his rather large protruding ears. No, he certainly wasn't a cowboy—he was too comic to fit my image of a cowboy, although later I saw so many strange-looking characters who were indeed cowboys that I would enlarge my understanding of who was a cowboy and who was not.

My ears were large, too, and I immediately recognized this a trait in our family. Uncle Martin made me think of the Bible, of Ezekiel. Ezekiel had shaved his head and beard, Ma read. Ma read the Bible aloud to me in the evenings. I remember in particular how I was terrified by the prophet Ezekiel. I had conjured up images of this great prophet who lived I don't know when. I dreamed that Ezekiel had hard bushy eyebrows set over these very dark eyes. The part I liked best was Ezekiel's prophecy to a valley full of dead, dry bones. I can recall the words, "And, lo, they were very dry," cracking and snapping around in my head. I was both fascinated and terrified as the bones came together with a noisy, rattling sound. Now I saw that very person here on the railway depot platform. Set in Uncle Martin's red puffy face were those very eyebrows low over the darkest eyes I had ever seen, even Ma's. He had wide cheekbones and sagging jowls with deep vertical creases down his clean-shaven face. He was talking now, telling me that we were taking the new Western Pacific train up into the mountains and it would take a full day. Then I realized that he reminded me of a puppet. He seemed mechanical the way that people are mechanical when they say the things they are supposed to say. Once during a puppet show in Huntsville I had become distracted by the marionette's lower jaw moving up and down magically by strings. Uncle Martin's upper lip hardly moved when he talked, just like the puppet's, producing a peculiar deep nasal effect. His gruff voice came in spurts—he tried to say everything he wanted to say at once. He had a noticeable Irish brogue, even after all these years—nearly forty in America—and the Irish twist to his speech partly accounted for the difficulty I had in understanding everything he said. His words came out like explosions, and he always moved his arms when he talked. He spoke with an edge to his voice as though you were being warned or scolded. I sometimes found myself staring rudely at the upper lip to see if it would move. It seldom did.

I was small and frail for my age. I prayed every night I would get bigger, but so far I was disappointed in God's response. I guess I took that part from Ma. I thought from the way Uncle Martin was eyeing me he was pretty disappointed in the package he had agreed to take on.

"That cut on your head minds me of your pa," Uncle Martin said.

"Train hit some cows in Utah . . . I never knew Pa."

"Hmmm? Yes . . . of course . . . he died when you were just a baby. Well, you've got somethin' of Tim in you, I think, but Lord, you need some weight. Tim, he was a stout fella, you know. He was a fine fighter . . . er, a boxer, I guess you know now, don't you? He whipped Blood Burns!"

I nodded. I would never be the boxer Pa was, and Ma never told me about Pa's whipping Blood Burns or the poster. I remembered that I never asked. Pa's voice so differed from Uncle Martin's that I thought surely it was all in my imagination.

"The Commander'll fix you up, I reckon. She's the best cook in the valley. We have an Indian cook, too. I spect the two of 'em . . . they'll fix you up all right."

"Indians?" I asked. I had never been around Indians.

Uncle Martin nodded. "Right. Indians. Maidu—some call 'em Diggers. I have fifteen Indians working on the place."

"Fifteen Indians, Uncle Martin?"

"Yes, yes—good cowboys, they are," he said, barely smiling again. "My foreman is Kenneth Joe Tracker. Blue Song, she also works with The Commander in the kitchen."

What strange names, I thought. *Who was The Commander? Who was Blue Song?* Doctor Brandt hadn't mentioned anything about The Commander or Blue Song.

"Who's The Commander?" I asked.

"Hmmm? Yes . . . well, yes, didn't Doctor Brandt tell you about your aunt?"

"My aunt's The Commander?" I asked, puzzled.

Uncle Martin raised his eyebrows when he saw my confusion.

"That's right, Aunt Hannah's The Commander. She's your Aunt Hannah all right, but we all refer to her as The Commander . . . of course, we don't call her that . . . we call her Hannah . . . but, well, she's just The Commander . . . you'll find out what I mean."

"Who's Blue Song?"

"Hmmm . . . you ask too many questions. You'll find all that out soon."

I felt better somehow now that I knew Uncle Martin was married even if he was married to a woman known as The Commander. Maybe I was, as Ma said, going to find roots.

After some business at one of the banks and some shopping for clothes Uncle Martin said I needed, we checked into a hotel for the next morning's train leaving for the mountains east of us.

The next morning was hazy and bright, terribly hot as we boarded the Western Pacific for Quincy, a 160-mile trip up the Feather River Canyon. It took us most of the day to get to Quincy in the American Valley because we made several stops along the way.

Except for the old Indian who boarded the train in Marysville and sat opposite me, the trip was long and tiring. I wanted to absorb everything that was new and strange, and my eyes and ears were working on a level that tired me too quickly. I had never seen an Indian in real life before. He was an old man, very old by the wrinkles on his face, but the hair coming out from underneath a battered old black hat was dark without a speck of gray. The hat had a mottled and striped feather in its rattlesnake band. He only uttered a few words all day, but he spent a lot of time running his dark calloused hand across John Thornton's head. Uncle Martin knew the Indian because he called him Mr. Charlie and said something about Yellow Eye and Kenneth Joe and a few other things I didn't follow. Uncle Martin remained awkwardly detached from Mr. Charlie, but the Indian seemed very friendly. The Indian had smiled and nodded as he sat across from us. He mostly grunted when Uncle Martin talked to him, so far as I could tell. He nodded toward me, and Uncle Martin told Charlie that I was his nephew and had come to live with them. The old Indian let out a long "Oooooh, I see, truly, I see" and smiled broadly. I noticed he didn't look directly at me. I thought briefly that maybe he was blind. His eyes were red and gray with little white peninsulas running out from the dark pupils. He wore a bright red cotton shirt, buttoned hard to his wrists, faded and torn blue jeans rolled up to his ankles, and he was barefooted. He carried his unlaced boots and set them on the floor beside him. His feet, I remember, were brown and twisted and bony and stuck out of his frayed blue jeans above the ankle. John Thornton took a liking to the old man and that made me feel a little easier.

I said, "His name's John Thornton."

The Indian smiled and nodded, but still he did not look directly at me. His eyes seemed to me like crystal balls, clear little worlds, safe. There were stories in those eyes, and they drew me closer. Uncle Martin did not tell me who the old Indian was, but I was to learn more about him later in another way. It was Uncle Martin's way with the old man that bothered me. Uncle Martin was not at ease, and he made this worse by being aloof.

For the last few hours aboard the train to Quincy all I could think about was Aunt Hannah's cooking, the old Indian, and the beautiful mountains we were climbing through. The train made several stops as it wound through the steep Feather River Canyon. Passengers disembarked at these times and wandered among the waterfalls and rock formations that make up the beauty of the Feather River. I got off, too, and spent my time observing trout rising in the deep black pools, but Uncle Martin, reading my excitement, told me it was better to fish the rough water as it comes together in the narrow channels. He pointed upstream to huge boulders rising out of tumbling white water. He said I should cast upstream and mend the line as it comes back downstream, bringing the fly near the lee side of the boulders. It was there the really big trout lay, he said. So I learned that Uncle Martin was a fisherman, too.

"Your Pa, he was the best fisherman I ever saw," he said. "Did you know that?"

"I guess, I do," I said, inwardly proud. Everything I knew about fly-fishing I owed to Pa. I knew that because I inherited his expensive handcrafted equipment.

I returned to the train, and I fell asleep to the swaying of the car and the heaving of the engine as it tugged against the weight. It was a climb all the way.

When I awoke the old Indian was gone, and Aunt Hannah was waiting for us at a little depot called Marston about 4 miles from Quincy. She was sitting in an open motorcar, a 1914 Imperial, although I didn't know an Imperial from a Ford in those days.

Chapter Three

TAYLORSVILLE

She pinned my arms at their side and lifted me off my feet. I was encircled, engulfed by her massive arms, and with no foothold I slid down the front of her dress until I came to rest—my face pressed tightly between her large soft breasts. Her perfume was overpowering, I remember, and she held me there until I nearly suffocated. Meanwhile, she erupted into rolling, convulsive laughter. John Thornton jumped in, too, and circled around her wanting the same treatment. The Commander was a large woman, considerably taller and heavier than Uncle Martin. I didn't know whether she was laughing or crying, but when she released me, her eyes were red, and her face was streaked with tears.

"My lord, Jim, we are glad to see you!" she said, standing back and holding me rooted in one place by the shoulders. She hovered over me and inspected my hair and ears and pulled me by my cheeks. It was all very humiliating, and I couldn't understand how she could be glad to see someone she had never seen.

"Hello, Aunt Hannah," I mumbled, catching my breath.

She eyed me up and down and with an appraising voice, announced, "Martin, this boy needs some cooking! Have you fed him anything in the past two days?"

Uncle Martin answered like a private summoned before a general.

"He had a large dinner last night at Maria's in Sacramento, and you know how big the feed is there, and he's had more sandwiches than I can eat on the train!" Uncle Martin said. I realized that much of Uncle Martin's peculiar speech habits, the explosive way he had of trying to get all the words out at once, was the result of his immediate compliance before Aunt Hannah's stern voice of authority.

"Well, he's going to fatten up in the next few months, I'll bet. We just need to get him home," The Commander said.

Uncle Martin grabbed my suitcases and Leonard fly rod tubes and threw them in the back of the seven-passenger Imperial. To my surprise, an Indian I hadn't noticed up to now came forward and took the driver's seat. Uncle Martin introduced Kenneth Joe Toby, the foreman of his ranch. While he had been more silent with Blind Charlie, he talked openly with this Indian.

"Kenneth Joe is known as 'The Tracker' around these parts, Jim, and he runs our ranch. You'll learn a lot from him," said Uncle Martin.

I was impressed by Kenneth Joe Tracker. He was dark and strong and very Indian. When he took the driver's seat, I wasn't sure whether he was playing the chauffeur or enjoying the opportunity to drive this fancy car. Either way, I felt a momentary pang of disappointment. The Indians I had read about were not chauffeurs.

Kenneth Joe Toby Tracker nodded. He didn't put out his hand. He smiled and greeted me with his eyes, and he looked to be about Uncle Martin's age, around fifty.

"Well, let's not stand around here in Marston. Let's get into Quincy to get our supplies before we head home," erupted Aunt Hannah. I was beginning to understand why she affectionately was called The Commander. She was the boss. The Commander had never had children. She couldn't, Uncle Martin said, and it nearly killed her. As a childless couple, Aunt Hannah and Uncle Martin made me their new center of attention.

Kenneth Joe Tracker drove us the 4 miles into Quincy. People along the road stopped to stare at the shiny new Imperial "54." We motored along faster than I had ever gone before, and we left a dense cloud of dust rising behind us. I saw fifteen or twenty other motorcars in Quincy. Uncle Martin told me that automobile traffic over the Oroville Road had doubled in the past year and that lots of people were driving in from Sacramento and San Francisco. I was surprised to find that Plumas County was much more prosperous than Randolph County back in Missouri. I had seldom seen a motorcar in Huntsville. The houses, the buildings, the streets—everything about Quincy—indicated a thriving economy. Quincy was as big as Huntsville. It had a bank, two or three hotels, livery stables, and two main streets loaded with general stores, assay offices, garages, barbershops, and saloons. From where I stood, I could see the Grand Central Hotel, all three stories of it, and farther down The Plumas House. While John Thornton waited patiently outside on the boardwalk, we went into the Ford and Lee Company, and The Commander bought me two pair of Headlight overalls for $1 each. Kenneth Joe Tracker and Uncle Martin bought several items from a long supply list. I hated overalls and I wanted to tell The Commander that right off, but I held my tongue. On the wall behind the counter was a large white metal sign that said in bright red letters, "Headlight Overalls, One Dollar—The best overalls you ever bought or your money back after thirty days!" I wondered how anybody could make that kind of quality comparison in thirty days. Overalls were overalls. Uniformly horrible. I wanted to give mine back right now, but if The Commander said I needed overalls, then I needed overalls. I was quickly becoming an enlistee in The Commander's army.

"These your size?" said Aunt Hannah, holding up one pair of overalls.

"I think so . . . I mean, yes, Aunt Hannah!"

Kenneth Joe Tracker was smiling. Uncle Martin was thinking of other things, his mind elsewhere.

Ford and Lee Company looked mostly like any other general store I had visited except there were tons of mining equipment for sale, pieces of wood and steel, picks, shovels, and all kinds of specialized tools I had never seen before.

Just before we finished, Mr. Guidici, the proprietor, carried out a new saddle and dumped it into the back seat. We were pretty well loaded when we left, and I began for the first time to realize that Uncle Martin and Aunt Hannah were rich. We left for Taylorsville and the beautiful Indian Valley where Uncle Martin and The Commander ran over 1,000 head of cattle.

I guess I was rich, too, although I wouldn't really need any money. Doctor Brandt was taking care of selling Ma's farm and all the animals. The money was to be forwarded to Uncle Martin and he would take care of my accounts and banking until I came of age.

A few miles from Quincy on the road to Indian Valley we came to the small town of Indian Falls, a mining town, but also a popular tourist spot. A man waved as we went by, and Kenneth Joe Tracker stopped.

Noel Pittman, the owner of the small hotel, began talking to Uncle Martin.

"Heard about the big rumble over at Lassen? They say it's going to blow for sure!"

"That's what I hear. Those men who've been working up at Big Meadows on the dam, they say anything when they passed through yesterday?"

"Yep. There's smoke comin' out the top all the time now. I'd sure like to go on up there and see it for myself."

We waved goodbye and The Commander told me all about the big volcano up north of there, Lassen Peak, which was about to erupt for the first time in several hundred years. It scared me to think the mountains were blowing up. In my mind I saw lava flowing down from Vesuvius and I didn't want to be in the Pompeii that Ma had once told me about.

We crossed the rusty steel trusses of Shoo Fly Bridge there on Indian Creek in the steep shadow of a canyon, and I saw again the stream where I would spend countless hours over many years casting an Adams or a Light Cahill or hundreds of other dry fly patterns.

Uncle Martin's ranch was just outside Taylorsville where he ran a few head of cattle on 200 acres. Most of his stock grazed on another 800 scattered in the high mountain meadows up on Red Clover Creek and near Kettle Rock. He had holdings in Genesee, too, a smaller valley about 8 miles up Indian Creek toward Antelope Valley, where he leased over 1,000 acres from the Hosselkus family. All of Uncle Martin's Herefords were in the mountains for the summer. In the fall he held a large roundup and drove them down to winter pasture below Table Mountain near Oroville, a gold mining community. Uncle Martin's ranch was much larger there, but with fewer buildings and only a small house. Uncle Martin, The Commander, and some of the Indians lived there sometimes in the winter, especially if the snow was real deep in the Sierra Nevada. Several of Uncle Martin's Indian workers stayed down in Oroville to look after the ranch all summer long.

The large house we drove up to outside Taylorsville was a grand white wood frame two-story estate, bigger than any house I had ever seen in Randolph County, except in photographs. The house was big enough to name. "Endemeo" with the Greek *endhmew*, was carved handsomely into a weathered board that was attached to the huge peeled pine gatepost at the entrance. Loosely translated, Aunt Hannah told me it meant "to be among one's people, to be home." Aunt Hannah's father, who was a missionary somewhere in China and understood the classical languages, had named the ranch when he visited here years earlier. Here, too, were three large barns, two ponds across the road encircled by cows, more outbuildings than a person could account for, and miles of three-row wood rail fences forming corrals and chutes.

Uncle Martin hadn't made his money in ranching. He was the owner of a prosperous gold mine near Greenville at the north end of the valley and he was an investor in the Engle Mine, the largest copper mine in California in 1914. I found Uncle Martin's business success strangely out of tune around The Commander. At home he didn't give orders. He took them, and I believe Uncle Martin liked it that way.

The Commander dragged me off to church every Sunday. Reverend Wenk and his daughter ran the show. He always spoke to us as if there were three or four thousand in attendance. His voice boomed off the walls behind the back row of pews and thundered across the narrow aisles, even when barely fifty gathered to listen. Miss Wenk, his daughter, asked me once if I was "saved." I knew what she meant because The Commander wanted to save me, too. Miss Wenk sang beautiful solos, and they were the highlight of the service for me. I think I was in love with Miss Wenk. She tried to save everyone else, too, but I became her most important project. I told her that I had already been baptized, that I already had been saved, and that Ma taught me the Bible. Aunt Hannah didn't take my past into account either. Everything had to be done over and she or Miss Wenk had to do it.

She loved to sing and she was an accomplished pianist. Her favorite song was one of Fanny Crosby's hymns, "Tell Me the Story of Jesus." Blue Song joined in, too, and they sang when they worked in the kitchen and when they worked outside in the garden. Singing like that became a habit for me. I remember humming the old tune even when I stalked the elusive rainbow trout on Indian Creek.

Taylorsville was a jewel of the mountains. Rising behind the small town to the south was Grizzly Ridge. Indian Creek wound through a small canyon below Grizzly and opened into Genesee Valley. Behind Taylorsville to the north above China Grade was the hard granite face of Mt. Hough and Arlington Heights. The forests above the town were a solid carpet of green sweeping up and over the tops of both ridges, and these vast expanses of pine and fir were interrupted only by two or three large faces of glacial moraine. The steep slopes behind Taylorsville cast a bluish shadow over the town even in summer. Dusk came two or three hours early on the west side of the valley when the sun disappeared behind the ridge. In winter, shortly after lunch, the mountain drew a shadow across the town, and the lights in all the homes sparkled through the curtained panes; and white smoke from every chimney formed a common layer of haze before nightfall. I've seen that picture from the back of a horse rounding up cattle on a summer evening, and I've seen it as I spent many a night on Indian Creek on the east side of the valley, working a fly through my favorite pools.

I had come to my new home in the mountains of California. I had my own pine-paneled room, one wall of colorful wallpaper, with a rock fireplace in a huge house next to better fishing streams than I had ever known in Missouri. A large framed painting hung on the wall behind my bed. I was drawn to the picture because the large black horse, the painting's subject, was running. Shocked, I could actually feel the movement. The hoofs seemed almost to beat against the turf. I saw that it was the horse of my dreams, the horse rearing high over my face, bent on crushing the life out of me. When I looked closer at the picture I saw that it was signed "York." I backed away, and from that day on the dreams of the black horse began to fade away.

John Thornton was at home on the floor at the foot of my bed at night or curled up next to the kitchen door, alert and ready at a moment's notice to go anywhere. And The Commander, along with Blue Song, cooked enough to fatten me up.

The kitchen was my favorite room. It was disproportionately huge for the house, with a gigantic wood-burning range some 8 feet long with four ovens. One of my jobs was to stack short pieces of oak in a box on the floor next to this mammoth black iron stove. The Commander or Blue Song fed these pieces I had cut or chopped endlessly into the jaws of a fire chamber set between two ovens with ornate nickel-plated bars. Pots and pans hung from enormous oval black rods over a large central refectory table.

Ma had read the description of Badger's kitchen in *The Wind in the Willows* to me a few years before she died. My first impression of The Commander's kitchen was that it was as warm and cozy as Badger's, but unlike Badger's underground domain, there were no tunnel-like corridors leading to The Commander's kitchen. It opened on to a large porch off the back with an overhanging roof. Uncle Martin and The Commander had furnished the porch with comfortable lazy Adirondack chairs, and one was invited to sit there on summer days. Like Badger, The Commander stocked her kitchen with nets of onions and herbs, and wire baskets of eggs rested invariably on the long hardwood counter. I liked to sit at the oaken refectory table and drink coffee with Blue Song—we called her Aunt Blue, although her legal name was Vivian—and The Commander in the mornings. They let me drink coffee and I was glad of that because Ma had always let me, too. A pot of coffee was forever heating on the stove, a huge gray porcelain pot with a curl of hot steam rolling from the spout. The kitchen was hot in the summer and warm in the winter. The ceiling was high, nearly 20 feet of exposed trusses and beams. Aunt Hannah and Blue Song had draped baskets and pans over these beams, and bowls and Mason jars filled with vegetables and fruits lined the shelves across the walls. Some of the baskets I saw were intricately and beautifully woven with dark designs on a lighter background. These were Maidu baskets that Blue Song had woven. I didn't know it then, but she was famous among the Maidu for her artistry. Two enormous oak iceboxes were filled with enough food to feed the ranch workers who came in at noon when they weren't out in the upper mountain meadows.

Blue Song was Kenneth Joe Tracker's wife. She was small with a nearly round, smooth, brown, clear face, framed by her long black hair. Her long black hair was nearly always tied in back like a horse's tail. They lived on the ranch in a snug log cabin no more than a hundred yards from the main house. Kenneth Joe Tracker and Blue Song often took their meals with The Commander and Uncle Martin, but I suspected that this was more on account of The Commander than Uncle Martin. Aunt Hannah loved Blue Song and Kenneth Joe Tracker. You could see that. As for Uncle Martin, I guessed that an Indian was still an Indian as far as he was concerned, although he relied on Kenneth Joe Tracker more than anybody. He employed the Indians but never had the slightest idea about who the Maidu really were. While The Commander easily saw them as brother and sister, Uncle Martin saw them as employees, Indian employees. Uncle Martin would not or could not deal with the likes of his dominant wife, so he meekly gave in to her wishes. As for Blue Song and Kenneth Joe Tracker—those wonderful people held Uncle Martin in no ill light for his feelings, although they must have felt his lordly manner. I became more and more bothered by distance between Uncle Martin and the Maidu as the days went by.

Kenneth Joe Tracker and Blue Song had three sons. Willis, who was two years older than I and attended the Bureau of Indian Affairs School in Greenville; Walker, who was in his twenties and on his way to Vancouver to join the Canadian forces in World War I; and York, an adopted son, who lived in a small shack behind Taylorsville with his grandfather, Blind Charlie. York was almost one year older than I and was working for Dutch Coder, the foreman of the Bacala Ranch up on Humbug Valley, the Tásmam Koyóm, when I arrived at my new home.

I learned that York was not Kenneth Joe Tracker and Blue Song's natural son. They had adopted him after a tragic, fairytale-like beginning to his life. York was nobody's baby. He came into the world unwanted and abandoned. The doctor who treated him said he was probably half Maidu and half white, although no one ever found the mother or father. One could guess why he had been abandoned, left to die along the banks of the Feather River near Oroville. Most likely, and sadly, it was because the child had been born crippled—one leg slightly smaller than the other, misshapen, bent and crooked because the bones had not formed normally. The baby's facial bone structure was violently different from a normal child's. The jaw structure protruded well beyond the nose and the forehead was wide and prominent, giving the newborn a distinct skull-like appearance. Worse, the baby boy looked to have a heart defect. He had difficulty breathing and was noticeably blue during much of his first year of life, a handicap that doctors would later describe as a defective heart valve.

The child may have come into the world screaming and crying, but when Blind Charlie and his friend Benjamin Kurtz came upon the tiny, whimpering bundle along a dirt path among weeds and scattered boxes, he was close to death. Blind Charlie had many Indian friends in Oroville, but on this trip he was with Benjamin. Benjamin was looking to purchase some agricultural land bordering on the Feather River and was inspecting the property boundaries along the river one morning in the spring of 1901. Blind Charlie came upon the child, cold and barely breathing, wrapped in old newspaper and burlap only a few feet from the river's banks under a willow. Blind Charlie picked up the child and held him out at arm's length, not really sure what to do with him. Both of these old men just stared at this creature for several seconds.

"What's wrong with it?" asked Benjamin.

"He is cold I thing," answered Blind Charlie.

"How do you know that? No, I mean look at him," continued his old Jewish friend, "he is deformed. His head looks like a skull."

"Ooooh, truly, this baby boy not gone be very pretty," Blind Charlie said, smiling.

"Alas, poor Yorick . . . I knew him, Horatio . . ." muttered Benjamin, looking down at the child.

"What be your talking about York?" said Blind Charlie.

"Shakespeare, a line from *Hamlet*. Some gravediggers discover a skull and they know who it is because they have buried him there many years earlier. His name was Yorick."

"They dig in somebody's grave, this York's grave?" said Blind Charlie, looking again at the child. "This child not come from the grave."

"No, Mr. Charlie, it's a story . . . a play from a great English storyteller—he wrote plays—named Shakespeare," explained Benjamin.

"I see . . . truly I hear before about that Shakes Spear," he said.

"What are we going to do with the child?" asked Benjamin.

"This Shakes Spear . . . then he be speaking in English?"

"He's from England, Mr. Charlie. He's been dead for four hundred years!"

"Ooooh, truly, then this Shakes Spear, he be gone tellin' stories for a very long time," continued Blind Charlie. "I hear bout him before."

"Yes, Mr. Charlie, he's known all over the world."

"We keep, I thing . . . we keep this . . . York, York, then!" said Blind Charlie finally.

"Yor-*ick*, Yor-*ick*, not York . . . you can't name him Yorick, Mr. Charlie. People who know the story of Hamlet will laugh," said Benjamin.

"No . . . no . . . truly, York gone be a good name . . . I like this York, I understand how be the story of York," said Blind Charlie with finality.

"Yor-*ick* . . . Yor-*ick*, Mr. Charlie!" repeated Benjamin.

"Yes, I know, it gone be York," ended Blind Charlie, not hearing or not wanting to hear the final syllable, exasperating Benjamin.

At least that is how Blind Charlie explained the story to me years later. I have to rely on his vivid memory for the details. Benjamin's explanation of how two gravediggers come upon the skull of Hamlet's court jester tickled Blind Charlie's narrative sense. York was his name, because that is the way the story unfolded. Blind Charlie saw everything in terms of a story, both the story he was telling and the story he was living in. He wouldn't have it any other way.

The Bureau of Indian Affairs was not amused that two old men wanted to adopt an abandoned child. The agent didn't know anything at all about Yorick or Shakespeare and Benjamin's explanations only irritated him. It didn't matter. The new baby, now named York, kicking and trying to scream between breaths—kicking strongly even with his skinny, crooked leg—had been cared for by a hospital in Sacramento before the legal entanglements involved in adopting the child could be completed a few weeks later by Kenneth Joe Tracker. The heart murmur complicated matters. The Bureau agreed that Blind Charlie could not adopt, but that Kenneth Joe Tracker and Blue Song could do so.

I have wondered many times through the years about Blind Charlie's discovery of York. How could it be that a great old storyteller of the Maidu would be the one to find this special child? Was it fate? Did it just happen? The Commander said that Jesus led Blind Charlie to York. That was a good explanation as far as it went, but I still could not help thinking about it, letting my imagination run.

Life at Endemeo was like an orchestra. I never thought about it quite in that way, but The Commander described it so. There were lots of workers and everyone had a part, and there was a harmony in the way they blended their work. We had two milk cows, one Guernsey and one Jersey. Priscilla, the Guernsey, was a docile milker, and I always enjoyed milking her during my morning and afternoon chores. But Cleopatra, the Jersey, was so darned mean, that nobody wanted to work with her. Kenneth Joe Tracker warned me to hold on to the bucket tightly with my knees and feet as I sat under her or she would kick over the bucket. The one Holstein I had milked back home on our Missouri farm was quiet by comparison. I spilled my bucket of milk more than once with Cleopatra, so even for a farm boy, it was like learning all over again. Kenneth Joe Tracker and I traded off with Cleopatra and Priscilla every day, but I never did arrive at a clear understanding with Cleopatra on who exactly was in charge. Clearly, she thought she was. One morning, for example, I was just about to finish up. The milk was full, nearly to the three-gallon bucket's rim. I remember I was pleased with myself for the tranquil morning I was enjoying without incident. The sweet smell of hay and manure reminded me of home and Ma. A single lantern illuminated the warm darkness of the barn, same as our barn back home. I was actually leaning my head affectionately on Cleopatra's flank, listening to the rhythmic barrage of milk streams hitting the bucket, when I found myself unexpectedly on my back. She had raised her rear leg with lightning-like speed and planted it firmly in the middle of my puny chest. Down I went, milk and all. In truth, I didn't just go down. I went out and down, sort of like being discharged from a cannon. Cleopatra had kicked me with such force that I flew out backwards, landing flat on my back about 5 or 6 feet from the cow. The imprint of her hoof became a black and blue memory for several weeks after. Kenneth Joe Tracker, of course, found the whole thing gleeful. He laughed so hard that he almost lost Priscilla's bucket of milk. And he told the story so many times in so many places that I was really worried that it might become a permanent part of Maidu legend. I realized Kenneth Joe Tracker was like a father to me. I could laugh and be myself around him. Uncle Martin was distant, both by the fact that he often was working away from the house and by his phlegmatic temperament.

From the cow barn we took the milk to a small shed we called the creamery. This was The Commander's favorite room, other than her kitchen. The creamery was very sanitary. Kenneth Joe Tracker had built it himself, with a concrete floor that sloped down to a drain in the center. The Commander took charge of keeping the creamery clean. She was forever washing down the walls with buckets of hot, soapy water and then running cold water through a hose connected to our gravity flow tank. The walls were all white and the room was always cool because it had been partially dug into the side of a hill next to the barn. The Commander had two cream separators in the creamery and shelves full of other equipment. She made her own butter with a large glass churn she kept in the kitchen. The cheese she made from several metal presses she left in the creamery. We only had that one cow back in Missouri, but Ma sold it when I was eight. Ma got her milk from a dairy down the road, so I was learning over again. I especially enjoyed pouring the buckets of warm, foamy milk into the Laval cream separators and cranking on the handle to spin the milk. The milk and the separated cream came pouring from two different spouts into large metal containers sitting on the floor. A door led to an even cooler room where Kenneth Joe Tracker placed these metal containers.

Endemeo produced more than cattle. Uncle Martin had about fifty hogs he kept in pens far removed from the main house. The Commander forbade me to work with the hogs. I think this was because she worried that I might get eaten by The Dashing Prince, the huge boar which reigned as king. The Dashing Prince weighed over 700 pounds and was rarely in good spirits. To enter his pen was a foolhardy act, so food was dispensed over a sturdy log rail. The Dashing Prince ate *anything*. Nearly all the farm garbage was given to The Dashing Prince. Cinderella was the sow. She was over 500 pounds but had such a sweet disposition that anyone could approach her. Her only problem, as it is with most sows, is that she had trouble keeping track of her litter. She lay on them as often as she fed them, so usually half of every litter ended up being recycled back through The Dashing Prince's feed dish. He didn't seem to mind eating his own children. We had two other sows as I remember, but since I spent little time near the pigs, I don't remember much about them. Our attention was centered on The Dashing Prince and Cinderella.

The ducks and geese were housed near a pond down by the road. Kenneth Joe Tracker had built separate pens and nesting houses for both. The pond also had an island in the middle where the ducks and geese generally lay tucked and cozy on sunny afternoons. When they were not sitting on the water or pecking and rooting around the pond, the whole flock of twenty or so found their way carelessly up to The Commander's back door. Out she would come with her broom, swinging and yelling, protecting her flowers. Blue Song's vegetable garden had an eight-foot fence that barred the geese with their clipped primaries. Another of my chores was to scatter grain, usually corn, to this brood of ducks and geese every day, although they seemed to do quite well independently—without my daily supplements.

Chickens seemed to be everywhere. We raised about a hundred of them for butchering and about another fifty for pullets. The pullets were transferred to an egg-laying house a good hundred yards from the main house. The Commander didn't like to hear the incessant cackling of the hens and wanted School Teacher, our giant New Hampshire rooster, to bellow his morning trumpet as far from the house as possible.

We had a large musty, leathery harness and tack room filled with straps and rings, saddles, and other working paraphernalia. Kenneth Joe Tracker and the other Indians worked with these things at times, but Uncle Martin had already gone to mechanized farm machinery for most chores, and the tack room had become mostly a museum and a place where we stored saddles, headstalls, ropes, and other gear for our herd of riding horses.

We kept about twenty to thirty good working horses on the ranch at all times. Once I could name them all. I knew my father, with all his ability to work with horses, would have been at home here with Uncle Martin. I was saddened by dwelling on what might have been. We used the horses to work the cattle all summer long and also to drive the huge herd down to Oroville in the fall.

Kenneth Joe Tracker, as foreman of the ranch, was about as good a man with horses as Uncle Martin could find anywhere. He had a special touch with horses that drew them to him. Dutch Coder, a cowboy up on the Bacala Ranch east of Big Meadows, drifted in from time to time at Endemeo, and he helped Kenneth Joe Tracker to raise, break, and train the horses. Uncle Martin, I knew, had once been a cowboy, and I learned that he understood more about horses than even Kenneth Joe Tracker or Dutch Coder. But the man I remembered from the photograph back home with Ma was not the Uncle Martin I knew now. His preoccupation with his mines and other business interests had forced him to give up this part of his life, except for fall roundup and the big drive.

The Commander was in many ways protective, but she gave me free run of the place from the moment I arrived. I had rules for this and for that, but mostly she wanted to give me my head. She didn't scold me if I was late for dinner, as usually happened when I was fishing. She might have nagged me—as I saw her do with Uncle Martin—to get up in the mornings. But I never could stand to lie around in bed. I was always up before light. With Uncle Martin away most of the days and with The Commander and Blue Song busy with the kitchen and their other interests, I was free to roam as I wished once I had finished my own chores. I liked to fish in the late afternoon and evenings sometimes, and Kenneth Joe Tracker milked both cows when I was lost in the grand world of fly-fishing. I think he understood, or at least he never said anything about it.

Ma had died only a month ago. It was early August of 1914. Uncle Martin had not fallen off the face of the earth.

Chapter Four

RATTLESNAKE!

"Get off me, you devil!"

I slapped my arms and face repeatedly, leaving slippery red smears and the flattened bodies of mosquitoes.

"There, how do you like that, you bloodsucker!"—flicking off the carcasses from my arms.

They were thick and bloodthirsty on Indian Creek that September, worse than August. They mostly ambushed me around the few isolated pools in the shady areas. I moved quickly on up the creek a ways where the woods opened up to more grassy banks. The mosquitoes didn't bother me in the sunlight. In Missouri we had mosquitoes, too, but usually just in the spring. After that, the chiggers and ticks took over and assaulted us like there was no tomorrow. In summer hardly a day went by that I didn't remove several big rusty ticks buried in John Thornton, and Ma searched me from head to toe when I came in at night. If she didn't find ticks, there were still the chiggers. They ate me up and left a bright red ring around my stomach and back. I could never see the chiggers, which Ma said were tiny larvae about to become harvest bugs, but when Ma rubbed me all over with benzine and a white lotion, the itching went away.

These Indian Valley mosquitoes were different. They rose in a cloud along the banks of the stream when I hiked ankle-deep through the grasses, and the grease The Commander gave me didn't help very much. I spent about as much time slapping my hands and face as I did working a fly out across the water. John Thornton's nose was covered. When I smashed them with my hand I left tiny patches of red and black on his fur. At the end of the day I was mad when I found vicious little lumps rising unevenly around his muzzle when I

36

ran my hand across his head. The mosquitoes seemed to know that the cold was coming on fast now, and the last big push for blood had to be made today. The mosquitoes could not lay their eggs to lie dormant through the winter unless they had eaten a blood meal. John Thornton and I were the blood sacrifice.

Lassen Peak was still smoking and erupting 25 miles to the north and overseas The Great War had broken out in great bloody battles that filled the weekly editions of the *Plumas National Bulletin*. School would start tomorrow, so I was spending all Sunday afternoon with John Thornton trying to catch one rainbow I knew was lurking in a pool just below where Montgomery Creek comes in. The Commander, like Ma, never neglected reading the Bible, so I had taken to naming the bigger lunkers after biblical characters. At first, The Commander did not find that amusing.

"Jim McLaverty, you mean to tell me you've named a *fish* after someone in the Holy Bible?"

"Yes, Aunt Hannah. But not just any fish—trout."

"Somehow that doesn't seem right . . ."

"You know, Aunt Hannah . . . that big 4-pounder I haven't caught yet out by Montgomery Creek . . . well, his name is Esau," I interrupted.

"Why didn't you name him Jacob?" she quizzed, sternly, deciding that my irreverent liberties weren't so bad after all.

"I already caught Jacob . . . a week ago, Aunt Hannah, in fact we had *him* for dinner, you remember?"

"*That was Jacob, the father of the twelve tribes of Israel?*" The Commander wailed.

"That's right, and I never use a name a second time. I figure I got thousands more to use."

The Commander looked at me in that stern way of hers and then threw her head back and laughed long and loud. I knew a hug was coming so I took a deep breath. I loved Aunt Hannah, but she physically overwhelmed my puny body. My lungs expelled all my oxygen when she squeezed me with those gigantic arms of hers.

I was wading upstream and finally came to the spot I had picked out earlier, about 4 miles south of Taylorsville. The previous winter of 1913–1914 had been a heavy one. Snow had fallen most of January and February, and Uncle Martin said 8-foot banks lined all the roads. As a result, the runoff in spring had been especially heavy, and during the summer, and now even in the fall, the creek had plenty of water. The water hadn't been as clear earlier, but now it glistened like crystal. The breeze picked up now and the mosquitoes disappeared.

The creek at this point is gray and shady on the west side where Grizzly Ridge and Montgomery Creek squeeze down between Indian and Genesee Valleys. The boulders jut out from the steep bank there, and the water is hidden by groves of alder and elderberry and cottonwood. It was impossible to cast from that side of the creek so I wandered slowly along the east bank, where Indian Creek was bordered by narrow meadows and marsh and low, grassy cutbanks. I was jumping over the tumbling pools between the rocks and rivulets and wading the gravelly bottoms. John Thornton knew better than to jump in ahead of me. He had learned to be patient and to suffer through long periods of inactivity as I quietly worked my line from pool to pool. I had scolded him more than once for jumping into the water and splashing around. That's a natural thing for a Lab to do, so there were still times when I had to tie him up to a tree. Because the stream flows swiftly through this canyon space, I was careful not to slip on the moss-covered rocks on the stream's edge.

My mind often wandered at times like these, especially back to Ma. It already seemed like long ago that she had died, and I felt guilty about the time passing so quickly. Ma would have loved it in these mountains. She just never knew about them. Then just as quickly I would crack myself back to attention. Fly-fishing is not something you can do successfully and dream at the same time. I wasn't paying attention to my footing, either. I teetered on a pointed rock, unbalanced, and came crashing down into the shallow water, but I was able to right myself with my outstretched arm as I found the bottom.

Pa's voice filled me with guilt. *Watch your step, boy.*

I looked around to see if anyone had seen my clumsiness. I imagined Pa on a black horse watching me. I felt uneasy for some reason—was someone watching? I looked around again, scanning the woods on the far side of the creek and the meadow grass on my side of the bank. But the sun was in my eyes when I looked up the sloping banks, and I turned back to my fishing. Pa wasn't watching even though I always wished he were.

I was casting a gray hackle into a dark pool where I had last seen Esau. I remember it was difficult to lay the fly down at first. The casting itself had been easy, and now the fly was poised in the air out in front of me, but I thought better of it. I quickly brought the rod tip back up and withdrew the fly, whipping the line behind me for another cast. I realized that I would surely entangle my fly in the brush overhead if I tried to force the cast in the targeted pool. I let the line down easily on the surface well back from under the overhanging willows. I was concentrating on trying to roll the line across the stream. I lifted my rod, and in that movement the line became a long arc from the tip down to my feet. When I thrust the tip forward, the line and tippet described a long graceful arc. The fly came back to me and rolled across the stream under the willows. For a second the fly was frozen in mid-air and then uncurled and rested on the silvery water like a dandelion.

Nice cast, Jim.

Sometimes I wished Pa's voice wouldn't follow me.

I studied the light hackle visible over the reflecting ripples. The fly sailed slowly in the lazier current near the far bank. A large white fir had fallen about 20 feet upstream and bisected the pool about 4 feet off the surface. Two weeks earlier I had scouted the pool by crawling on my belly out across the log. It had been a hot August afternoon and I was just learning to read the creek. I had carefully looked over and down on the pool for signs of trout. That's when I saw Esau. I could see his dark green back under the shadow created by the log. He wasn't feeding. He was just purling against the current, but I knew that in the morning or evening I would have a good chance. Dragonflies and caddis flies skimmed the surface, but no trout were rising. Downstream water ousels darted here and there, and a single spotted sandpiper was hopping over the rocks and pebbles next to the cutbank. I rolled the fly again and again without result.

Today my eye caught a movement up and to my right. A bald eagle soared down low over the middle of the water and disappeared around a bend in the creek to the south. The bird was gliding at astonishing speed, and its great white-hooded head seemed to swivel as it looked for prey in the water. I suspected that Esau saw the eagle, too, and I was uncertain about the chances now of catching the large rainbow. He saw the great bird with its massive wingspread, twice as long as he was. John Thornton sat back and let his tongue hang out, not a very dignified thing to do. John Thornton just didn't match up to the bald eagle's majesty and he knew it.

The stream was not silent. The water poured over the rocks and down into pools. It wasn't a roar like the plunging water down at Indian Falls, which seemed always to be boiling. Here the cataracts were more like simmering pots, repeating endlessly in countless ways a sound more like a chuckle than a roar. The creek laughed at me.

Retrieving my line, I worked my way past the log upstream. My hip boots were getting hot, so I pulled them off and removed my stockings. I rolled up my Headlight overalls and I tied a no. 16 Adams on my 4-pound tippet. I set the fly on the water just upstream from the log and played the line out as the current carried the fly downstream toward Esau's hole. I saw the fish rise and take my fly, and I hooked him solidly, pulling back on the rod horizontally and parallel to the log. The fish broke the surface several times and raced for the other side of the pool. My drag sang in a steady clicking whine.

"Ya-haaa! I have you, now!" I yelled, and my voice echoed up and down the stream almost in violation of the peace.

If the stream were laughing at me, I was going to do my laughing now. My bamboo rod was bent in a close arc and the tip kicked and quivered. I had the rod on its side so as not to rub the line on the rough bark bulging around the underside of the white fir.

I saw immediately that I was in an awkward position. I couldn't continue to play the fish under the log and keep the rod tip up. With the rod down like it was the line could easily snag any of several protruding rocks between me and the fish. I needed to get under the log and around to the downstream end of the pool. I splashed into the water recklessly and my bare feet suffered against the sharp rocks. I waded in under the log. John Thornton went down to the end of the pool and watched the trout. I was in waist-deep now, and the cold water filled my overalls and inflated them like a balloon. Against the warm day the icy shock took my mind momentarily off the trout. As my line slacked, the rainbow broke the surface frantically again, twisting and dancing to lose the fly. My heart was beating, and I was in a panic—I retrieved the line. He was still on, but I saw that he was about 2 pounds, no Esau.

As I neared the bank, walking backwards and keeping my eye on the trout—I was running various names for the trout through my mind from Reverend Wenk's sermons—I heard a distinct rattle. The sound made no impression on me in the excitement of the moment, but I knew that it was not the click of my Hardy's drag. It was near and loud and threatening, but I continued to concentrate on the trout. The shrill chattering grew louder, and I looked down at my reel. Uncharacteristically, John Thornton ran toward me and barked, and the noise stopped as quickly as it began. The trout exploded through the surface once again.

"Agag!"

At the echo I looked up. Again, I felt watched.

The Reverend Wenk's sermon that morning had been a story from 1 Samuel about King Saul's failure to destroy a bad king, as he had been commanded to do. I thought it was a smashing good story but disappointed that Reverend Wenk spent twice as much time *talking about* the story than *just telling* the story. Amalek was the name of the people King Saul was battling and Agag was their king. All this flashed through my mind as my newly named rainbow began now to play a slower tune on my reel's ratchet. The clicking was noticeably slower. Agag was tiring.

It happened as I stepped up on the grassy bank. The 5-foot rattler had waited, deep in a dark recess where the log had made a depression. It struck swiftly at the bare white calf of my left leg. I saw the strike—a dark flash out of the corner of my eye as I reached the bank.

"What . . . what?" I said, calmly at first. Then the pain hit me. I watched as the head fastened on to my leg and then released—like a door hinge opening.

"Yi-yi-yi! No-no-no!" I yelled. I dropped my fly rod on the grass and stared at the two small red holes in the muscle. The rattler had withdrawn into the shadows and was striking wildly at John Thornton now. The rattlesnake was tan and brown and gray in a mottled symmetry with a flattened, puffed head. I stared stupidly at the western rattler as it struck repeatedly and unsuccessfully at my most precious possession, John Thornton. I saw the pit, a crater set between its menacing wide-set eyes and nostril in its broad viper head. I was angry now.

I could feel the presence of someone else there even before the shadow loomed from behind. John Thornton had quit lunging at the snake and backed away in the same moment. John Thornton was looking at something and cowering. As I turned to see what or who was behind me I saw a brown arm release a huge boulder above and across my left shoulder and into the space where the rattlesnake was coiled.

The stone hit its mark. The rattler's tail flipped and jumped in its death spasms, its head embedded beneath the large round river rock. I was hypnotized by the gyrations of the rattlesnake's horny ringed tail until it slowed to a sluggish roll.

I looked up then and squinted into the bright blue sky. The Indian came around to face me and knelt to look at the fang marks in my leg. Already the bite was turning an ugly purple and the soft muscle tissue was rapidly swelling. Frightened, I sucked in my breath. I was scared not only by what the snake had done to me, but also by the boy who now examined the wound. I had never seen such a boy. He was not exactly ugly, although some would call him that. His face was drawn tightly over his high bony cheekbones and his eye sockets were deep-set recesses, black shadowy pools below his protruding brow. I thought of Gagool, the hideous prophetess in *King Solomon's Mines* and was ashamed of myself in the next instant. I have always had nightmares about Gagool.

My fear passed quickly because I knew this boy was not a monster. His skin was smooth, unmarked, and clear, and his eyes shone like dark highly polished obsidian.

"I been bit," I gasped. The bite was very painful now.

The boy, who was about my size, but very muscular in a thin, wiry way, looked at me and just nodded. He was breathing, wheezing heavily, unnaturally in spurts. He didn't look away in the diffident manner some of the Maidu did when I first met them. But he stared at me vacantly as though he were looking through me to someplace faraway. Behind this vacant stare was a fierce anger, I thought. But this detachment didn't keep him from setting to work immediately.

He rolled up my overalls beyond my knee. He took off his cotton shirt, soaked it in the stream, and tied it gently around my leg just below the knee. He knew what he was doing. I learned later that it wasn't a tourniquet that was needed, just a slight constriction. He put his fingers between my skin and his shirt to see that it wasn't too tight. Satisfied, he felt around behind my calf for a pulse.

"Knife?" he asked, catching his breath.

"No!" I said, thinking stupidly that he was asking for my permission to cut off my leg. I was hyperventilating now. Together we sounded like two winded runners at the end of a long race.

"I need your fishing knife," he repeated calmly, "to bleed the wound." Again, the dark black eyes took charge. He was lighter than most of the Maidu I had seen and looked to have European blood in his background. He didn't talk in the way I had imagined an Indian would talk. I'm not even sure I had ever thought about it much, but I suppose I expected some sort of foolish Indian talk I had gathered from reading James Fenimore Cooper. But I knew my reading of the various adventures of Natty Bumppo in no way prepared me for the real Indian I now faced. This Indian was not like that at all. He spoke with a calm authority, intelligence, and precision—but as an Indian at home in the wilderness, not as a professor from an east coast college. He was about my age, I was sure, but he sounded so much older than I.

"O.K., right . . . in my bag, there," I said, somewhat relieved.

I always kept my knife razor-sharp. Cleaning fish was easier that way. The Indian now ran his thumb across the edge.

"The knife is very sharp," he said. "It will do."

I nodded.

"Put your foot into the water, here," he commanded.

I scooted over the bank and placed my wounded leg into the water up to the knee. The water felt soothing and cold, and the pain lessened. The Indian ran his fingers across the wound and tried to clean it the best he could. He then lifted my leg out of the water and stretched it out on the grass.

"You can watch, if you wish," he said. "I'm going to make several small cuts now. They will hurt." He stopped again to catch his breath. I knew he was suffering in some unspoken way.

"O.K." I assented, but he had already begun.

He made several short incisions near and through the fang marks, across the bite and vertical. He made no cuts against the grain of the muscle. The cuts bled in long running streams down my leg, around my ankle and under my foot. I thought I was going to die, but the speed of the Indian's movements and the confidence he placed in his actions left me quiet and assured. John Thornton was calm, too. He lay next to me as quiet as if we were on a picnic.

My heart was pounding like a piston. I had thoughts about the venom moving rapidly through my body. I was becoming a bit nauseous. I had read in some book that I wasn't supposed to become excited, and now I was more excited than ever in my life.

He squeezed my calf muscle with both hands and began sucking on the incisions and spitting as he took a mouthful of blood. I was surprised by the amount of blood he purged from his mouth at each quick movement of his head. I felt like throwing up. He worked this for several minutes. I was too scared to do anything, too scared to cry.

When he finished, he noticed the trout on the line. It was dragging the rod, so the Indian stood quickly and picked it up. He reeled in Agag. He had no idea what he was doing and the tippet snapped before he beached the fish. He took the rod apart at the center and packed the reel in my utility bag. I noticed that he walked with a severe limp and that he leaned heavily to his left side.

"Anything else of yours besides the bag and pole?" he asked. I flinched at his calling my rod a "pole," even in my present distress.

"Hip boots . . . socks . . . I guess that's all," I sputtered.

"I've got to get you back to the doctor," he said. He reached down and cut the rattles off the dead snake and put them in his pocket.

"Twelve rattles," he said. "You faced Palawäiko himself!"

"Who's Pala . . .? What's your name . . .? Who are you?"

"C'mon, we've got to go now. We can talk about this later."

He whistled shrilly, and as if by magic, a huge black horse appeared at his side. I neither heard it coming nor understood where it had been concealed. Later, I marked this up as part of my confusion and nausea. The horse snorted and pitched and stomped around. John Thornton backed away, and I thought the noise was mysterious for a horse so silent in its coming.

It was then I knew that here it was again, my horse! I tried to yell and pulled back. The Indian only smiled.

"Stand, Black, stand!" he commanded the horse. "He is safe," he continued.

The Black quieted, but I saw that his eyes were alert. The horse was entirely black, save a white star on his face.

"I'm York," said the Indian, looking at me with those penetrating eyes. "Up . . . let's get up on the horse . . . Meshuga will get us back to Greenville fast."

"No! I can't . . . Greenville! Isn't that . . . 10 miles or more?" I asked, frightened, stupidly standing on one leg, not at all wanting to get on that horse.

"No argument. Get on . . . there's no doctor in Taylorsville."

"York . . . then you're York Toby?" I asked, weakly. "We have to go all the way to Greenville?" I said again.

"No doctor in Taylorsville. We have Sophia, Sophia Taylor—she delivers babies and helps with the fever, but you need a doctor. Got to go to Greenville."

We both were about the same height. Maybe he was slightly taller. The great black horse towered over both of us. I looked up to the horse's bare back and wondered how in the world I was going to get up there. Before I could answer, York picked me up like I weighed nothing and threw me up on the tall black horse and led me over across a dirt track, while I grabbed for the mane. He was obviously much stronger than I was, yet I saw that York was not in good health. He spoke with a heaviness of one who was not well, and he looked like he might be in pain.

"New to the McLaverty place, aren't you, Little Jim McLaverty? You're supposed to help me with the cattle drive next month . . . I hope you're strong enough . . . I've been watching you for the past hour. I'm drawing today and I have you in my sketchbook." He walked the great black horse near a tight group of trees and picked up a leather case, pushing his pencils and a book inside. He slapped at the mosquitoes on his bare arms and shoulders. He untied his shirt from my dangling leg and pulled it on. I was too sick with the snake-bite to be angry with the "Little Jim," even if he was about my size.

"Don't feel so bad about the snake—it's a great story to tell—it's

Palawäiko, you know." He smiled briefly, as though it were difficult to break a face etched in stone into a smile, but I was again unnerved by his appearance and his heavy breathing.

"Meshuga, he will get back soon enough, I think, but . . . then, maybe you will die, anyway. But I think Meshuga will get us back quickly. Watch out and lean forward while I get on." He jumped on the bare-backed horse behind me. Obviously, the deformed leg and the marked limp didn't hamper his ability to ride.

"Let me warn you now, Little Jim—hold on! You understand?"

"Yes, I think so."

"Go, Black!" he said quietly but with authority.

The great black horse exploded beneath us. The horse's speed was breathtaking. I was feeling a little woozy, but York held me by one hand as he guided the Black's reins with the other. We stormed down the dirt road toward town as the trees, the rocks, the road—everything—became a vibrating blur. I was nearly 10 miles from Greenville when the snake's attack had occurred, and I was sure the horse would slow to a walk soon. I had been on a horse only a few times in my life up to that moment, and then only on draft animals used on our farm. Never had I ridden a horse that ran like this one. The picture in my room of the running black horse mingled with the thin black line of Ghost Horse and his herd I had seen from the train window on the Nevada desert barely a month ago.

I was sick with nausea, but I grabbed the Black's mane for all I was worth. We never slowed or walked so far as I can remember. I only recall the steady beat of the horse's hoofs on the hard packed gravel road. Somehow, York was able to hold me, my rod, my bag, and his drawing equipment at the same time. Poor old John Thornton was left in the dust, but he got to town an hour later. The last thing I remember was sliding off the horse and lying down in Doctor Rutledge's infirmary in Greenville.

Chapter Five

BLIND CHARLIE

Blood was oozing down my leg and all over the clean white sheets. Doctor Rutledge took a long look at the cuts he had made with his scalpel, made several more incisions, and began suctioning out large amounts of blood with a rubber cuplike device. No one had been bitten by a rattlesnake for quite some time, and my story made the county newspapers. I was in a very bad way. There really wasn't much else Doctor Rutledge could do, except give me liquid and rest. He got me out of my wet clothes and put me to bed. I don't know what happened to York. He didn't to talk to white folks much, except to Uncle Martin and The Commander—and to Uncle Martin only when he had to. He told the doctor what happened and rode off to get Uncle Martin and Aunt Hannah. The snake's poison made a balloon of my leg, scaring me with the swelling, and the leg was red and inflamed around the dark purple section of the bite. The doctor didn't tell me then, but he feared that gangrene might set in and I might lose my leg.

"Happened to Tom Peters four years ago," he said, when the danger had passed.

I was in fever for three days and during this time was moved to my room at Endemeo. I don't remember Uncle Martin and The Commander coming to get me because I was delirious and only semiconscious. I dreamed bad dreams, dreams of a flattened viper's head swaying back and forth . . . waiting to strike. I dreamed of Gagool's sinister smile and her great skull-like head. I cannot recall if the dreams were before or after Blind Charlie's story, but it doesn't matter.

A few days later I was sitting up in bed and feeling like I wanted to get out of bed and go fishing. I saw my fishing rods leaning against the cabinet over in the corner and my fishing bag hanging on the wardrobe. I couldn't get Ma out of my mind then. When I was alone I shook and wept more often than I wanted to. My feelings were breaking loose. The Commander and Blue Song were in and out of my room like it was the kitchen. I tried to control myself when I heard them coming up the stairs. That was probably the loneliest time of my life. You would think that the three weeks I lived with Doctor Brandt back in Missouri after Ma died would have been my roughest time, but it wasn't. I would lie in bed here at my new home and stare at the ceiling and the walls with little control over my thoughts. I counted wildflower petals on the wallpaper above the half-pine wall at the end of the room and reckoned on reasons why I should feel sorry for myself.

I had bowls of fruit and bread on the table next to me, and they served all my meals in bed. I said I wanted to get out of bed, but The Commander gave me such a threatening look that I didn't even dare protest using the bedpan. The only good thing about being in bed was not having to suffer through The Commander's formidable hugs. But I received about a thousand kisses in exchange for that loss. York came to visit me once during my delirium, they said, but had gone on back to school and hadn't returned.

If I thought that missing school that first week was a reward for snakebite, I learned otherwise very quickly. The Commander wouldn't neglect my lessons. She took on the responsibilities of my education herself. She became my tutor for up to three hours a day, which was about all I could stand. The Commander had been well-educated at a school in the East, Mt. Holyoke College in Massachusetts. Her interest in books was obvious from the hundreds of volumes that lined all the walls of our library at Endemeo. The Commander had been well brought up in the East. She had come out west to be a teacher just after the turn of the century and had met Uncle Martin when she took a position in Quincy.

The Commander drilled me with a vengeance. In the first place, she was somewhat annoyed that my speech habits had deteriorated over the past few weeks since my arrival. Used to speaking correct English in my home because Ma insisted on it, I seldom indulged in slang or sloppy language. Now here, out west, I surprised even myself as I lapsed into constructions such as, "Me and him, we are on our way to . . . ." The first time I did that I thought The Commander was going to have a fit.

"What kind of English is that, Jim McLaverty?" she asked, irritated.

"I know, Aunt Hannah . . . I forgot . . ."

That and other mistakes, specifically double negatives such as "I don't have no . . ." forced The Commander to give me what she called "elocution lessons." She nearly had apoplexy when I used double negatives. She would launch into remembrances of her father at such times. I knew I was in dangerous waters when she invoked the name of her father. I wondered if her father could match up to my father.

"My father, Henry Marshall, would be getting out the rod if he heard those words come out of my mouth!" she would say. I never knew Henry Marshall of Lenox, Massachusetts, but I think I understood how he felt about double negatives.

These drills in correct and precise English so tired me that I made a much stronger effort to speak correctly, even in the company of my friends.

We pored over mathematics and science texts. Since I was a good student in mathematics, The Commander quickly centered my attention on algebraic equations. Her science lessons were mostly classifying and memorizing, which I found detestable. Later I would be grateful for the practical applications of science that York would teach me, but without the drill and memorization The Commander forced on me I would not have been capable of appreciating York's commentaries.

I learned that Admiral Nelson fought a brilliant battle at Trafalgar and that Martin Luther was asked to retract his teachings at the Diet of Worms in 1521. I was more fascinated in the title of the conference than I was in the subject, but The Commander was well prepared to give me an interesting account of both.

She introduced me to Dickens and to Shakespeare, although Ma would have done that if she were still alive, I was certain. In *David Copperfield*, I was shocked to find Uriah Heep to be exactly like one of the suitors who came courting Ma, the one from Kansas City.

I was frightened by the specter of Tungay, rod in hand, marching with his wooden peg leg up and down between the rows of desks at Salem House, daring anyone even to look up from his work, while the violent headmaster, Mr. Creakle, looked on from a distance. I was angry that Tommy Traddles was so reduced by the fear of this man that his scholastic output was nothing more than drawing skeletons at the back of the room. David was an orphan like me, whose mother had died when he was young. I remember feeling relieved that no Mr. Murdstone lurked about my life.

Even after I returned to school The Commander continued with a relentless schedule of literary study.

When she began on *The Iliad* and *The Odyssey*, she had my rapt attention. I was mesmerized by Achilles. As a reader of James Oliver Curwood and Jack London, I found this old classic more to my liking. She told me about Homer and how he had lived about three thousand years ago, even before Jesus. But when she got into the part about Helen of Troy and the Trojan Horse, I was hooked. Together we started reading Homer's epic. By the time we got to the one-eyed Cyclops eating Odysseus's men on some island in the Mediterranean Sea, I was used to the verse and was reading on by myself. I was always something of a reader. Ma had seen to that, but The Commander was well on her way to making me into a bookworm. I finished *The Odyssey* in two days and was beginning a story on Jason and the Argonauts when I received a new visitor.

The Commander came into the room to tell me that Mr. Charlie was downstairs.

"Mr. Charlie seldom visits nowadays," she said.

"Blind Charlie?" I asked.

"I think he is pleased that York was able to help you."

I nodded.

"York is not well, Jim . . ." she continued.

"I don't understand."

"York was never well. He has grown strong because he works hard, but he has a mysterious illness. The doctors are not sure what it is, but it has to do with his heart. He was born with it. I just want you to know this . . . but don't talk about it with Mr. Charlie. He knows, but he doesn't talk about it."

This new information was no sooner digested than my aunt rushed from the room, and I heard footsteps on the stairs. I had the impression that there was more about York's health than she was willing to tell me. I was afraid of the worst.

Blind Charlie seldom visited because of the tension between York and Uncle Martin. I began to wonder how much like Uncle Martin my father must have been. I would probably never know.

I realized Blind Charlie was honoring me. He came in and sat down in the maple rocking chair next to my bed. The Commander went downstairs to the kitchen to make some tea. John Thornton immediately stretched and sauntered over and placed his head in the old Indian's lap. I never saw anything like the way John Thornton warmed to Blind Charlie. He grunted in his characteristic way and leaned back. John Thornton yawned and rubbed his head and ears on Blind Charlie's leg. He smiled broadly. He was no longer barefooted, wearing laced boots, and wore the same red shirt and blue jeans I noticed on the train. I hadn't seen Blind Charlie since that day he boarded the train in Marysville, but I knew by now that he was York's grandfather, the father of Kenneth Joe Tracker. And I knew that York lived with Blind Charlie, not at home with his adopted parents.

He sat facing me, framed in the illumination of the window open to the afternoon. His face, as a result, was dark and only the reflection of my bedside light reflected off his red and gray eyes. Again, he didn't look directly at me, just as before. I learned he wasn't blind as his name indicated, but his eyesight was extremely poor, the result of some white man's illness he got from the Spanish when he was a boy, the scarlet fever probably. But that wasn't the reason he was called Blind Charlie. I learned that he saw with his heart and could see things I could never see. He was coughing this morning. At first he said nothing, just stroked John Thornton's head, and tried to expel some terrible congestion from his lungs and throat with repeated, desperate coughing. I felt suddenly foolish lying in bed.

When he recovered, he pointed at the two new pictures hanging on the wall, one a black and white drawing of me casting on the pool where I was trying to hook Esau. The other one, a painting in subdued colors, showed a coiled snake under the fallen log. It was the rattler, and I was thrilled by the memory York had given me. He had caught the tension of the scene beautifully with John Thornton pulling back and barking and me grabbing my white bared calf. I had missed the first week of school, but that didn't upset me much. I had spent quite a bit of my time just looking at the pictures.

Blind Charlie still wore his black hat. The feather, I learned later was from a red-tailed hawk, and was held by the rattlesnake band as I had noticed on the train.

Blind Charlie was old now and not in good health, as I saw from his repeated coughing. His Maidu tribal name was Too-Noo-Tar-Kee, "The Black Hat," a name he had inherited as a young boy by the Big Waters when a Spanish rancher had given him the hat at a trading post.

That was eighty-odd years ago now, before the Gold Rush of 1849, when California was a Mexican territory. He still remembered the trip—he was only four or five. He and his father had hiked over Carter Mountain, the mountain the Mill Creek Indians had always called Copper Peak. There he had met Yellow Eye, one of the leaders of the Maidu on the Yuba River. In the Maidu language, *Yuba* meant "Maidu Village." Years later, the chief, as he was mistakenly called by the settlers and traders in the area, would become call "Big Injun Mister." That was in the 1850s when Marysville was still a crude dirt street and a few wooden buildings. The white men called each other "Mister," he said in one of his drunken stupors, and he became the unfortunate butt of several bigoted newspaper editorials. The new Californians were quick to ridicule the natives. "Big Injun Mister," alias Yellow Eye, then slipped into perpetual drunkenness and Blind Charlie hadn't heard from him again.

They had stayed at Yellow Eye's lodge by the river, where the two big rivers of the feather met, and the chief had told the boy many stories of the Great Rattlesnake, of Raccoon, and of Coyote. The Spanish rancher had visited—he was a friend of Big Injun Mister— and the saga of the Black Hat had begun in Blind Charlie's life. The hat had been much too large for him then, sagging down over his ears and nose, and covering his eyes.

No one called him Too-Noo-Tar-Kee as the weeks went by because a new name seemed never to go away.

"Winnee-squee-a!" he yelled when anything new or exciting was going on in the settlement near Taylorsville, the "Yodawi" group. "I want to see, I want to see!" he yelled, running around naked, except for his black hat.

The tribal elders looked at him with the black hat down over his eyes, the hat he would not take off, and they would say, "Look at Tabar's son—he is always wanting to see . . . Winnee-squee-a. . . ."

He became known as Blind Charlie. Charlie was a popular name among the Maidu, and other California Indians as well, and now the two words connected gracefully in the lyrical patterns of their language. Blind Charlie did odd jobs around Endemeo for Uncle Martin but continued to live in his little cabin about a mile away where the old Tosi-Koyo and Ta-Si-Dum settlement used to be. The remains of the sweathouse were still there.

He was wearing that hat now, ancient and dusty and worn, as he sat near me. He, himself, seemed even older now. His eyes were red, crusty, and teary.

"Oooooh, hi, Jim . . ." he said.

"Mr. Charlie," I said. The Commander had always referred to him as Mr. Charlie, and I did the same.

"How you feelin'?" he said in his soft high voice. As usual, he did not look directly at me, but stared slightly away from my eyes. This, as I said, was a peculiarity of his poor eyesight and not a shyness on his part.

"I'm all right, I think . . . now . . ." I said. "York saved my life."

"Ooooh, truly, York, he a good boy, yes a good boy."

"He killed the rattler!" I said.

"Truly . . ."

"He saved my life, Mr. Charlie . . ."

"How big the rattler, you say?"

"About 5 feet long, twelve rattles . . ."

"Who get the rattles?"

"York, he cut the rattles off just before we took off on Meshuga."

"Ha . . . that big dam horse is no good. Your Uncle, he don't like that big horse. I be not sure about that big horse neither . . . he be gone to kill somebody someday, you jes watch . . . stay way from that crazy horse!" Blind Charlie said, raising his right hand and drawing a circle in the air. He did that often, but I never knew what he meant by the gesture. He smiled as he said this, and I thought it strange that a warning should carry his smile.

"But . . . Meshuga got me to Greenville so fast . . ."

"I don't doubt . . . you coulda get killed too . . . York he nuts over that horse . . . you know he get it from that crazy cowboy up in the Big Meadows close by to Tásmam Koyóm, Dutch Coder . . . no, you stay way from that big crazy black one," he said again, still smiling.

We were both quiet for an awkward moment.

"I like your grandson . . . York, I mean. What is wrong . . ."

"Yeah, ooooh, I hear it old Palawäiko, he say . . . you know, rattlesnake, we call them 'Chi-ta-ta-cum' and the big one, he called Palawäiko," he said ignoring my question, not allowing me to finish. Mr. Charlie was like that. He would become preoccupied with another thought and you might just as well be talking to the chair. I was going to ask about York's black horse when he interrupted me. I think he thought I was probing into York's illness and facial distortions.

I was about to ask about this Palawäiko and Chi-ta-ta-cum when my aunt returned.

Aunt Hannah, The Commander, burst into the room through the open door with a tray full of tea. Uncle Martin, Blue Song, Kenneth Joe Tracker, and York trooped in from behind. The Commander set the large platter on the table and served tea to everyone while they sat around the bed.

"Well, how are you doing today?" asked Uncle Martin. He had just returned from Engle Mine. It was nice to see his round bald head and protruding ears. I had grown used to his rapid speech and puppetlike face.

"Good . . . a little sore."

"Tell us the whole story," said The Commander.

"Ooooh, yeah . . . give us the story of old Palawäiko," said Blind Charlie. "Then I tell you more about old Palawäiko."

"Mr. Charlie can tell stories, Jim, but you won't sleep afterwards," said Kenneth Joe Tracker.

"There's more about rattlesnakes than any of us know except Grandfather," said York.

Everyone looked at York and was surprised at this outburst. It was unusual for York to say much of anything. He was as silent as stone most of the time. Uncle Martin laughed, but it wasn't a laugh.

"Jim, I guess you and York know the story of that crazy black horse of his and how fast you got into Greenville," said Uncle Martin. I think everyone else in the room thought the black horse was a hero. Uncle Martin's words hung heavily in the air.

"I don't think that horse is crazy, Uncle Martin," I said, feeling uncomfortable. York looked at the floor.

"Ha! The horse is crazy . . . I'm just glad you're alive," emphasized Uncle Martin. "Just ask your Aunt Hannah." The Commander ignored the remark.

"Well, if Mr. Charlie is going to get going on one of his stories, I'm going back down to the piano. I'll wait for Jim's story later," announced The Commander, breaking the silence and grabbing Uncle Martin's sleeve. She pulled him from the room. Blue Song and Kenneth Joe Tracker left the room too.

"It is not the right time, Grandfather," said York, alone now with Blind Charlie and me.

"Ooooh, I know it's not fall time yet, and I can be waiting—maybe we tell the story when we be driving the cows down the mountain. Then I tell about ole Palawäiko," said Blind Charlie. "Ooooh, you know, I feel the winter it's coming on pretty soon this year."

York nodded and sat down. He seemed tired and his breathing was heavier. I thought about Uncle Martin. He would be catching it from The Commander just about now for his remark about the black horse. No one talked back to The Commander. Then he would settle back in his chair and stuff his pipe.

The afternoon was still light, but in September the sun goes down behind Mt. Hough earlier. Downstairs The Commander began hammering away at the piano playing something I had heard once in church. The shadows would begin arriving earlier today as the fall approached. I looked at the snake picture hanging on the wall. It seemed almost real.

Blind Charlie, too, looked again at York's picture.

"Jes maybe, I tell you how that snake got there, how he bite you, Jim. I think I know all about that snake . . ."

"How do you know about Little Jim's snake?" asked York.

"Ooooh, truly, I know about all the snakes, about ole Palawäiko."

I wanted to say that I would like to hear the story now, but it wouldn't be polite to ask for it. The Indians believed it had to be fall or winter, especially night, before the telling of these legends could commence. I knew Blind Charlie was the tribal storyteller and that he was a medicine man, or shaman, of sorts. I heard he told stories which scared a body half to death, as Kenneth Joe Tracker had said.

Blind Charlie sipped his tea. In the silence, while we waited, the wailing of Canada geese from out across the marsh broke the tension and told a different story. Some animal, a coyote perhaps, was stalking the pairs of geese even as the afternoon was still light in the shadow of Mt. Hough.

Blind Charlie broke the spell with his coughing. When he recovered he said, "You come to my place some night. I tell you this story. I got it all in my head."

Chapter Six

PALAWÄIKO

Grizzly Ridge rose like a giant behind Blind Charlie's small log cabin on the outskirts of Taylorsville. There was no electricity, plumbing, or any other of the modern conveniences that were rapidly coming to Taylorsville in that fall of 1914. Most folks couldn't wait to get a telephone, although years later there were as many as twenty parties on a line. Much of the day was punctuated by waiting to hear your ring. Of course, you heard everyone else's ring, too. Long-distance communication came by Western Union telegraph. Mail was the reliable source of long-distance communication.

Mr. Charlie's cabin was built in the center of the old Ta-Si-Dum village. The remains of the sweathouse, all sunken with a partial roof, stood near the road only a few yards away. Children played there now, both Indian and white, running through the old remains, yelling and screaming, kicking up the dust inside, mocking history.

The cabin was tiny, not more than 12 by 15 feet, with two bunks and a woodstove. Simple shelving holding books and kitchenware. A large metal tank of water in one corner. There were two windows that opened on hinges from the top. On warm days and nights, he would swing the windows up from the inside and hook them with pieces of wire hanging down from the exposed log beams. Blind Charlie had built the cabin himself with the help of Benjamin Kurtz. Nothing more would have been done to it if Blind Charlie had anything to say about it, but Blue Song had put up some plain white curtains and set down colorful braided rugs to give the bare wooden furniture some company. One easy chair was all the comfort he could squeeze into the tight space, and another rocker was out on the porch. Blind Charlie spent hours sleeping on the porch in the summer. Dominating the center of the cabin, between the two bunks, was a large easel, currently holding a large oil painting of a bald eagle in flight. The floor showed the signs of spilled paint. Brushes, knives, spatulas, and containers in many colors occupied shelves over both Blind Charlie's and York's beds. Leaning against the wall were stacks of canvasses and large sheets of heavy paper. Drawing tablets were everywhere—on the table, across the bed, on the arm of the chair. A ladder next to the door provided access to a small attic where York stored his many drawings and canvasses. It must have cost hundreds of dollars to buy the inventory of art materials I saw in that small cabin. Later I would ask The Commander about this. She told me that some unknown benefactor in San Francisco who had seen York's drawings had provided him with an open account at a large mail-order house. York simply had to order the materials he wanted and the bill was paid. I considered this part of the mystery of York, but I could certainly understand why it was done—considering the wonderful work he had produced.

Over in one corner was a small table with a single drawer. Here York had placed a microscope, an awkward-looking monster of huge proportions that Benjamin Kurtz had obtained from a friend of his in Berkeley. Glasses, small boxes, and botanical specimens littered the little table.

Blind Charlie and York did most of their own cooking, but occasionally came to Endemeo to eat with us—usually when Uncle Martin was away on business.

This was poverty, of course. In comparison to the grand house Uncle Martin had at Endemeo, Blind Charlie's simple cabin was too plain for words. In fact, however, I have never experienced a greater feeling of "home" than I felt at Blind Charlie's small table.

I was there one evening a few days later. Blind Charlie's cabin was only a ten-minute walk from Endemeo. John Thornton knew the way, brushing back and forth in front of me, causing me to stumble. The night was chilly and dark, moonless, with a million stars in the clear Sierra. A coyote's voice broke across my path, so far yet so near. A dog barked in the distance, and I heard laughter down at the saloon.

Blind Charlie, York, and I sat at the small table under the light of a lantern, our faces three light ovals against the darkness. John Thornton was sprawled across the front door like a guard, and York had brewed a pot of tea. The three cups steamed up in wavy strands below the light of the lantern.

"What kind of rattler was it, York?" I asked, holding my cup of tea.

Although he didn't think of himself in that way, York was a young amateur naturalist. He habitually learned the scientific and common names of just about all the plants and animals he came across, although I wasn't aware of that when I asked the question that day.

"He's a *Crotalus*," York said. "It's here in one of my books. He walked over to a shelf against the wall next to his bunk, withdrew a large green volume, and returned to the table. He spread the book flat under the lantern. York and I stared at the black and white drawings surrounded by fine print. York pointed to *Crotalus*.

Blind Charlie got up from his chair. He was too old and stiff to stand up perfectly straight. He walked slowly over to a drawing in the darkness away from the table. It was another drawing of the snake, the actual working sketch York had made on the day I was bitten. Blind Charlie put his face against the wall.

"*Crotalus atrox*, western diamondback rattlesnake," York announced, looking up from the huge book. "Look, here's the drawing."

Blind Charlie returned to the table, and we huddled together, three heads over York's book of natural history. I don't think Blind Charlie could read, although I never asked him that. I was certain he could barely see the tiny illustration in the text and would have preferred one of York's grand colorful drawings to this fine pen sketch. We learned that *Crotalus atrox* grows to a maximum length of 5 feet and that he has a thick girth of up to 5 inches. Although the rattlesnake was only a blur before York had killed it with the boulder, I remember distinctly the broad head and narrow neck as it warned off John Thornton. York's book said that the neck was a distinctive part of the snake, that it was easily noticed behind the broad flat V-shaped head and the thick body. It made me shudder.

"Ooooh, truly, I thing I know all bout ole Crot-al . . . what's he name you say, York?" asked Blind Charlie.

"*Crotalus* . . . Cro-tal-us, . . . *Crotalus atrox*, Grandfather," he said. "*Crotalus* is the genus and *Atrox* is the species . . . we call it a scientific name . . . Grandfather," York said tentatively, not sure that Blind Charlie was following the scientific explanation. York looked around at me and withdrew into himself as he had done at Endemeo, momentarily embarrassed by his talking.

I was impressed with York's knowledge. Indeed, York almost seemed to lose himself in his enthusiasm for the subject. As an artist, York had learned the importance of biology and botany to his work.

"Are there any other kind of rattlesnakes?" I asked.

". . . Well, yes . . . we have *Crotalus viridus*, a dark western rattler. In other places we have, let's see . . ." he said, as he paged through his book. "*Crotalus oreganus* is another western rattler, a large snake, found in California and to the north of us," he continued. York gave us a whole lesson on the various rattlesnakes in the United States.

York doubled over in pain and held his chest.

"What is wrong, York?" I asked.

"Nothing, nothing . . . it is nothing," he whispered.

Blind Charlie looked away.

"Ooooh, O.K., we call his Crotalyus, yes, Crotalyus." Blind Charlie emphasized the last syllable with a "y" sound as in "yes." Blind Charlie looked at York. "And do you have the rattles?"

York, recovered now, produced the link of twelve rattles from his pocket and handed it to Blind Charlie. He then set the rattle down on the table in front of him. We were three faces around the table, a young white face with protruding ears, an old, weathered face, and a face shaped hard by bones and cartilage in all the wrong places.

We both listened as Blind Charlie began.

Blind Charlie moved his right arm in a circle. Blind Charlie spoke in his peculiar, clipped English, his storytelling language that heightened his Maidu accent. His voice rose and fell with the various tensions of the story.

"My mother, Jim, she be proud of that snake that bite you. She was almost bit by a big Crotalyus, too. My mother, she was name Hoo-Roo-Chook-Maragi, Needle Leaf. She almost stone Crotalyus one day. I was just little, more little than you, Jim, and I watch that Big

Rattlesnake, big Crotalyus. Needle Leaf, she come upon me and the Big Rattlesnake.

"She tremble all over like the leafs and lift a large stone . . . she walk toward me, toward Crotalyus. And she try to throw the big stone on Crotalyus. It remind me of you and York and your fish-rattler. But my good friend, Moon Man, he stopped Needle Leaf. And Crotalyus, he slide away into the night.

"And now I thing maybe Crotalyus, he come back for you, Jim."

Here was the connection to Blind Charlie's story. The same rattlesnake coming back. I knew that was impossible, but all things were possible with the story, and that is what Blind Charlie was doing . . . telling a story. Blind Charlie saw everything as reeds woven into one basket.

"How he come for you that day and what he do along the way is a new story now, Jim. The diamondback slide along the mountain, like a man hunting very slow. He goes with rhythm like the sycamore kelemi drum. Now, Jim, you get bit in the afternoon last Sunday, and I know you are out on the creek fishing. But, Ooooh Crotalyus, he come down long before. He is good at waiting and at being very quiet. He slide and slip under cover of darkness most of the time, under the yellow pine and the cedar tree and the fir tree. All along the ridge above Montgomery Creek, for you know he come down from Grizzly Ridge, way up there."

Blind Charlie rolled his arm, turned and looked at both of us.

"It is dawn, and Crotalyus is heavy today and he has gone up and down the slopes. He has followed the criss-crossings of the deer trails, the ancient deer trails, and now the very darkness of the mountain is coming into day. All is shadow and outlines and shapes. It is dark blue and the sun coming in the morning is begin to give color to all that is wild around.

"He stop and he look all around. Very, very . . . slowly. He has twelve rattles all strung on his tail and they curve up and he is very proud of the rattles. He lift his puffy flat head and look everywhere. He doesn't move now trying to listen like the snake listen . . . with the feelings inside him, for Crotalyus, he can feel all the little feet in the forest, all the leafs when they fall, and all the noise in the ground.

"And now he feel the bumping of tiny feet way off faraway but still he can feel it . . . so Crotalyus, he do not move. He like a rock, except his eyes, they move and they see everything when they get close. Crotalyus, he like ole Blind Charlie, he cannot see so good . . . he see just a little way.

"Crotalyus know something is very near. Soon the little patter of feet cross the path in front of him. Crotalyus, he has shining eyes. They burn like the fires so he know he must hide his eyes.

"He is listening and watching . . . yes, the little patter of feet and he follows the sound and the movement with his burning eyes. Then the large raccoon . . . what do you book say about Raccoon, York?"

". . . uh . . . *Procyon lotor*, Grandpa . . ." said York.

"Ooooh, truly that is very hard name. To the Maidu, Raccoon is Pha-to-toc-a, Pha-to-toc-a . . . can you say that, Jim?"

"Pha-to-toc-a, Pha-to-toc-a," I said quickly, wanting to get back to the story.

"So, as I say, Raccoon, Pha-to-toc-a, is come right across where Crotalyus is waiting and Crotalyus does not coil . . . he is still hiding his burning eyes and he being very, very quiet.

"Pha-to-toc-a comes with her four kits, not even 10 feet away, and then they quickly go away into the heavy deer brush and man-zanita. They do not know the danger for they have not seen the burning eyes of Crotalyus. Ole Crotalyus, he follow where they go until they disappear into the dark. Again they are just sounds in the night, just the patter of feet.

"Pha-to-toc-a and her kits have been on the raid again. They have been down to Uncle Martin's chickens, here at Endemeo. They are after the big red ones and this time they don't get any . . .

"Ole Uncle Martin, this time he get Kenneth to rebuilt the chicken house and Pha-to-toc-a, he come away with nothing." Blind Charlie laughed, and we also laughed with him.

"But . . . ," and Blind Charlie slapped his fist into his palm again, and we all jumped, "ole Crotalyus, he is hungry, too, and he is thirsty. He must take his skin off again and he know it is easier when he is not thirsty. Crotalyus is not eating for eighteen days . . . eighteen days! Thing how hungry he must be!

"It has been so long that he has come across something to eat. He remembers now . . . it was when he come to the little hole in the rocks and dirt high up on the ridge, way up on the Grizzly Ridge. The little animals were sleeping . . . what were they? Ooooh, truly, they were little Deer Mouse, what the Maidu call Jum-boom. Jum-boom.

"Ooooh yes, the little Jum-boom were sleeping in their little holes, and ole Crotalyus, he sneak up and know they are sleeping. He can hear their little breathing in the holes. He has very good nose and he smell the little warm, furry bodies down there sleeping. For all the many, many year of his life he do this, and now he will do it again. He will creep and crawl up to little animals who don't know Crotalyus, don't know when he comes . . . and . . ."

Blind Charlie slapped his palm with his fist again. I just about came off my chair, I was so startled. Blind Charlie laughed.

". . . He bite one of them when they come out to see what's there—poor ole Jum-boom, he does not know up from down . . . but soon he is going down, down into Crotalyus belly.

"And . . . so your Crotalyus is not so hungry. He is crawling and creeping now down to your fishing place . . . where you go to catch the trout on last Sunday.

"Ole Crotalyus, he glide like smooth over the broken leaf but he is going very slowly now, very slowly, because he is so full of Jum-boom. He find the oak leaf good to hide in because nothing can see ole Crotalyus in all the leaf. The leafs are cool in the hot September and he know soon the hunters will come here. He is here before and he remember that he need water from the creek. He will go down to the creek where you are fishing last Sunday, Jim.

"Crotalyus, he bunch himself all together and then push. His heartbeat is slow. He slip under the brush, all the pine needle, through the little bushes and down through the fern, the Maidu call Soo-la-la, Soo-la-la. He can feel the water running, the creek falling over the pools and rock.

"Crotalyus is go on new way today. He is never going this way before, and he travel to the east. This is all new place, new trees. Crotalyus is not afraid of this new place. He look around, everywhere he look and then come to the water. He cannot get to the water on this side of the creek, so he thinks maybe other side will be better.

"Ooooh, Jim, you member the fallen log?"

I nodded.

"Well, Jim, ole Crotalyus, he go across the fallen log to the other side of creek. He smell everything now, all the living things, and so he explore by feeling, by listening, and by smelling. He drinks the water and knows he can now take off his skin. Crotalyus does not like the grass bank, the pebbles and the sand. So he go under the log and wait. He crawl into his hiding place in the dark of the log. He wait there for you to come, Jim, only he does not know what you are doing there.

"Ole Crotalyus, he must wait now and cool down. He is hot and Crotalyus cannot be hot. His little heart is not ole Charlie's heart. My heart is big and strong and has many part. Ole Crotalyus, he has the little heart with not so many part and now he must be rest. Crotalyus must cool to the air all round him. He must be jes like everything around him, all the air round him."

So Blind Charlie had listened to York as he told us about Crotalus out of the white man's book, I thought.

"Temperature, Grandfather, Crotalus must be the same temperature as the air around him," said York.

"Yes, jes like I said, ole Crotalyus must be same temashure as the air all around him," continued Blind Charlie.

"And so he rest underneath the log and he wait. Along come Jim, here, with his fishing big pole. Crotalyus is coil now and Jim here he comes close in under the log. York, who draw pictures from the trees, does not see Crotalyus under the log yet, but he can hear the Chi-ta-ta-cum of the rattle."

Blind Charlie picked up the rattle off the table and waved it around so York and I could see it. John Thornton jumped up from his nap at the door and tried to wrench it from Blind Charlie's hand. We laughed. It seemed to grow larger as he shook it. We waited. Then he set the rattle back down and resumed the story. John Thornton lay at Blind Charlie's feet.

"Jim he take off his boots before he fish under the log and that make him easy to bite. Crotalyus watch as Jim get close . . . real close with that long fishing big pole. He wiggle his tail like mad snake now and still Jim, he keep on coming . . .

"And now that black dog, John Thorn-tawn, he makes all of noise at Crotalyus and Crotalyus does not like the John Thorn-tawn doing this. He look at Jim step on the grasses next to where he rests and . . ."

Here Blind Charlie lifted his foot and slapped it with his open hand. We both jumped again. John Thornton looked up into his eyes, and let his tongue hang out under rapid breathing. He must have known this part of the story was about him.

John Thornton barked. We all laughed and then fell silent again before Blind Charlie continued. I held John Thornton's ears.

"Hi-yi-yi . . . Ole Crotalyus, stab his fangs into Jim's soft leg. Crotalyus has bite man before and he does not like to do it. Now he watch as another man come. Crotalyus like quick get into his coil and wait . . . but the other man he lift this big rock and a shadow pass over Crotalyus as he lay under the log. The shadow passes over Crotalyus more quick than the rock and then . . . the rock and the shadow meet Crotalyus head at same time."

Again Blind Charlie slapped his hand.

"York's first blow kill ole Crotalyus and his eyes deep into the head. It mash all the stripes on his skin and break his bone. It split his tongue even more and the brain is pushed down into Crotalyus throat. Ole Jum-boom he come out all over the place. He is all like the mash of the Acorn.

"Crotalyus is gone."

Blind Charlie had ended his story and he looked at me, grinning his few brown teeth set along mostly empty gums.

"That is how ole Crotalyus get down to where you were, Jim?" he asked. He phrased the question as a statement of fact.

"I think so, Mr. Charlie, I think so," I said.

"York, you thing it is good that Jim here have the rattle?"

"Yes, Grandfather, I took it for Little Jim. It belongs to him."

"Good, then you shall have it, Jim."

He handed me the rattles and I took it in my hand. I wrapped my fingers about the cold, slick surface, but I remember to this day that I really didn't want it.

John Thornton and I walked home. The darkness spoke to me now. Crotalus was out there. There would always be Palawäiko. I was a regular visitor to Blind Charlie's cabin after that. Uncle Martin called it a shack, but to me it was much more than that. The cabin is gone now. It burned in the thirties.

Chapter Seven

SPIDERS AND BATS

Doctor Rutledge came to the house every day on his rounds to Taylorsville, but even though I was feeling well enough to escape the bed briefly, Aunt Hannah made me get in bed when he visited. He continued to worry out loud about "gang green." The leg was terribly discolored, but I still had it. His fretting scared me to death. Doc Rutledge seemed almost to delight in expecting the worse.

"Hope you don't lose that leg, Jim," he said.

I just stared stupidly down at his hands massaging the still swollen muscle.

"Jim Peters lost his to gangrene, you know." He told me that every day. The same story of the logging accident. The same man. I didn't even know him. I felt sorry for Mr. Peters and the way his plight was broadcast around the valley.

I didn't pay as much attention to Doc Rutledge's peculiarities this morning because I was amazed by Blind Charlie's story—it seemed he had told it as though he had always known the story. How could that be? That morning, while three of us sat in the kitchen, I told The Commander and Blue Song about Blind Charlie's talent with stories like that, and to explain to me how he was able to do it.

"He knows many, many stories, Jim," Blue Song said, as she sipped her coffee. "Some of them have not been told yet, like the one he told you and York last night."

"Old Mr. Charlie has wild, imagination, Jim," added The Commander. "Did he tell you the one about the snake?"

"He told us about Palawäiko, only he changed the name to the western rattlesnake's scientific name, *Crotalus atrox*, and the story

66

was all about how the rattlesnake came to bite me. It was scary. It was like he was there when it happened."

"Oh, Grandfather is like that. He knows all the stories, even the ones that haven't happened yet," said Blue Song.

"So he didn't tell you how ole Palawäiko got his fangs?" asked The Commander.

"No," I said.

"Well, you might just hear about Palawäiko and the fangs one of these days," smirked The Commander. "I've heard that one once, and it rose the hackles up my back—even me, and I don't scare that easy."

I looked up at my Aunt Hannah, all 6 feet and 200 or more pounds of her, and knew that she probably wasn't scared of very much. After all, that's why we all called her The Commander—not to her face, of course.

But that night, after a full day of studying science, geography, and a generous reading in *The Odyssey*, I found out that she was deathly frightened of a very small thing: a bat.

Of course, I already knew she hated spiders. The second day after arriving at Endemeo I found out how much she was alarmed by them. We had lots of spiders in our home back in Missouri, too, especially black widows. Seems like I was always on the lookout back in Randolph County for the "Widders." They often spun their webs across the doorway leading into the cellar. Whenever I would forget and run in to get some jar of beans or peaches, or whatever for Ma, I would let out a yell if I got tangled in a web. I knew it was one of the black widows. I would search frantically all over and brush it off as quickly as I could. If I couldn't find it, I figured it must have gone on down my neck and was at that moment somewhere on my back. I always could feel the itch of the bite and the tickle of its eight legs. I would run into the house and tear the shirt off my back so Ma could give me a complete inspection.

We didn't have any black widows in the mountains of northern California—at least I never saw one. But we had plenty of other varieties. One spider in particular, a large brown species, invaded our house in great numbers. Every morning I would find one of the hairy 2-inch spiders in the bathroom sink. When it wasn't there it was probably in the folded towel. At night they appeared in the kitchen sink. They didn't bother me any, though. They weren't poisonous like the black widows. I just squashed them and forgot about it.

Not so with Aunt Hannah, The Commander, I soon learned.

"There it is again!" came the shriek from downstairs. I wasn't used to such noises back home. Her voice echoed through the huge house, down the halls and up the stairway. I had been reading in my room. It was late and I was nearly ready to doze off to sleep. I jumped out of bed and ran into the hallway to listen.

"That big damn hairy spider is in here again, Martin! Do something!" demanded The Commander. Apparently, Uncle Martin and The Commander were downstairs in the kitchen.

"It's just a spider, Hannah," said Uncle Martin, sputtering out his words in rapid-fire succession.

"Godalmighty, I don't care about a biology lesson," spat The Commander back, "just dispatch it—it's big enough to name!" The Commander generally forgot religious temperament in these emotional moments.

I ran downstairs to join in the conference and see what all the fuss was about.

"What's wrong, Aunt Hannah?" I said, entering the kitchen.

"There!" she said, pointing to the kitchen sink.

Uncle Martin and I peered into the sink and there spread out about 2 inches across the white basin near the drain was a large hairy brown spider.

"Aunt Hannah, you know these spiders are helpful. They aren't poisonous, like the black widows back in Missouri," I said, hoping to ease my aunt's fears. Uncle Martin frowned and didn't say anything.

"I know it's no black widow," The Commander said, "but it bites. It crawls. It's ugly. Its sole purpose in life is to get *me*. Get rid of it."

"What do you want me to do with it?" I asked.

"Kill it!" came her immediate response.

I put my hand down into the sink and coaxed the brown spider onto the back of my hand. It crawled slowly up to my wrist, and I walked over to the door. The Commander backed away to the far wall, put her hand to her huge heaving breast. The Commander was breathing in shallow bursts. I thought she might have an attack of some kind, so I quickly threw the spider out into the darkness.

"I wouldn't do that for all the tea in China!" she said, almost fainting.

"Harmless. What kind of spider is it?" I asked.

"Blind Charlie calls all spiders Chop-pem," she said, relieved. "That's what I think we should do with all them, Chop-pem up to pieces."

"Blind Charlie doesn't kill them, Hannah," said Uncle Martin.

"Lord, he probably eats them for all I know," she said.

I learned soon enough that all winter long we would have those big brown spiders in the house. The Commander was always harping on Uncle Martin to do something about sealing up things better. Uncle Martin did try. He had two of his Indian ranch hands caulk and seal every room in the house, around the floorboards, up in the attic, everywhere. Then the men hammered down molding strips over the caulking. When they found out why Uncle Martin had dragged them away from the cattle to do these domestic chores, they laughed. Uncle Martin never knew and wouldn't have been happy about the way his Indian cowboys laughed and snorted over his wife's fear of spiders. They couldn't imagine The Commander being afraid of anything.

But nothing worked. Webs filled every corner almost as fast as we swept them down. Of course, The Commander had nothing to do with this. She always called on me or Blue Song or Uncle Martin, anybody who was handy, to get rid of them.

Now as I was recovering from the snakebite I became well-adjusted to The Commander's outburst about the spiders, but bats were something new. We had lots of bats in Plumas County. When Uncle Martin and I sat on the porch in the early evening and watched darkness settle on the valley, the bats joined us. I didn't think anything about it. They were part of life as far as I could tell. York would explain to me later how many mosquitoes and other insects they ate in one evening, but for the time being I rather enjoyed their graceful flight—outside.

It happened that very night. It must have been around ten o'clock.

I heard footsteps pounding on the landing outside my room. The Commander was screaming again and Uncle Martin was running after her. I was thinking how quiet a Sierra night is. It is really quite difficult to explain in words. You must experience it. In the middle of this reverie came the outburst.

I sat up straight in bed. I listened.

"Do you see it?" shrieked The Commander.

I knew she couldn't possibly be running away from a spider.

"I'm afraid to look! I can't stand bats!" she continued.

From the safety of my bed, I could tell The Commander was busy turning on all the lights in the house, lighting lanterns, and the soft glow worked its way beneath my closed door. Electric light bulbs in those days were big and stout. She had pulled the switches on the stairway, in the hall, and the parlor. Still, I couldn't see or hear the source of her alarm. But somewhere out there was a bat.

Ma once began a book about Dracula, but stopped when she couldn't sleep at night. It was Bram Stoker's *Dracula*. She read me some stories, too, from Edgar Allan Poe. Now Aunt Hannah's screams had a . . . *Fall of the House of Usher* quality. My thoughts trailed back home to Missouri, to books I had read and to stories I had heard about bats. Not just ordinary bats, Vampire bats. Did they have Vampire bats in Plumas County? I didn't know the answer to that question. Dracula was probably hovering over some unsuspecting victim with an exposed white neck in the moonlight. Boy, what Blind Charlie would do with that story.

While The Commander and Uncle Martin's voices faded off downstairs somewhere, in the darkness of my room I began to picture myself with two little red holes at the base of my neck. Blood was oozing out in two streams and down into one red pool on the white sheet. I saw the fang marks from Crotalus's bite in my imagination. The Commander was going to find me here in the morning dead and stiff. Blood, fangs, teeth, Dracula, wooden stakes, the hydrophobia: horrible thoughts danced uncontrollably in fleeting images across my mind. I pulled the covers tightly around my neck. John Thornton slept quietly at the foot of my bed, not at all disturbed yet by The Commander's commotion downstairs.

I couldn't hear The Commander and Uncle Martin now at all.

Had they caught the bat? Had they opened the door to let him out? Silence.

I thought I heard something. Was that just ringing in my ears or was it the sound of a soft, plump Vampire circling around the room ready to attack? My God, my window was open! I leaped from the bed and slammed it shut. I imagined that something had landed on my head and was clinging to me while I was running around trying to get it off. Aunt Hannah was coming back up the stairs.

The Commander threw open my bedroom door.

"Jim, have you seen the bat?" she yelled, not bothering to find out whether or not I was awake.

At that very moment a dark shadowy object flew silently into my room. John Thornton now rose with explosive speed to watch the bat. I dived for the covers.

"It's in here!" I yelled with the blankets now tightly over my head. John Thornton was on the bed now, leaping into the air and falling clumsily on me at each unsuccessful leap, pounding me into the mattress. The bed groaned. Soon Uncle Martin joined The Commander in my room. She jerked on the electric light bulb. Bedtime was over.

There circling about the room was a bat. I allowed the covers to slide ever so slowly down to my eyes. We all three watched as it circled about the room, always staying comfortably out of John Thornton's frantic reach. We just watched it for a few moments, three pairs of eyes riveted on its silent glide, mesmerized.

The Commander had a broom, but that paled by comparison to Uncle Martin's L.C. Smith double-barreled 20-gauge shotgun. I had admired the gun just that morning as it lay enshrined in his gun case. While she was swinging the broom in sporadic careless arcs all over the room in desperate, wild attempts to bring the bat to bay, Uncle Martin cocked both shiny Damascus barrels. Click. Click. I stared at the muzzles.

What in the world is he going to do with that shotgun? I thought.

My eyes swung back to the bat. Maybe it's the fur. I thought maybe flying creatures shouldn't have fur. Why was I so upset with the bat and so entranced with the bald eagle I had seen on Sunday while fishing? Maybe it's the shape of the wings. We watched as the bat dived, banked, darted, and navigated the close confines of my bedroom. The Commander slammed my door shut. I wondered why she did that. I didn't want the bat in my room, not with Uncle Martin and his L.C. Smith.

"Open his window, Martin!" she commanded.

My window snapped open again.

"Get out of here, you wretched beast!" The Commander screamed, swinging the broom barely over the top of my head, hitting John Thornton and knocking him to the floor. The bat continued to ignore all the threats hurled in its path. It also stubbornly refused to exit by the window.

Uncle Martin raised the shotgun and waved it around trying to get a bead on the tiny flying creature.

"I'll get you, you son . . ."

"Martin!" screamed The Commander.

"Don't shoot, Uncle Martin! You'll hit John Thornton!" My dog was leaping frantically from the bed trying to land his foe.

"*Shoot, Martin!*" commanded Aunt Hannah

"*No!*" I yelled. Aunt Hannah opened the door a bit and looked out.

We didn't see the bat fly through this small space and into the hall.

"*Get to the parlor!*" yelled The Commander.

I jumped out of bed and followed The Commander and Uncle Martin down the stairs, John Thornton following. We had lost track of the bat but assumed that it was still in my room after Uncle Martin had closed the door.

Downstairs we waited, Uncle Martin turning and circling like a big-game hunter. He was in his robe. With his ears sticking out under a bald head he didn't strike anyone as a menace with the gun. No sign of the bat. By this time, Blue Song and Kenneth Joe Tracker were knocking on the door, wondering what all the commotion was about.

"A bat!" yelled Uncle Martin. "There's a bat in the house!"

We all stood in the parlor looking around at the ceiling and walls. The bat suddenly swooped down just over our heads and into the kitchen. Back and forth it flew the length of the house while we ducked and watched in fascination.

Uncle Martin raised the gun and fired. These were low-power black-powder shells, not like the shells of today. My ears rang as plaster dropped from the far wall and ceiling in great chalky slabs. White powder filled the room as the ceiling sections crashed on The Commander's coveted blue Persian rug. I coughed in the smoke and dust. The room quickly smelled of cordite.

"Look—another one!" pointed Blue Song, plugging her ears and dropping to the floor.

"No, that's the same one!" said Uncle Martin, waving the gun across The Commander's breast.

"*Point that gun at the bat, not at me, dammit!*" The Commander grabbed the muzzle, pushed it up, and crouched behind.

The bat swooped down and across our heads again.

"Looks bigger to me!" I said, pointing. Nothing this exciting had ever happened back home. I heard Pa's voice. *This is crazy, Jim.*

Uncle Martin fired again. The explosion inside the parlor tortured our ears. A giant hole appeared overhead, exposing wood joists and wire.

"*Stop shooting, Martin, for God's sake—you can't hit it!*" shouted The Commander. "*My ears hurts! It's going to take two months to clean up this mess!*"

"I'm out of shells anyway," Uncle Martin said.

"*It's a blessing!*" replied The Commander, standing up.

John Thornton raced around the room, nose to floor, trying to find something that might have been winged by Uncle Martin's shots.

"There it is again!" said Kenneth Joe Tracker.

"Is that the same one?" wailed The Commander, pointing to a large bat heading straight for us from the upstairs hallway. We hadn't seen the bat go upstairs, so this was probably another one.

"Open all the doors!" she ordered.

Blue Song, Kenneth Joe Tracker, and Uncle Martin opened all the doors. We then all scattered to the windows. A dense layer of smoke hovered above our heads. We opened the windows. Our big parlor clocked chimed eleven o'clock. An hour had gone by. The Commander turned on more lights. John Thornton now sat by the parlor door, discouraged by his efforts and confused by Uncle Martin's shooting. He, at least, was going back to sleep. The entire house was awash with light now.

"Bats don't like light," The Commander announced.

"How do you know that?" exploded Uncle Martin, exasperated.

"They live in the dark, don't they? They live in caves, don't they? They only fly around at night, don't they?" She snapped.

We waited for another few minutes. No bat. Surely it had flown out one of open doors or windows in the house. I was tired.

"Jim, you get Blind Charlie to tell you about Bat-Man," said Kenneth Joe Tracker. In the panic of the moment, this suggestion seemed completely out of place.

"I'm not the least bit interested," said The Commander. "Why anybody on this good earth would want to actually hear a story about *bats* is more than this God-fearing Christian can understand. They are of the devil!"

"Mosquitoes are worse!" I announced.

"Bats eat mosquitoes . . ." said Kenneth Joe Tracker, smiling and looking at the holes Uncle Martin's shooting had made. Debris lay everywhere about the room.

"Yes, of course, the devil knows his own! Are we going to have another biology lesson in the middle of the night? Lord, it's a good thing York isn't here—he'd have all his books out by now and be explaining bats' feeding habits until two in the morning!" interrupted The Commander.

We all took that as our cue from the voice of authority to get back to sleep.

"Well, I want to hear Mr. Charlie's story, anyway," I said, and went upstairs to bed, followed by a now thoroughly bored John Thornton.

Soon the panic stopped, and from the silence of my room, I thought about bats, eagles, snakes, and rainbow trout in a crazy mix only dreams can raise. Life in Plumas County was good. Pa was right, Uncle Martin was crazy, Aunt Hannah is actually afraid of something, and I wished Ma were here. She would have found it a place to send down roots. Ma would have loved The Commander and she would have understood the bat. I wished Pa would get off his horse whenever he talked to me.

I was sad that Ma had dropped off the face of the earth.

Chapter Eight

LEARNING

I had fully recovered from the snakebite and would start school on Monday. The bat was gone—at least for a while. A carpenter quickly repaired the buckshot damage to the parlor, but the room still smelled of nitrate and sulphur for many days. I was looking forward to this last full afternoon of freedom because Kenneth Joe Tracker and Blind Charlie were riding out to work some of Uncle Martin's cattle and they wanted me to come with them. It wasn't just that I wanted to go—I certainly did. But more important to me was the thought that they needed my help.

The Commander, of course, had to give her approval, but she always did when she was calm. I was standing there in the parlor feeling silly with my skinny white legs shooting out of my shorts like Ezekiel's bones. John Thornton sat and watched. He had a way of hanging up his upper lip over a tooth. I could swear he was smiling.

"My lord, you need to fatten up, Jim," she said, as she carefully looked at my leg and scars where the snake had struck. She looked at my eyes, too. I don't know why.

"I think I'm getting bigger," I said.

"How do you feel?" The Commander asked.

"I been feeling better for days now, Aunt Hannah. I been doing the milkin', haven't I?" I blurted.

"Let's not forget your grammar, Jim McLaverty. It's not 'I been.' It's 'I've been,' you remember that now!"

"Yes, Aunt Hannah—I've been, I've been, I've been—I won't forget."

Looking down at my leg, I could see that the bruises were gone, but I still had the two small fang marks and the tiny hair-thin scars criss-crossing the wound where York and Doctor Rutledge had made their cuts to suction out the venom. I felt completely well. When I had passed The Commander's inspection and received her reluctant approval, I raced upstairs to get my jacket and vaulted back down the stairs three at a time and out to the barn to meet Kenneth Joe Tracker and Blind Charlie. John Thornton thundered his 80-pound body up and down with me.

They had three horses ready to saddle and ride out to the river. We had about a hundred head of cattle grazing down there about a mile away. We also needed to cut about ten calves from the steers and drive them back to an upper pasture for branding and castration.

Most of the other hands were cutting the last of the hay and storing it in two large barns, out of sight at the very end of the property around the point where a large rocky drift fingered its way down from Mt. Hough into the valley floor. I remember I was happy not to be haying. It was the hardest work we had to do at Endemeo.

This wasn't the first time I had gone riding since my arrival at Endemeo, but it was my first day of actual work as a cowboy. Kenneth Joe Tracker had selected a beautiful sorrel mare for my mount. I recognized her as Uncle Martin's horse. She was about ten years old and as gentle as one of the Missouri draft animals I had ridden back home. She wasn't one of those horses I had tried earlier that you had to maneuver with brute force. I came to learn that Kenneth Joe Tracker had given me these difficult horses at first because they couldn't be ruined by a poor untaught rider. This mare, however, had a delicate touch. She turned out to be my regular saddle horse for several months. Her name was Moon because of the nearly round star on her face. Kenneth Joe Tracker explained to me how to saddle her and to make sure there was plenty of space between the blanket and the withers, because Moon liked to be comfortable. If her cinch was too tight, or if the saddle blanket rested on her withers, she would toss her head wildly up and down. Kenneth Joe Tracker demonstrated how to place the edge of my hand underneath the blanket and the saddle just below the saddle horn to loosen up the blanket so it wouldn't bind.

Kenneth Joe Tracker saddled her once while I watched, then asked me to do it. Lifting the saddle high enough to get it over Moon's back proved to be embarrassingly clumsy for me. I threw it up there and it came crashing down on Moon hard enough to make her jump. The stirrup followed in a wide arc and slapped her opposite flank. By contrast, Kenneth Joe Tracker had saddled her quietly and efficiently. In my hands the saddle seemed to be all loose straps, cinches, flailing ropes, and four or five stirrups flying through the air in various orbits. As this mass of leather and wood finally settled down on Moon, I was standing spread-legged next to her on the left side. When she moved, she lifted her front foot and set it stiffly down on my boot. Moon weighed about half a ton, so I figured I had at least a fourth of that on my left foot. She looked around at me and I looked at her. Kenneth Joe Tracker and Blind Charlie looked at my foot. They both apparently wanted to see how long I would stay in this predicament. My foot was on fire with pain.

"Yeoooow!" I yelled. Moon remained stationary. First snakebite and now horsefoot.

I pushed on Moon, but she stayed where she was. She looked back at me again as if to verify the presence of such an inept rider. Finally, Kenneth Joe Tracker lifted her foot and I extracted mine quickly. That was my first lesson in saddling Moon. It took me quite some time to improve on my technique.

I hardly ever had to use the reins. Generally, I just let them dangle loosely in my left hand. I became overconfident and cocky, but I don't remember ever having a problem with Moon. For good measure I should have been thrown at one time or another. I had taken riding for granted—anybody could do it—and my vanity deserved a bruised backside. I would get that treatment, all right, but not at the hands of Moon.

I learned to transmit commands to her with just a touch of my hand or legs. She was a wonderful horse, trained mostly by Kenneth Joe Tracker and Dutch Coder. Heretofore she had always been Uncle Martin's favorite, but when he found out how much I relished riding her, he never let on how much he would miss her himself. He had just purchased a new four-year-old light gray Arabian stallion from a ranch down in Stockton. Sudan was a show horse. People came from all over the valley just to see him, and the *Plumas National Bulletin* carried a long story on his bloodlines. I know Uncle Martin paid a fortune for him, but the horse had been professionally trained as a riding horse, and he was a joy to watch. Stallions, I learned, aren't the easiest horse to keep, but Uncle Martin said that Arabian stallions can be very gentle. He would use the purebred stallion to improve the stock at the ranch, although as far as I could tell we didn't have very many quality mares. People said that because of his Arabian blood he would be an outstanding endurance horse. No one except Uncle Martin and Kenneth Joe Tracker was allowed to ride him. But Uncle Martin was gone so often that Kenneth Joe Tracker had to saddle him every so often just to keep him sharp.

All our horses except two were kept together in a large field that ran all the way down to Indian Creek, about a half mile distant. During the late summer and fall when the horses were worked more regularly, two large holding pens or corrals were used to keep the horses nearby. Meshuga and Sudan were kept apart from the others, Meshuga because of his unpredictable disposition and Sudan because he was a stallion. Meshuga was a strange one, all right, distinctly unlike the other horses, not particularly sociable, and preferred to be penned up alone. York kept him in a large corral near the cow barns. I could see Meshuga from my bedroom window, and I talked to him as Kenneth Joe Tracker and I went by his pen on the way to milk Cleopatra and Priscilla in the mornings. Since Sudan was in an adjoining pen, he often had his head leaning over the fence nose to nose to Meshuga. We wondered at first how that was going to work out. Uncle Martin didn't like Meshuga and was about to move Sudan to a special paddock. But eventually they warmed up to each other on either side of their fenced border, guarding their small countries like heroes, Sudan the pale gray and Meshuga the shiny black. I think that for all of Meshuga's arrogance he recognized in Sudan a horse worthy of his company, although Uncle Martin would never believe that. They were there for different reasons and had strangely different backgrounds, but each was a very special horse in his own way. I wondered how Sudan would fare against Meshuga in a race. I couldn't imagine any horse beating York's big Black in any race at any distance. I said so once to Uncle Martin at breakfast.

"Uncle Martin, I think Meshuga would beat Sudan in a race."

Uncle Martin was mounding one of The Commander's biscuits with Blue Song's raspberry jam. He dropped the spoon back into the jar and set his biscuit back down on his plate. Then he looked at me.

"About the only thing that big Black is good for is hauling York around, Jim. There's no way that half-breed mustang grade horse can beat my Arabian. Sudan is a fast horse, Jim. He's in the Book. You'll come to understand more about horses later on."

"I'm not sure . . ."

"Well, I'm sure. You've been around York too much. Just make sure to stay clear of the big Black!" he said with finality, going back to his biscuit and jam. Everyone warned me, it seemed, to stay clear of the big Black.

The Commander listened to this exchange without interference, but I could tell she disagreed with Uncle Martin.

Meshuga was much the taller horse, nearly seventeen hands, while Sudan was barely thirteen. To watch them standing in the pens, you would think that neither was particularly spirited. But if you looked closely into their eyes—there was something deep and magical in their crystalline darkness that was absent in the others. I wanted to read those eyes, to penetrate their mystery. Put a saddle on either of these two—they would explode with speed and energy.

Except for the heroic ride to Greenville after my snakebite, no one except York and occasionally Dutch Coder, however, could even get on Meshuga, let alone ride him. Aunt Hannah had learned a lesson about riding Meshuga. So it was a safe request for York to make: that no one was to ride Meshuga and he was to be left alone during his absences at school or with Dutch Coder. Kenneth Joe Tracker, however, led Meshuga down to the field every afternoon so that he could run. The speed of Meshuga was thrilling. I often interrupted whatever it was that I was doing to accompany Kenneth Joe Tracker down to the field with the big Black. We both watched him run. An hour later, Meshuga would be returned to his pen, hardly spent. It became a daily routine.

This afternoon Kenneth Joe Tracker, Blind Charlie, and I were riding lazily out to the creek. Blind Charlie's burro, Hercules, walked sluggishly behind us. John Thornton and Kenneth Joe Tracker's kelpie, Hamstring, trotted along with us to the road expectantly, but I wanted John Thornton to stay. Hamstring was a cow dog and would help us cut the calves from the herd. I was afraid John Thornton would get in the way, so I commanded him to go back to the house. With his tail between his legs and with a lowered head, he turned and walked away, hurt because he was second fiddle to a kelpie. Hercules did as he pleased, so we ignored him.

The gray sky was closing in on us from the northeast across the valley, turning the grand white cumulus formations so common in the early fall into an unbroken ferment. In another hour the peaks on Keddie Ridge would be obscured by the weather. It might begin raining, but it was still mild. The wind, which was gathering, muffled the sounds of the cattle, but we scattered some Canada geese and ducks on the way out, setting off a chorus of racket underneath the rush of air brushing my felt hat. The ever-present white-tailed deer, feeding in the timothy stubble like stone statues from afar, watched us warily for any movement in their direction. All three of us had on denim jackets, jeans, and boots. My jeans were the dreaded Headlight overalls. Were it not for my size, an observer would have thought me just another cowboy on Uncle Martin's ranch. I hoped I would grow up soon.

Typically, Blind Charlie said little, if anything, when he was riding. He was an old man, and he rode as an old man might ride. He was humped over the saddle horn and the way he cupped his shoulders reminded me of a man in some pain.

Kenneth Joe Tracker and I were discussing dinner—what The Commander was having for dinner that night. I noticed that dinner, in fact all meals, was an important topic in Kenneth Joe Tracker's repertoire of conversations on any given day. He was always giving me a complete description of breakfast, dinner, and lunch. If we had pancakes, then he exclaimed on the virtues of pancakes and how wonderful they were, how light and fluffy The Commander had built them. That was another peculiarity: to Kenneth Joe Tracker, cooking was described as "building." The Commander "built" a wonderful meatball tonight. The Commander "built" the best apple pie I ever ate. The Commander, she and Blue Song, they "built" a man's breakfast, didn't they? They understood just how to "build" a nice thick steak. It made little difference that I, too, had been there and had also enjoyed what they "built." Kenneth Joe Tracker would not be happy until he dramatized both the "building" and the eating of the dinner.

"Blue Song, she says we're havin' chicken catch-a-story tonight," he said, expectantly.

"What's that?" I asked.

"Oh, what . . . Jim, you mean to say, you don't know what chicken catch-a-story is? That I cannot believe. Why The Commander, she builds the best chicken catch-a-story that ever be built . . ." he continued.

"Yes, Kenneth Joe, but what *is* it?" I asked, interested now.

"O.K., I tell you . . ."

"Are you gone tell every toot and tot bout how they be makin' it, an how it be taste like usual, Kenneth?" interrupted Blind Charlie, not bothering to look up.

I giggled to myself, but Kenneth Joe Tacker didn't lose a beat. He launched into a long and unabridged report on the building and eating chicken cacciatore. We weren't spared any detail. We learned that The Commander always used two whole 4-pound chickens that Blue Song had slaughtered. It used to bother me some that one of the chickens I had been feeding I was now eating. Since I had the simple habit of naming all the animals on the place, I was afraid to ask Blue Song if this were Penrod or Dexter or Proserpine or any of the other dozens of names I had given the chickens as they were being fattened before butchering. I would not have been able to eat them if I had known. Aunt Blue used a machete to chop off their heads. It was a fearful thing to watch—the chickens screamed and the feathers flew, but the huge machete always found its mark across an old stained pine stump.

The chickens were cut into pieces and giblets were set aside to sauté. Here Kenneth Joe Tracker launched into the discussion on the virtues of sautéed mushrooms, garlic, and onions—which preceded the giblets into the pot. Although it crossed my mind to ask him what it meant to "sauté," I dismissed the thought for fear that this conversation might become a speech. On he went, expansive now with his hands explaining the efforts going on in the kitchen.

"Then we throws in the giblets and they get sour-teed up with the onions and garlic and mushrooms. And sometimes The Commander, she throws in some peppers and celery."

"What next?" I asked politely. Blind Charlie started coughing fitfully, and we had to wait for his throat to clear.

"Then The Commander, she puts in the chicken pieces to brown up a bit, you know what I mean?" He looked at me sideways. Blind Charlie had not lifted his head, but continued on in front of us. He seemed to have cupped his shoulders even more and humped over his saddle horn—more broken than earlier.

"Next . . . well after the chicken, it cooks, then The Commander, she throws in the tomaters, whole tomaters from Blue Song's garden, and then the olives, and then . . . uh . . . the herbs. The Commander, she likes to use lots of herbs—basil, oregonno, and rosemary."

Kenneth Joe Tracker pronounced basil with a short *a* as in the same man's name and "oregano" like "Oregon" with an added *o* but I didn't know the distinction in those days.

"Are you gone be tellin' bout the dee-sert, too?" chimed in Blind Charlie.

"I can't help it, Mr. Charlie. You know how I like to talk about food and cookin'," said Kenneth Joe Tracker. He called his father Mr. Charlie like everyone else.

"Well, I can't wait for dinner, then," I said. We all fell silent as the horses moved across the grassy field toward the creek. Overhead a red-tailed hawk was circling under the overcast sky.

I was watching Blind Charlie when he pulled up his horse and stopped. Moon pulled me up also. Hercules stopped and sat on his haunches. The horses' tails switched the mosquitoes off their sides and tossed their heads, aggravated. Kenneth Joe Tracker followed his father's gaze out across the creek. Uncle Martin's cattle were on the other side of the creek as we neared the rocky ford. Hamstring sat whenever Kenneth Joe Tracker stopped. That kelpie had the most alert eyes I had ever seen in a dog and uncanny intelligence. He knew exactly what Blind Charlie was watching, and he, too, looked in that direction.

"Mull-o-cum," muttered Blind Charlie.

"Yes, Mr. Charlie, I see it . . ." said Kenneth Joe Tracker.

"What is it?" I said, quietly.

"Mull-o-cum," repeated Blind Charlie.

"Mull-o-cum?" I asked.

"Great blue heron," said Kenneth Joe Tracker.

"Truly, ooooh Mull-o-cum," continued Blind Charlie.

"Where? I don't see anything," I said.

"Anything, Jim? How can you say you don't see anything? Look all around you. What do you see?" teased Kenneth Joe Tracker.

"Well, I mean I can't see what you're looking at, the Mull-o-cum, whatever that is . . ."

Taking my cue from my two companions I stared in the area where they were now looking. Still I could see nothing. I shrugged.

"You are look at everything, but you are look at nothing. Jim, you should look at *something* and not *everything*," he said in that quiet, peaceful voice of his. I had an idea what he meant. I knew Blind Charlie's eyesight was poor, and now I was upset that I, with my excellent sight, could really see very little of what was going on around me. I had no eye for the detail that Blind Charlie found important.

I concentrated. The first thing I noticed was how much my foot hurt where Moon had stepped on it. Then, forcing that out of my mind, I began to disassemble the bank in the distance. Against the tall blue, green, and yellow grasses I saw a shape begin to materialize—a greenish-gray shape, a large bird standing perfectly camouflaged in the creek. I had never seen such a bird. And now it impressed me with its invisibility against the brush and grass. It stood barely in the water on the far side, its long muddy-colored feet forming a wave where they broke the current. I now saw its dark striped eyes and the crown of black feathers that streamed out behind in a plume. The heron was fragile but in some mysterious way fierce, too. Even in its motionlessness, its eyes cast a devilish gleam. The great bird was looking directly at me.

"Ooooh, truly, Jim, you not look at Mull-o-cum before?" asked Blind Charlie.

"No, Mr. Charlie, I haven't seen one at all since I've been here," I replied.

"There be many of the Mull-o-cums in this valley, Jim," he said.

He told me they were important to the Maidu because they indicated how plentiful the food supply would be. Of course, Young's
Market had always supplied enough for everyone since 1862. If the
great blue heron did not become skinny and die, then food would be
plentiful for the Maidu in that year. In that sense the bird was very
important to Blind Charlie, even if the Maidu people did not live as
close to nature in 1914 as they had in centuries past.

Blind Charlie urged his horse ahead. As we followed, the giant
bird took flight in a graceful flapping motion. It was a silent ascent,
with its neck still in its characteristic S shape. Its long legs trailed
out behind as it flew on down the creek and across the valley until
it disappeared from view.

"Mull-o-cum be more important than to talk bout dinner, Jim,"
he said. "Ole Mull-o-cum, he tell us if we be havin' any dinner for
Maidu."

Kenneth Joe Tracker laughed.

"What he means, Jim, is that the heron tells the Maidu whether
there's going to be food for the winter. If the heron is skinny, we
don't eat much. If the heron dies, we are going to die."

"And . . . ?" I asked

"Well, that heron looked pretty fat to this old Indian. I think
we're going to have big batch of chicken catch-a-story tonight."

I was struck by how little I could see. I hadn't seen the rattlesnake.
I hadn't noticed York drawing me from his perch in the woods
while I fished. It had taken a great commotion in the house for me
to see the bat. Now I had missed the great blue heron, and it took
two Indians to show one little white boy what to look for. It was
all a matter of training. Blind Charlie and Kenneth Joe Tracker saw
nature differently—as if they were part of it. It dawned on me that I
was seeing nature as a visitor. What a fly-fisherman might I become
if I could see nature in the same way as Blind Charlie and Kenneth
Joe Tracker! Blind Charlie saw everything as part of a pattern.
Everything was part of a story. The great blue heron was part of
his story. Meshuga was part of his story. The bat was part of his
story. With a shock, I realized I was a part of his story. For Blind

Charlie, all of nature—the great mosaic of land, of trees, of water, of animals—was a seedbed of plots, some told, but mostly untold. He was the tiller of that fertile ground. Everywhere in nature there were countless stories unfolding, both peaceful and violent, both full of quietness and abounding in discord.

I had been satisfied with the occasional wild visitor to The Commander's back porch. Once in the very middle of the night when I should have been soundly asleep, I awoke to the sound of scratching below my bedroom window. John Thornton and I sneaked quietly downstairs in the darkness. I carefully raised my head to the window. There by the light of the moon I saw shadows eating apples out of a bushel basket on the porch. Even in the darkness I saw the thin black masks across the eyes of several raccoons. Cautiously I moved over to the open back door to get a better look through the screen door. The raccoons heard me and set into a low throaty growl. Two or three of them moved off the porch to watch me from a distance. The larger ones continued on with eating apples. John Thornton growled, but I grabbed his muzzle with both hands and firmly shook his head. He lay down. I wished the raccoon would come back in the daylight so I could see them better, but I knew they were nocturnal animals. I would have to content myself with these middle-of-the-night spectacles. Apples were spread out and tumbling across the wooden floor of the porch. What a mess. The raccoons would take one bite and then go for a fresh apple. The Commander would be out for blood revenge in the morning.

Early one evening I was returning from the woodshed with wood for the kitchen stove. As I stepped up onto the porch I saw a huge shape peering into the light of the kitchen. Stunned, I saw that it was a large black bear peeping into The Commander's kitchen just to see what was going on. Perhaps it was hungry, maybe it was curious. I never knew. So engrossed was this bear in the activities of the kitchen that he didn't notice me at the end of the porch. I froze, fascinated. I had never seen a bear before. Inside I could hear Uncle Martin blurting out a speech of some kind about work at the mine that day. The Commander was telling him what to do about it, although she knew nothing about mining. I thought, *Surely this bear cannot be interested in Uncle Martin and Aunt Hannah*, when one of the pieces of wood I was carrying fell out of my arms and onto the wooden porch like a pistol shot. The bear turned in my direction. I was ready to run when the bear beat me to it—in the opposite direction. There was a small overhanging shed adjacent to the porch that was filled with old buckets, a washing tub, and other miscellaneous tools. There wasn't a door on either side of this shed. It was just a continuation of the roofline and open on both ends. The bear could easily have avoided this jangle of junk and debris simply by going around it. But the bear decided on his destination and that is the way he departed. Into the shed, over the washing tub, through the buckets, sending brooms, shovels, and boxes of jars across the grass as he went. Everything in his way was trampled, smashed, or scattered as the large round bear blazed this new trail. I was simply amazed. You cannot imagine the racket his exit produced. Soon the kitchen was emptied of Uncle Martin, The Commander, Blue Song, and Kenneth Joe Tracker.

"What in blazes is going on out here?" screamed The Commander.

"Jim, are you all right?" asked Uncle Martin.

"It was a bear!" I said.

"On the back porch? Are you sure, Jim?" asked Kenneth Joe Tracker.

"Yeah, it went through the shed, knocking over everything. Why did he do that?" I asked, laughing now.

"Oh, that's bears for you. They go in a straight line. Once they make up their minds where they're going, then that's the way they go," said Kenneth Joe Tracker.

"Where'd he go?" asked The Commander.

"Out there, that way," I said, pointing toward the mountains that rose above China Grade behind Endemeo in the blackness.

We listened, but we couldn't hear anything.

"Well, Jim, you must have scared him to death!" said Uncle Martin.

I thought about the bear and the raccoons. There are some animals I can see. They just have to be right under my nose. But I wanted to see more than raccoons and bears on my back porch. I wanted to be more than just a visitor. I wanted to have Blind Charlie's gift. Sending down roots here was more than just being here. I was here, but Blind Charlie and Kenneth Joe Tracker's roots were down deep. I wanted to be more than a visitor.

Soon, we moved into the herd of cattle and began the work of cutting the calves. They weren't spring calves. Those had been branded in the summer. These were summer calves and were nearly three months old now. They could dart and run very quickly. But not fast enough for Hamstring. As Blind Charlie and I watched, Kenneth Joe Tracker and Hamstring went to work. Blind Charlie and I were to pick them up when the dog shepherded them in our direction. The kelpie followed behind the running calves, nipping their back feet and forcing them our way. In just fifteen minutes Kenneth Joe Tracker and his dog had separated all ten calves from the herd. We drove them back across the ford and on up to the corrals for branding the next day.

On the way back the sky loomed ever darker. By the time we crossed the road, the rain was a light sprinkle. At the corrals it turned into a heavy, soaking downpour, each drop exploding little puffs of dust. Soon the dry ground everywhere gave into the torrent, turning into dark puddles and rushing ruts of water. We hadn't brought our slickers and I was getting wet to the skin. It wasn't cold, but I was worried about Blind Charlie's cough and saw the water running in little waterfalls off his black hat. That black hat had to be over a hundred years old. I wondered how many times it had shed rain like this.

We didn't hurry. We carefully drove the calves into a large pen next to an overhanging roof from the barn. The calves looked at us stupidly and stood out in the rain when they could have moved under the roof. Soon Blind Charlie was throwing down hay into the feeding troughs and the calves, more sensibly, moved into the dry area of the pen to feed.

A few minutes later we had unsaddled the horses, stored the tack, and were having coffee in The Commander's kitchen. Blue Song ushered me immediately upstairs to change into dry clothes, while Blind Charlie and Kenneth Joe Tracker sat wet to the bone next to our huge Home Comfort cast-iron woodstove. When I returned to my mug of coffee, Blind Charlie was talking about the bat we had in the house last night.

"So Bat-Man, he been here last night?" he asked.

"Yes, well, we didn't get much sleep, Mr. Charlie," said The Commander.

"Yeah, he . . . ole Bat-Man, he don't be give anybody much sleep," Blind Charlie said, giggling.

Chapter Nine

THE BLACK HORSE

School days and workdays became one. My chores had to be done before school, so I was up well before dawn to help Kenneth Joe Tracker do the milking. Priscilla was still giving over three gallons at each milking, but Cleopatra had dropped off sharply. This was not expected because Priscilla had calved a month earlier than Cleopatra. At least Cleopatra hadn't kicked me lately, and I hadn't spilled any milk.

Since the cattle drive would begin in two weeks, York and I worked hard sorting out ropes, tack, and other supplies both before and after school. The drive would take three or four days over the Buck's Ranch Road, east of Quincy through Meadow Valley and Tollgate. Willis, York's round-faced grinning brother, came back from the Indian Mission School at the Rancheria to help move the horses to the upper corrals near the house. He brushed, shod, and fed the horses an extra measure of grain. The other Indians who worked for Uncle Martin, headed by Bobby Berry and Gilliam Scogg, were busy driving cattle the 20 miles down from Genesee and Lone Rock and putting them in the pasture near the creek. Bobby and Gilliam had worked faithfully at Endemeo for many years now, and they would run the Table Mountain Ranch in Oroville in the winter season. Uncle Martin wasn't moving the family down to the Sacramento Valley in the winter of 1914–1915. The Commander had grown too attached to Endemeo. She said she never wanted to leave again for the winter. Soon, Bobby and Gilliam would have nearly eight hundred head of Uncle Martin's cattle dotting the grassy pastures between the house and the creek a quarter mile away.

Both Meshuga and Sudan both were eager to go. Each regularly circled his pen now, jumping and cavorting in the enclosures as Willis brought the saddle horses near the barns. Uncle Martin always took off from his other responsibilities at Engle Mine to go on the annual cattle drive, and he was looking forward to using his prized new stallion on the 90-mile trek over to Oroville.

Meshuga was seven years old and in his prime when I came to the valley in 1914. Other than Dutch Coder and York, only one other person dared ride him: Aunt Hannah, The Commander. She only rode him once and Uncle Martin told me it was a "damn fool thing to do." She herself told me that upon finishing the wild ride, she yelled at York, between breaths, "*My lord, it was a serious mistake, York—you'll never get me on that horse again!*" That, in part, accounted for his name. There had to be a reason why no one besides York and Dutch wanted to ride him.

"He's a crazy horse, a lunatic," said Benjamin Kurtz, who preferred burros to horses and found York's big Black entirely unpredictable and dangerous.

"Meshuga . . . meshuga that horse is," he said, in his characteristic way of naming things—as he had named York. He explained to us that *meshuga*, in Yiddish, meant crazy or mad or demented. Up to now, York had simply called his horse "Black," but so liked the feel of the ancient word as it rolled across his tongue that he immediately bestowed Benjamin Kurtz's slander upon his spirited mustang. At first he called him "Meshuga Black," and finally just Meshuga.

The incident with The Commander occurred when Meshuga was three and will help to explain why York's horse came by his new name honestly. Old timers still call it the "Lone Rock Run." Uncle Martin told me that it happened on one August day in the summer of 1910. He, York, Kenneth Joe Tracker, and The Commander were working cattle up near Lone Rock, about 15 miles east of Taylorsville. The Commander seldom worked the high meadows so far from home, but she was an excellent rider who enjoyed spending full days in the saddle when the mood struck her.

They had packed a picnic lunch and were eating and relaxing under a grove of trees when The Commander took notice of Meshuga.

She knew a good horse when she saw one and got the urge to give the big Black a go. York was surprised and in his diffident way immediately consented. Uncle Martin, who never was fond of the Black, was unsure. But The Commander did what she wanted.

York never rode his black horse with a saddle, preferring bareback riding. He did use a handsome bridle with a severe spade bit, but he was gentle with his touch.

The Black did not protest when The Commander threw on her saddle blanket and stood entirely still when she smoothly placed the saddle on his back and tightened the cinch. She slowly pulled the reins back over his ears, while Meshuga looked straight ahead. He didn't appear to be a compressed package of dynamite. The others all sat and watched.

"Watch out n-n-now, Miss H-H-H-Hannah," said Dutch.

"Seems like a gentle horse to me," she said, placing her left foot in the stirrup and laughing.

But when she got on the horse everything changed. He bolted into a dead run, bending poor ole Aunt Hannah flat over the cantle. Managing to right herself, she was still helpless, even with all her riding experience, and the bite of a severe bit. Meshuga carried her beneath several cedars with low overhanging branches that she managed to avoid at the last instant. Later she would say that being knocked off would have been better than the pains she suffered later.

She yanked, she pulled, and she tugged on the reins, but the big Black ignored her commands. The Commander was a formidable woman, a force to be reckoned with in any other encounter. But to York's horse she was nothing more than an uninvited intruder. She wasn't Dutch or York. Uncle Martin jumped up and tried to halt the fleeing horse but had to jump out of the way.

York's horse then broke into a breakaway dead run—for Endemeo and Taylorsville. York, who was only nine, watched in dismay and ran after them, whistling futilely for his horse to return. This was not what he had expected.

The others mounted their horses and pursued The Commander, who by this time was going headlong down the dirt road toward home.

As I heard the story, the pursuers followed nothing but clouds of dust. They never did get a clear glimpse of the running horse. Some said he got too much of a head start. Others said no, it didn't matter. By the time they got to the valley floor, miles from Lone Rock, the Black had a 2-mile lead.

The horse ran the entire 10 miles to Endemeo in roughly thirty minutes. The Commander must have presented an unusual sight to the ranchers as she galloped at full speed past each house. People on porches waved. Farmers tilling the soil looked up. One motorist pulled his dusty Model T over to the ditch. Aunt Hannah streaked past. The horse splashed his way through Lights Creek, took a shortcut across Beardsley Grade, and jumped two fences. It was all she could do to hold on. Right through the main street of Taylorsville they galloped, past Young's General Store and the saloon. By the time people ran out to see the ruckus, she and the horse had vanished around the bend.

When The Commander arrived at Endemeo, the Black decided to stop. He stopped at the large metal water drum to get a drink. He was just as calm as when she had mounted him up at Lone Rock. She slid off the saddle. Aside from a little sweat and foam he seemed the very picture of obedience and composure.

The Commander was in terrible shape. Every bone in her large and ample body was shaking. She could barely stand up. She staggered over to a bench next to the corral and sat down. The Commander was not one to cry very much, but she told all of us that she cried then. She just broke down, as Blue Song came running down to her. York's horse, of course, was unmoved by this scene and remained exactly where she left him.

The others staggered in an hour later, saw the black horse by the water trough and The Commander sitting on the bench. She waved weakly and Uncle Martin helped her into the house. Soon York led his guilty black horse back to his paddock. Dutch looked on, uncertain of whether to leave or stay but decided to help Kenneth Joe Tracker unsaddle the horses and put them away.

In the days that followed this incident The Commander was able to laugh about it. She even spent time patting the newly named Meshuga on the nose. But she never again entertained any ideas about riding him. Blind Charlie once told me that Uncle Martin, however, held a grudge against Meshuga and York.

"I thing he gone shoot that horse," Blind Charlie said.

"That horse is crazy . . . Meshuga," Benjamin Kurtz said.

What went on behind closed doors no one could ever guess. The Commander set Uncle Martin straight on the matter and explained to him, no doubt, the truth that he already surely knew: that York and the black horse were inseparable. It was more than just important for York to have Meshuga.

Blind Charlie knew something else. He knew that Meshuga and York were part of a story, a story that was unfolding day by day—and not merely unfolding either; it was getting larger. What would happen next, only Blind Charlie would understand. He must have grinned about that.

I pieced together Meshuga's story from Kenneth Joe Tracker, Dutch, Blind Charlie, and York over the next few months. Meshuga came to be the valley's most famous horse. He was an unlikely hero among the valley's legendary cowboys, old farmers, the Indians who never forgot, and the miners and loggers who came here to work.

Meshuga, they called him, after Benjamin Kurtz's slander.

Meshuga was so black he shone, reflecting the brilliant blue sky. He was the foal of a storied mustang stallion and a tired gray-white Percheron mare. Olivia, the Percheron, was a 1,700-pound draft horse, popular in western France, used mostly on the Bacala Ranch for pulling Louise Bacala's wagon. Percherons have prodigious strength and stamina, matched with an unusual intelligence. Old Louise, nearing ninety, hated most modern things, especially automobiles, and besides, she couldn't bear the thought of not using Olivia. When she died in 1906, the finer automobiles were just coming into Plumas County. Perhaps she would have changed her mind if she had driven one of the large touring cars.

When Louise died, Olivia's usefulness was questioned. She had become surplus stock on the Frank Bacala Ranch. Dutch Coder, the foreman, was running a herd of horses over on the Smoke Creek Desert in western Nevada. His idea was to haul Olivia over that spring for breeding stock. He'd already corralled one excellent mustang stallion the previous summer for use on the ranch, and now he was intrigued by the prospect of a mustang-Percheron cross, particularly with another mustang—the best mustang out there—Steel Dust. Olivia was huge, but she was gentle. She would be easy to handle. But more important, Dutch knew that she had great strength and power. She was quick, too, for her size, but it was the brute power of Olivia that he wanted in her colt.

Olivia was twenty years old then. Her last foal would be Meshuga. The sire was no Golden Stallion or Great White Pacer or Blue Streak, one of those mythical beasts grown larger through countless lies and half-truths, but he was called Steel Dust by the Paiutes who lived in the high Nevada desert near Smoke Creek. Naturally, when they told me that Meshuga was sired by Steel Dust, I thought back to the stranger on the train and the long streak of dust raised by Ghost Horse. Dutch knew all about Ghost Horse, a white stallion, who was sometimes called Great White Pacer. Dutch told York the legend had gone on so long that now Ghost Horse might have been fifty. They both must have laughed.

Steel Dust roamed over thousands of square miles of high desert sagebrush with his herd of fifty to sixty mares. Supposedly he was shot one summer by a rebel mustanger. The killer, a simpleminded Bostonian, who owned two saloons in Reno, was wearing fancy Wellingtons with their low heels. When he fired his .30-.30 caliber lever-action rifle behind his horse's ear, the animal bolted. His foot slipped through the wide bell-bottom stirrup, and the crazed horse dragged him over pebbles, jagged boulders, cactus, and sagebrush to a pulpy, screaming death down the dry rocky basin of a Smoke Creek tributary. When Dutch Coder heard what had happened, he was furious. The incident had taken place near his corrals. He had planned for weeks to capture the famous stallion for breeding with Olivia. When his boss, Frank Bacala, told him about the shooting, Dutch asked not about the man who died, but about the health of the horse that dragged him to death. As it turned out, both the mustang stallion and the Bostonian's horse survived.

Dutch Coder was a wild young wrangler when he first came to the Bacala Ranch in 1899. Dutch was a mustanger, and he spent two or three months of every year away from the Bacala ranch near

Big Valley to round up mustangs. He broke the animals, bred them, and in so doing helped to build up the stock of the Bacala Ranch's workhorses. Frank Bacala was never convinced that Dutch's experiments were worth the effort, but mustangs in those days were not only wild—they were of unknown value. It was at least worth trying to find out how valuable they could be.

Dutch's problem was that he preferred to be alone, and mustanging is better done with several men. Dutch hated to talk, mostly because he stuttered. As a result, Dutch was considered antisocial, when perhaps he would have preferred the company of other men. Dutch covered this up with long months by himself. When he did run across others, his speech was peppered with grunts and groans because he never knew how the words would come out. Occasionally, he would complete a sentence and a thought without interruption. At other times, he stammered until he had to give up what he wanted to say. So Dutch had learned to deal with this humiliation by avoiding all talking. Then, too, his teeth were mostly brown, crooked, or missing. When he opened his mouth, he revealed five well-aired teeth, three on the bottom and two on the top.

In the spring of 1907, only a month after Louise Bacala died, Dutch tethered the old Percheron and several other mares to the back of his wagon full of supplies, and rode over Fredonyer Pass into Susanville. From there he drove north and east into the Smoke Creek Desert just across the border of California into Nevada. This was plateau country, high desert, under a forest of sagebrush broken by empty rock arroyos, box canyons, and rocky volcanic outcroppings, white with the droppings of partridge and sage hen. Jackrabbits jumped from virtually every bush and coyotes roamed fearlessly. In the spring, when the rains still dampened the parched white soil, the smell of sage was nearly overpowering. The strong scent so dominated this wild country that to define it was to begin and end with the gray shredded bark of the desert sage.

Dutch had built a small shack many years before in a box canyon of reddish-brown sedimentary rock. It was a fabulous place, quiet except for the afternoons when strong winds blew through the sagebrush. The wind howled, and tumbleweeds rolled and jumped across the desert floor. Dutch's corrals were filled by June. He had several mares, three strong mustangs he had broken from a herd a few days earlier, and Olivia and the other horses from the Bacala Ranch. He did all his own cooking in a low shack that seemed to blend with desert. The ceiling was barely 6 feet high, and you had to duck to enter. From a distance you could see smoke curling from the galvanized smoke pipe rising crookedly from the tin roof. For two weeks that spring Dutch searched the desert for the great Steel Dust. Several mustangers and miners that he ran across told him they had seen him, but he found only empty canyons and spring-dampened arroyos on every lead. He returned to the Bacala Ranch in May, leaving the Percheron and other horses in the care of a Basque sheepherder, Antonio, who had been a friend of his for many years.

In June, Dutch returned to a disaster. Antonio, in his broken English, explained how he heard a roar in the distance one afternoon. He saw a huge herd of horses on the horizon and had hurried back to the shack to check on Dutch's horses, especially the Percheron. Using a mix of sign language, Basque, and English, Antonio told Dutch that the corral was empty and the gate, broken. Dutch spent several days tracking the horses but without success. Dutch gave up and returned to the Bacala Ranch for the remainder of the year, convinced that the whole project had gone to ruin. But there was always the chance that he could pick up the trail the following year.

Through Dutch's dealings with Uncle Martin and Kenneth Joe Tracker, he met York one summer. York was only seven. Dutch reached out to the broken and grotesque young boy of mixed white and tribal parents such as no white man had ever done. They formed a unique friendship that lasted through all of York's life, but actually began a year later, when York became part of Dutch's plan to breed what he called "a s-s-s-super h-horse."

When York was very young he didn't like to talk much, either. So when Blind Charlie and Blue Song agreed to allow York, at the age of eight, to work with Dutch Coder the next summer, they had brought together two crippled, lonely personalities.

In the spring of 1908 Dutch took York with him over Fredonyer

Pass and on into his beloved Smoke Creek country. The snow was still 4 feet deep over the pass, so they picked their way along the rivers and creeks, through a difficult heavy growth of manzanita and black cottonwoods.

Maybe the Percheron was dead, Dutch thought. For two weeks York and Dutch tracked the mustangs up and down the sagebrush of Smoke Creek country. Dutch knew that many of the mares would have foaled and that the young colts would have difficulty moving at the speed that he and York were moving, day after day. The mares generally foal from March to June when young spring grass breaks through the winter freeze on the high desert. Dutch also understood that the mares instinctively know when they are going to foal and leave the herd to find some secluded spot, usually a place where the mare feels at home. Dutch knew all this and thought it probable that Olivia returned to an area not too far from his shack.

Early in May they found the herd. It was raining as they came upon a small canyon. Dutch knew he had found Olivia.

"I-I-I think we will f-f-f-find them now, York," he said.

The herd was tranquil as they rode toward it. The magnificent black stallion mustang was far off, watching York and Dutch approach. The horses milled about as York and Dutch drew closer to Olivia, but Louise's old mare remained calm. Dutch saw that she had foaled, a black colt, a large colt with gangly legs that stood rigidly braced as they drew near. The colt ran in circles and kicked as they moved even closer. Both Dutch and York saw that he wasn't going to win any horse shows with that bowed nose. So ugly he was cute.

"I-I-I-I be d-d-damned, York, lookee th-th-there!" Dutch said, pointing at the black colt at the Percheron's side.

York smiled as Dutch slipped his rope around Olivia's neck. They rode off, leaving the herd and ducking and pitching black stallion far in the distance. Perhaps it was Steel Dust, perhaps not. But Dutch said that he had never seen such a fine horse. He would go after him another day. As for the Percheron, he had been able to approach her while others in the herd had kept their distance. The stallion's dominance over Olivia had not entirely replaced her affection for Dutch.

The legend of Meshuga had begun. York and Dutch got the mare and colt back to his shack and enjoyed several days of the colt's antics. Dutch saw that he would be an unusual horse, but he had no idea how unusual.

Meshuga was now seven. Sudan was four. Their eagerness seemed wasted on something as common as driving cattle down to Oroville. I thought back to Meshuga's beginnings. I wondered how it would turn out if Meshuga and Sudan raced. I would eventually find out.

Chapter Ten

SCHOOL

I was no longer the new student at Taylor School. One other student, Ridder Burns, had enrolled after me, and I was grateful for the shift in everyone's attention. Ridder was a bully with a tough background. I didn't know it then, but Uncle Martin had brought Ridder and his father to Taylorsville.

I had been a celebrity when I arrived at Taylor School a few weeks earlier. The story of my snakebite had reached every corner of Plumas County through the columns of the *Plumas National Bulletin*. The retelling of the story had increased the rattlesnake's size to an impossible 10 feet. It wasn't just the rattlesnake. It was York's amazing 10-mile ride on Meshuga all the way to Greenville. The students had already quizzed York before I ever arrived, but York, in his typical way, said very little about it.

I was surrounded by everyone on the front steps. Heads and shoulders pushed in from a tightening circle to see. The first thing they demanded was that I roll up my Headlight overalls all the way to my knee so they could get a firsthand look at the wound. I was willing to do this because I thought their attention might be diverted from the dreaded overalls, which I detested. A pretty blonde girl with blue eyes came up to me and asked if she could touch where I was bitten. I just stood there, mouth agape, and said nothing. She was beautiful. When my rattlesnake bite was heroic in her eyes I should have had more presence of mind, but I just nodded. She reached down and touched the rough scar tissue and she sent a tremor through me I can remember to this day. All you could see then was the purplish holes and several scars where York had made his cuts. But these lines and blotches were the stuff of legend. At least in her eyes. I didn't ask her name that first morning, but she would sit next to me in class.

Mrs. Jesse Eldred, my teacher in that fall of 1914, was a killer. She worked us to death, but at the same time eliminated boredom. She was a stern old woman, ageless in the way longtime schoolteachers can become, with big baggy arms and a shrill voice. Behind her back we called her Mrs. Gray, gray as the old, oxidized metal roof above our heads. She invariably wore a gray dress with long sleeves to hide her flabby upper arms. A gray dress with a round white collar. A gray dress with a pointed collar. For variety she wore a gray dress with huge blue flowers. Her hair was gray, which she pinned up in tight, unimaginative curls. Even her pale face appeared an ashen gray in the subdued light of the afternoons, broken only by the rouge she rubbed on her round, puffy cheeks and the red lipstick. Her personality was anything but gray. Her voice trumpeted across the room. I can still hear the echoes of her high-pitched, scratchy voice as it bounced off the high ceiling with just a twinge of an echo. Her voice was red, full of energy and wit, as red as the lipstick smeared unevenly over her small thin mouth.

"Jim McLaverty," she would say, lifting her head in her peculiar way and looking down at me down over her cheeks, "do you want to grow up all crooked and bent over?" She always addressed her students by their first and last name.

She was a stickler for posture. Indeed, much of her day seemed to be marked out by periodic outbursts on the virtues of good posture. We were commanded to sit up, keep our backs straight, and assume a correct writing position for our penmanship. This was unfortunate for me because out of all the students in that class I was the worst offender. I usually slouched or bent over with my back rolled into a ball as I leaned over my work. Mrs. Eldred predicted more than once that I would be as crooked as a swan if I didn't improve my posture, that I wouldn't grow up properly, that I would never reach my full potential, and that I would have to endure a lifetime of back problems. The only frightening thing about all this was the thought that I might not be the flycaster I wanted to be. This scared me more than a lifetime of Mrs. Jesse Eldred's warnings.

"Jim McLaverty, you are going to stunt your growth and retard the development of your brain," she said. "And, Jim McLaverty, you have a good brain, such as it is at your age, so let's not be slowing its growth."

I bolted from my slovenly droop into a position of ramrod rigidity. But the pain of this awkward and uncomfortable adjustment gradually weakened my will to improve my posture. I finally sank back into my previous sins. If I was a hopeless case, Mrs. Eldred never let on. She seemed to take a regular interest in my well-being, and I learned that she had infinitely more patience than I.

For Mrs. Eldred, just about anything could stunt your growth. Bad posture ranked at the top. Telling a lie was a close second. Eating too fast was way up there. Not eating all your food was another. Even incomplete assignments had bad emotional and physical effects on growth. But bad posture was the pinnacle of infamy. It resulted in inferior brain development, sloppy penmanship, bad study habits, and poor grades.

I never liked the word "stunt" and I didn't understand "retard." There was something sinister and evil about anything that would "stunt" one's growth. Perhaps it was because the word rhymed with "runt," which I was sure described my current condition. When Mrs. Eldred first delivered these warnings, I shrank back in horror that my classmates would agree with her and that I would be the butt of their jokes. But as I looked about the room, I saw only indifference in my plight. Or perhaps it was relief that I was the target and not themselves. I saw students who shared similar reproaches for a variety of pet misdeeds to which Mrs. Eldred took a special interest.

She was born to be a teacher. She saw everything. She heard everything. I think she knew everything. Although the Taylor School was a one-room schoolhouse, the main room was large. In this spacious cavern Mrs. Eldred heard the slightest whisper. She noticed the most carefully planned movement. It mattered not a bit whether her back was turned to the blackboard, scanning one of the many maps across the walls, or if she was hovering over a student's desk helping with a problem. There were desks enough for thirty-six students, grades one through eight. The height of these wooden desks rose and fell like canyons and valleys of iron and wood from the worn oak floor. Some were close to the ground for the tiny first graders, while others angled heavily from their cast-iron frames for the older students. But Mrs. Eldred could negotiate this forest of desks and spy out any activity which she considered "an unwise use of your time."

Only sixteen students attended that year, and we lost two of those before the year ended. Miners left with their families when their fortunes changed. Gold mines opened and closed with disheartening regularity. Boom times when they opened. Bust times when they closed. By 1914 more mines were closed than open. The economy was rapidly changing from mining to timber and recreation. The southland around Los Angeles was already looking for ways to utilize the north's water, where the giant rivers plunged from the northern Sierra Nevada and southern Cascades.

The Taylor School was already old, even in 1914. It had been constructed of brick in 1863, and the corrugated tin roof was growing discolored. John Morden, who lived in town, made each brick by hand. The nails were pulling out from the wooden roof boards, the result of expansion in decades of freezing winters followed by the hot drying sun of the following summers. Now the metal roof lifted and curled with neglect. Inside, the wood-paneled walls absorbed most of the sun from the three windows on each side of the room, but this subdued light contributed to the general coziness I have always associated with the Taylor School. Outside a huge belfry rose from the front of the slanting hip roof. Mrs. Eldred let us take turns ringing the bell to begin the day.

Inside, Mrs. Eldred prowled the aisles like a sentry. The school still exists, but Mrs. Eldred would leave after ten years in 1924. Even so, she taught longer at Taylor School than anyone in its 127-year history. I was reasonably sure that Mrs. Eldred *would* live forever. She rarely sat down and only stood still, in one place, when she read stories aloud to us. This she usually did in the afternoons when we had completed most of our written work. Then, on winter days, when the huge Acme "Oak Leaf" pot-bellied stove radiated a hot wood fire, she read to us wonderful tales. My favorites were from the *Thousand and One Nights*, stories from the East, exotic lands that Ma had never told me about. "Ali Baba and the Forty Thieves" so arrested me that I spent one whole evening telling Blind Charlie and York the entire story, York for the second time, since he had heard the story from Mrs. Eldred with me in the classroom. Mr. Charlie, as usual, punctuated my telling of the story with "truly."

Mrs. Eldred was different from Mrs. Dovey, my former teacher in Missouri. While Mrs. Dovey was very tall and angular and bony, Mrs. Eldred was round and barely taller than I was. Mrs. Dovey was hard. Mrs. Eldred was soft. Mrs. Dovey always used a stick to punish us, a round ash rod about 3 feet long that she applied frequently and without hesitation to our backsides when we had misbehaved. Mrs. Eldred never punished us physically—no spanking, no paddles, no willow switches. While Mrs. Dovey needed to punish to keep control of the class, Mrs. Eldred seldom had need to keep control—at least I don't remember any problems in class, apart from Ridder Burns, a huge eighth grader who had just moved to Taylorsville from Chicago that summer. Ridder was a troublemaker from the start, a child in a man's body. But there was an air of authority in Mrs. Eldred that even Ridder understood. When she spoke, you listened. There was something magical in that high-pitched voice of hers, a strength we all recognized—a shrill voice of authority that took us and held us in its grip.

Despite my slumped posture and the lingering fear that my brain never would develop to its full potential, I was a good student. Not as good as York. No one was as smart as York. But I got better grades than York did because I attended to the daily ritual of completing lessons and studying for examinations. York seldom did that, only doing what he had to do to get by, mostly doing the work that held his curiosity. York was interested only in biology and art, in that order, although he had a passing concern for other subjects if they somehow related to biology or art. The Commander couldn't do anything about York's inconsistent study habits, but she made sure of mine. Between Mrs. Eldred and The Commander, I guess I was in a pretty tight place.

York was one of three Indians in our small class. The others were Tommy Peters, a primary student, and Gilbert Young, a fourth grader. I don't remember too much about them because they were younger than I, but I still can see York working with them, helping to solve math problems.

York, a seventh-grade student in 1914, was as different

intellectually from the others in that class as he was physically. York's gruesome facial features and heavy limp, in another time and place, might have given him a name like Quasimodo from Hugo's *The Hunchback of Notre Dame* or some other cruel label. But Quasimodo had poor eyesight and was deaf, whereas York had strong eyesight and extraordinary hearing. That October, during one of our last Saturday baseball games, Ridder Burns called him "Bonehead" when he came up to bat. He was facing York's blazing fastball, mostly relying on leaning far back before releasing the ball. Ridder hung his huge head out over the plate, the bright red cap looking silly on his mop of uncombed hair. York threw the ball right down the plate, and Ridder had to drop flat to the dirt to avoid being hit. York smiled at Ridder as he got up brushing the dirt from his pants.

"Strike one!" the umpire yelled, adding a second insult to Ridder.

York had then thrown a second strike and yelled, "You ever heard of John C. Bender? He was an Indian just like me—York Toby. He was big, red, round, and ugly. Great pitcher. He carried a knife on the mound, and he died before he'd give it up. You want the knife or the ball?"

The rest of us on the team didn't have any idea what York was talking about. I couldn't even hear him because I was behind him at second base. But he did things like that. He was hard to figure out.

York struck him out on three pitches, and Ridder walked back to the bench a different person.

York had grown up in Taylorsville and everyone except Ridder knew him for what he was, a remarkable boy with unusual skills. They did not pity him. He rose above that by his talent. Something "inside" him must have produced the pictures he drew and painted. Most people knew that it was a miracle he was alive and that he suffered from a congenital heart defect. Blind Charlie called it "a gennelman's artifact." I did not know it then, but York's differences were marked by two extremes: he was a genius, and his heart would not support what his active mind demanded of his body much longer.

Despite his physical prowess, York grew tired more quickly than any of us. He was warned by Doctor Rutledge, and a specialist he had seen in Sacramento added that he was not to participate in any sports. Blue Song was consistent in warning York about this, but she got no support at all from Blind Charlie. He seemed not to care. Inside, Blind Charlie cared more about York than anything, but he believed that York had to be given his life.

York would not have listened, anyway. He was an excellent baseball player, although he could not run fast enough to beat out anything hit to the infield. His limp was not the reason. He could move remarkably fast, even with this handicap. But breathing was another problem. If he ran all out for first base, he had difficulty recovering his breath. I had seen him more than once doubled over on the ground, gasping for breath, Mrs. Eldred leaning over him and asking the others to keep back. But usually he had learned to discipline himself and to control the level of his effort.

He was a pitcher. The same wiry, muscular arms that had thrown the heavy rock at the rattlesnake could propel a baseball toward home plate with unbelievable speed. He took a long time between pitches, breathing deeply and heavily between each throw. He had a jarring motion, the result of his crooked leg coming off the mound unevenly. The clumsy movement acted like a lever. He threw strikes, one after another. York's favorite pitcher was, of course, Chief Bender of the Philadelphia Athletics, who that fall lost the World Series to the upstart Boston Braves. But the Chief was on the mound for the last time in the Major League in 1914, and there never would be an American Indian who would win over 200 games in York's lifetime. York took an unusual interest in the World Series. After the Athletics lost, the Chief retired to the shipyards to help with the war effort. York lost interest in baseball for the remainder of his short life.

York liked to tell the story of Chief Bender's brother. John C. Bender was a minor-league pitcher who once pulled a knife on his manager during a game in South Carolina in 1908. No one remembers the argument, but John C. Bender stabbed his manager, not seriously, and was banned from baseball for two years. Later, he turned up in Canada for some little remembered team in the northeast in 1911.

As York told the story, "John C. Bender, Chief Bender's brother, died on the mound throwing his best fastball. For a pitcher there could be no better way to go." Outside of York's wild imagination, John C. Bender died in obscurity, but his famous Indian brother,

Chief, would be installed in the Hall of Fame in Cooperstown, New York, after it was established in 1939.

By the middle of October rain and mud put an end to baseball, and the days were growing shorter. By afternoon, the sun sank behind Mt. Hough. As Mrs. Eldred read stories aloud to us, we could rest our elbows on the desks, cradle our chins in our hands, and watch the sharp shadow crawl behind the sliver of light as it retreated from the floor and disappeared through the windows to the east. In just minutes the glare faded, and we were left in a gloomy unlit chamber, which sometimes enlarged the tale. The Taylor School had no electric lights or gas lamps. We relied on the natural light that streamed through several large windows, adjusted by the uncertainties of weather. On cloudy or wintry days, we worked in a gray dimness that perfectly matched the subdued tones of Mrs. Eldred's dresses. As the day grew darker, the subtle flickering light from the stove would catch my eye, and I would come under its spell. It was a marvelous thing to look up from our desks and to see green mountains, snowcapped in the winter, from the windows on three sides of that room.

York followed his own curriculum. Mrs. Eldred understood that she had a genius on her hands and never thwarted York's peculiar interests. She encouraged his artwork, sending him outside to draw and to paint. I can remember whole mornings and afternoons York sometimes spent outdoors following his own special pursuits while the rest of us labored over our studies. We never minded this, again with the exception of Ridder Burns, because York was not secretive about his work. He shared what he had done with the rest of us. Mrs. Eldred put some of his pictures on the walls as York consented. Others she stored in a closet off the front of the room. We had an outstanding library at the back of the room, filled with stories, biographies, and picture books. York spent hours poring over the books on science, especially those on botany and zoology. He was forever making notes in little notebooks he carried in his pocket. He must have filled volumes of those little green books.

"How come he gets to go out and do pictures?" complained Ridder, the first time York was excused from his regular classwork.

"That's the work I want him to do, Ridder," replied Mrs. Eldred politely.

"Is he too dumb to do anything else?" Ridder said, looking around the room for approval.

The rest of us didn't even look at him. York was a very popular boy in our room. We knew Mrs. Eldred would have an appropriate way of handling Ridder's sarcasm.

"No, Ridder—he's too smart! He's also smart enough to know how rude it is to say unkind things to others!"

York squirmed. He didn't like to be defended.

Everyone snickered. We couldn't help it, but Mrs. Eldred stared at us in that disapproving way of hers and we quickly went back to our work. Ridder glared at all of us. This was all very new to him.

But York was not my favorite person in that school room. Lucy Barr sat on that pedestal. She was the girl who touched my scar on that first day. Lucy was twelve, same as I. She was taller than I was by several inches, and this certainly frustrated my attempts to make her notice more about me than my now famous snakebite. Really notice me, I mean. I was new at this—I mean I had never thought about anybody, especially a girl, noticing me, in this case not noticing me. I was in love with Lucy, only I didn't call it that. I had been pretty upset with women in general ever since I read the account of Mercedes in *The Call of the Wild*. That wretched, whining female deserved what happened to her as far as I was concerned. I conveniently forgot the brutal and barbarian treatment of Buck by the man with the club. My disgust with Mercedes was tempered by Ma, The Commander, Blue Song, and the other grown-up women in my life, but somehow I never thought of them as girls. Mercedes I thought of as a girl. Now, with Lucy, my remembrance of Mercedes was rapidly fading.

As seventh graders, Lucy and I sat across the aisle from each other. We often worked math problems together, but Mrs. Eldred was a stickler for individual work during most of the day. I couldn't concentrate on nouns and adjectives half the time with Lucy's long blonde curls only a few feet away. To complete my misery, it seemed to me that Lucy was working without any distractions at all.

One of our subjects was Civics. During this hour Mrs. Eldred taught us everything she knew about government, the Constitution, and participation in a democratic society. It was during a lesson we had on individual rights and responsibilities that I first found myself in a real conversation with Lucy. Unfortunately, Ridder was part of our group. We three had been assigned to work together and to answer the question, "Can there be liberty without law?" Ridder contributed little more than a few grunts, but I noticed that he, too, was interested in Lucy. While Lucy and I worked to answer the question using our text, Ridder spent his time teasing Lucy and making me look foolish.

"That's a stupid answer, McLoverly," he whined, mocking my name.

"My name's McLaverty," I replied.

"Yeah, that's what I said . . . McLoverly," he repeated.

"We're not going to get this assignment done if we don't get on with it," interrupted Lucy.

"Well, what do you think about the question, Lucy?" I asked.

"We didn't ask you, McLoverly," continued Ridder. "Lucy, let's you and me walk home after school."

Lucy ignored Ridder, but he persisted. Not only was the assignment not getting finished, my stature with Lucy was declining rapidly. Or, at least so I thought. Then I did a foolish thing.

"Leave Lucy alone!" I said firmly, as if I were the most confident person in the world. I must have inherited that recklessness from Pa. This was the first time I ever really noticed that taking the initiative was part of my personality. It just happened and I was amazed at myself.

My left hand was spread out on my desk holding a sheet of paper flat. Ridder's movement was so swift I barely knew what had happened. He raised his fist and brought it down hard on my knuckles. Hearing the loud thump over the room full of voices, everyone looked over at us. I was sure he had broken my hand. Lucy stood and Mrs. Eldred came over to our group. York took one step toward us.

"Sit down, Bonehead," said Ridder.

"That will be enough, Ridder Burns," said Mrs. Eldred.

Bent over my desk, I was holding my left hand between my legs. Mrs. Eldred, as I said, knew everything that went on in the classroom and was even then politely informing Ridder, who was now standing, that he would spend another hour after school with her working on his unfinished work.

"I'll get you," he said under his breath, "Bonehead, too!"

"You will get no one, Ridder Burns!" said Mrs. Eldred.

I looked up at Ridder and Mrs. Eldred. The scene was almost comic as I look back on it now. At the time, my hand hurt too much to think about it. Ridder was much taller than Mrs. Eldred, but he knew when to shut up. He sat down and looked up at Mrs. Eldred as she stared down at him. She had a command over everyone, including Ridder.

Lucy walked home with me for the first time that afternoon. My hand wasn't broken, but I couldn't close my fingers into a fist. Several times during our walk home Lucy asked if she could see my hand. I obliged her request each time, if for nothing else to keep her from looking at my Headlight overalls.

"Does it still hurt, Jim?" she asked.

"No, not really. I just can't bend my fingers."

"You shouldn't have said that to Ridder, you know . . ."

". . . I meant it!" I said, with that same confidence that was really beginning to surprise me.

"He's a big bully . . . be careful with him, Jim," she finished.

Lucy had a way of pitching her head to one side as she talked. She told me that the vision in her left eye was not as good as her right, but that she hated the idea of wearing glasses. Before she finished high school, she would be wearing them at least to do her classwork.

"How old are you, Lucy?" I asked, already knowing the answer, but wanting to make conversation.

"Twelve. How about you?"

"Twelve. But I'll be thirteen in February."

This was not exactly a romantic conversation, but it was the beginning of our friendship. I told her all about Ma and Pa and Missouri and fly-fishing. I said I would take her fishing with me some time, that I had extra equipment. I was absolutely amazed that she was interested in learning to present a fly.

"What does *present* mean?" she asked.

"To cast the fly in a way that makes it appear real to the fish," I said.

"Oh."

"In other words, casting."

"You don't use worms, then?" she said, relieved.

"Never!" I snapped, too seriously.

"I'll bet Ridder uses worms!" she said, laughing, understanding immediately the low esteem I held for bait casters.

"No question about it," I said, laughing with her.

Ma had drilled that into me for as long as I could remember that Pa looked down on bait fisherman from his supreme perch as an artist in his craft.

"Ridder's a fighter, Jim . . . I mean his father's a famous boxer or something . . . I'd stay away from him . . ."

It was like being slapped.

"What . . . say that again," I interrupted.

"Ridder's father is a boxer, or was one, I guess . . ."

"Blood Burns?" I asked, shocked. "I don't believe it!"

"I don't know his name, but I don't think it's *Blood*," she emphasized.

"No, no, Blood would be his boxing name, of course . . . I don't think I really know his actual first name," I said, staring rudely at Lucy. "It's on the poster . . . his real name, I mean . . . I've always thought of him as just Blood. . . ."

I turned away. My heart was pounding at this new bit of information.

How could this be? I thought.

"Do you know Ridder's father? What's all this about blood? What poster?" Lucy pleaded, wondering what was going through my mind.

"Nothing, Lucy, it's just that I think that maybe Ridder and I have a common past—in a way," I said, trying to unravel my emotions. I wanted desperately to talk to this Blood Burns—to learn more about Pa.

"Where does the Burns family live, Lucy?"

"I don't think he has a mother . . . they live over at Donnenwirth's, above the general store. He works for Mr. Donnenwirth and has a mine out in Genesee someplace where he works on weekends."

Something extraordinary happened that afternoon, and we both knew it. What we actually said to each other in conversation took a long second place to just being together. For the rest of all my school years and college I would walk with Lucy Barr.

I had a bigger mountain to climb in the person of Ridder Burns. After I dropped Lucy off, I walked home and decided to pay a visit to Mr. Burns at the Donnenwirth General Store. I couldn't bend my fingers and they were turning a dark purple. But I knew I had to go.

Chapter Eleven

BLOOD BURNS

The world was changing for me with the passing of the season. My memories of Ma and the stone gravesites she and Pa shared back in Huntsville were fading as quickly as the golden leaves were blowing from the black oaks near the end of that cold and windy October. Pa continued to talk to me as often as ever, but I never told anyone. Blind Charlie, maybe he would understand. While others in my little mountain valley in 1914 were consumed with the growing war in Europe and President Wilson's concerns in the weekly paper, for me time was measured out by school and Lucy, The Commander's relentless lessons, my daily chores, long evenings reading books from our library, and tying new patterns for next spring's fly-fishing—and trying to live up to my pa.

In some ways time stood almost still around the parlor fire at Endemeo. It wasn't quiet in Europe. The weekly paper was giving more and more space to the hideous war that raged in France and Belgium. Blue Song and Kenneth Joe Tracker's oldest son, Walker, was there now with the Canadian forces. He was with a cavalry unit somewhere getting ready for a battle near Ypres. If there was something unreal and remote about the words in the skinny columns, the words in black and white that described the agony of the suffering and the noise of artillery, it was because even with my imagination I could not see or hear men actually spilling blood in the trenches over there. Not while living at Endemeo. We were too insulated from that world. Only Walker, whom I had never seen, connected us to the distant battlefields of France and Belgium.

My own troubles with Ridder increased the next day. He was waiting for me as I walked to school with John Thornton. I walked toward him, tense. I told John Thornton to go home. I wanted to talk to Ridder but didn't know quite how. My heartbeat was increasing by the second. I held my books loosely under my left arm. It was raining that morning and I carried the books wrapped in several sheets of paper. I walked right up to him and stood my ground. I seemed to be at least a foot shorter. John Thornton didn't go home but walked over to Ridder with his tongue hanging out.

"That your dog?" he asked.

I looked at his fists. They were doubled up and hanging tensely at his side.

"McLoverly," he said, "I have something for you!"

I didn't say anything. I just looked at him, determined to muddle through any problem the day would bring.

He pushed me. John Thornton growled.

"Ridder, I . . ." I faltered.

"Don't talk to me, you little . . ."

He didn't finish the sentence. I rarely heard vulgar language and his restraint seemed to slap me. He worked on my imagination. I could supply my own word.

He tried to punch me in the stomach, but I blocked him with my books, moving my left arm upward. I had never been in a fistfight, and I was finding my own way.

John Thornton grabbed Ridder's pants and part of his leg, too. Infuriated, he swung wildly with his right hand and caught me on the forehead as I pulled back. He ignored John Thornton completely. For all of John Thornton's weight, he couldn't hold on to Ridder.

I dropped my books. He missed several more times, swinging at me as I moved backwards. I had no idea what I was doing at all, but I realized that I was much quicker than Ridder. Several students had come up to us by this time, had grabbed John Thornton, and were shouting at Ridder to stop. I turned to see who was behind me and then turned quickly back. Ridder hit me squarely in the middle of my face. I felt the bones in his knuckles splatter my nose with a sickening dull thwack, sort of like a hammer falling on the end of a log. I fell down, trying to hold my face together. I thought I was coming apart.

He stood over me then, fists doubled up and sneered. I looked up at him—standing there in the rain with his bushy hair flattened by the downpour. I looked down at the dripping of blood discoloring the tiny puddles in the gravel.

"That's for yesterday!" He looked up at the others. I thought it strange that he didn't hit me again. And then he did something very strange. He turned away quickly and walked away, but he was heaving and shaking. I was sure he was upset, trying to keep from crying. But I wouldn't know because he was gone.

My nose was bleeding worse now and I was sure it was broken, so I walked on back home with John Thornton to The Commander and Blue Song. Some of my school friends wanted to help me, but I said no. It hurt to walk too fast. Even the slight jarring up-and-down motion of walking sent shocks of pain up my nose and between my eyes. Blood was running down around the edges of my mouth and dripping onto my freshly ironed shirt. But I was determined to go to school just to show Ridder that I was tough, too. The Commander took one quick look at me and drove me into Greenville to see Doctor Rutledge.

"How'd this happen?" she asked as we bumped along the road.

"Ridder," I mumbled, holding my nose under a towel.

"Who?" she demanded.

I didn't want to talk about it, but she finally managed to drag the story bit by bit out of me.

"You know, your uncle Martin brought that boy and his father to Taylorsville," she went on, looking at me sideways.

"Uncle Martin?" I responded, surprised by anything now.

"Yes, your uncle Martin has known Burns for many years. He was a friend of your father's, you know . . ."

"I know."

"Well, your uncle will tell you the story sometime. I'm sorry this has happened," she added. She seemed to be crying.

"You're keeping me in business, Mr. McLaverty," Doctor Rutledge said when he saw me. "What now?"

He said there wasn't much he could do about a broken nose except to put some white adhesive tape across the bridge to keep it from sliding crookedly across my face.

The Commander was not happy about this. If she had had her

way, she would have stomped into the classroom, grabbed Ridder by the ear, and trooped out with him in tow. But The Commander didn't want her way. She knew I had to solve the problem for myself, and she understood things about the Burnses that she had learned from Uncle Martin. I was grateful to The Commander that she had the wisdom to see it that way, and inside I could barely conceal a growing excitement in learning more about Pa.

I walked into the classroom later that morning, once again the center of attention for wounds I had suffered. Lucy looked over at me as I took my seat and concern lined her face. I will never forget the feeling of satisfaction I had as I bravely started my work. Mrs. Eldred interrupted her lesson in composition to wish me a good morning.

"Good morning, Jim McLaverty. I'm so glad you could join us," she said, smiling.

I just nodded. I noticed a peculiar difficulty in swallowing and a dull pain across my cheekbones. My eyes were already deeply recessed in two puffy blue caves. I could glance out and down from these swollen caverns and look across a dark bridge between heavily bruised cheeks. I was in no sight able to impress Lucy, and my headache throbbed so badly that I didn't care anyway.

Doctor Rutledge had given me some pills to ease the pain, but they didn't seem to help much. Ridder wouldn't look at me, although I tried to gain his attention. He didn't find much to gloat about. In fact, he seemed angry that I came to school and captured everyone's sympathy. Then Ridder did the unexpected: he wept. He covered his face with his arms and lay his head on the desk. We all knew that Ridder's life was different from ours, and I learned that day that a broken nose was a small price to pay. Something worse than that was hurting Ridder Burns.

After school I took a tube from the wardrobe, unrolled Pa's poster advertising his fight with Blood Burns in Chicago in 1904, and tacked it to my bedroom wall. I hadn't looked at it for months now. I studied every detail. It was a colorful poster with a bright red band around its borders over a white face. Large block letters in blue announced the main event at the top. Underneath the box in layers of increasingly smaller letters the preliminary fighters were listed. But Pa's name was headlined at the top along with Blood Burns's:

EXHIBITION MATCH
MAIN EVENT
Sponsored by the Police Athletic League

Timothy "Bronco" McLaverty
Huntsville, Missouri
UNDEFEATED IN 39 AMATEUR FIGHTS
160 Pound Middleweight

vs.

Geoffrey "Blood" Burns
Chicago, Illinois
UNDEFEATED IN 15 PROFESSIONAL FIGHTS
198 Pound Heavyweight

As I stared at the names, I realized that Ma had been wrong. Pa had turned professional in this one fight. For the first time I began to think that this was the fight that caused Pa to stop fighting. Pa had died of a ruptured appendix or ruptured something a few weeks after his fight with Burns. He never fought again after he met Geoffrey "Blood" Burns. Why? My emotions were all tangled now, and inside I was eaten up by a desire to know.

I finished my afternoon chores early because Kenneth Joe Tracker figured I wouldn't be in any shape to do the milking. Kenneth Joe Tracker was like that, always quietly thoughtful.

"What do you think you're doin', Jim?" he said. "I'll finish up your work out here. You go on now."

I told Kenneth Joe Tracker where I was going and why and to tell The Commander to keep my dinner in the oven. I would be back late.

I took Pa's poster off the wall, rolled it up under my arm, and walked down to Donnenwirth's General Store. John Thornton came along for the walk as always. I told John Thornton that I had no idea how I would approach Mr. Burns, but I was gathering my courage along with my wits as I neared town. Trotting along beside me, his nose to the ground, John Thornton looked up at me repeatedly as if he understood. For some reason that I didn't at all understand, I was no longer afraid of Ridder. When Ridder had wept in the classroom that afternoon, I knew his pain was worse than mine. I didn't fully realize it yet, but there was something in Ridder's life that drew me to it, to make things fit.

The Burnses lived upstairs, and I could reach their rooms either from inside the store, up the wooden stairs to a horseshoe-shaped mezzanine—where Donnenwirth's displayed long lines of clothing on racks—or from a set of narrow stairs behind the building.

I looked in the window to see who was working the store behind the counter. I saw Mrs. Donnenwirth and no one else. The store would be closing soon. Maybe Mr. Burns was through for the day and was upstairs. John Thornton and I walked around the back. I knew Mrs. Donnenwirth wouldn't appreciate John Thornton in the store and, besides, I didn't want anybody else to see the frightful condition of my swollen face. And I knew I wanted John Thornton with me when I saw Mr. Burns.

A spiral of smoke poured out of their brick chimney, so I figured someone was home. I knocked on the door, and after a short delay the door opened, and I looked up at Ridder.

He didn't say anything. He just stared at me and I back at him for several seconds.

"Hello, Ridder."

He just stared at me.

"Ridder, I'd like to talk to your father . . ." I said quickly and firmly, although my voice sounded sandy and hollow inside my crushed nasal passages. John Thornton looked up at Ridder and whined.

"No . . ."

"I mean, I think I know your father . . . I don't exactly know him, but my pa, he knew him, I mean . . ." I tried to explain.

He didn't reply. He seemed to be frozen in place.

"I know you don't like me, Ridder . . . but if I could just see your father . . . it's not about this." I pointed to my face.

From the inside a voice bellowed, "Ridder, who's ever at the door don't wanna stand on that tiny landin' out there. Don't you know nothin', *ask 'im in*!"

With a start, Ridder moved aside to let me in. He did not talk. I walked slowly past Ridder and I noticed that he kept the door open so that John Thornton could come in, too. The terrible Blood Burns was sitting in a chair next to a kitchen table. I don't know what I expected exactly, but I was definitely not ready to deal with the "Mr. Burns" who sat a few feet away from me.

Geoffrey "Blood" Burns wore a black patch over one eye and his left arm dangled nearly uselessly at his side. As he got up to greet me, he reached across to his left arm and moved it off his knee. It was a graceful movement, something he had done thousands of times before. But I thought this huge, now gaunt, and hurting man could not have been the heavyweight fighter who was the stuff of legend and myth in my imagination.

"Dad, this is Jim, Jim McLa . . ."

"McLaverty, Jim McLaverty," I finished.

Blood Burns walked stiffly over to me and shook hands with me, all the time looking me over. His one healthy eye was a brilliant blue. It seemed to radiate energy, even now with his obvious handicap.

"And where are you from, Jim McLaverty?" he asked with the beginning of a smile forming on his puffy red face.

Ridder sat down and rubbed John Thornton's forgiving head.

"Missouri . . . Huntsville . . . we had a farm in Randolph County," I said. "Been here since August. My ma died of influenza in the epidemic back east this past summer. I live with my uncle Martin now and Aunt Hannah about a mile west of here just below Mt. Hough . . . at a place called Endemeo."

"I know the place. Beautiful spot. We only been here a couple months ourselves," he said. "We come from Chicago. I worked at odd jobs back there. Sometimes gardenin', sometimes storekeepin'. I can do quite a bit with this useless arm of mine. I can move my fingers, but I can't move the arm much . . . Sorry about your ma . . . uh, you didn't tell me about your pa."

"Mr. Burns, that's what I came to ask you about. I think maybe you knew Pa better than I did. My pa's Tim McLaverty."

Blood Burns paused, seemed lost in thought for a few moments, and looked down.

Then looking up he said, "I know, Jim. I knew it when Ridder here started sayin' your name. Your uncle Martin and I have known each other for years. It's a long story about the death of your pa and Martin's interest in boxing. He's helped me out many times over the years, and now he found me this job here in Taylorsville. I think, maybe, it's 'cuz of you, but I didn't know it till now.

"Like I say I coulda said your name if you hadn't said it first. I knew it even with the bruises and your swelled-up nose. I once saw your pa with a face like that. Ha, it's like a miracle! You're just exactly the image uh Tim."

Ridder was confused. He looked from me to his dad. He knew something uncommon was happening for his father, so he probably wanted to keep quiet and continue stroking John Thornton, who was closing his eyes in that ecstatic doggie way of his when he was getting the treatment he felt he deserved. Suddenly, Ridder jumped up.

"Dad, I did it. I mean, I beat up Jim . . . I did it to him . . . I broke his nose. I'm sorry now I done it. I . . . I . . ."

"Yeah, well now I already figured that out for myself, Ridder," Mr. Burns interrupted, "but that don't matter now, does it? Just sit down." He looked at Ridder and back at me. "But I'm proud of you, boy, for up and tellin' me about it without me havin' to ask you."

Mr. Burns asked me to sit down and I unrolled the poster and spread it across the table. We put unopened tin cans down on the corners to keep it from curling. He took the patch off his eye and I saw that the eye was dull and dead below a fallen lid lapping half of its blue pupil. Ridder came over to sit with us around the table and looked at the poster.

"I can see just a little bit with this bad eye. I can't look at nothin' with than patch on, but I don't like to make folks feel uncomfortable. It's not very pretty to look at."

I didn't reply.

"Look at that, Ridder!" He said, admiring the poster. "I used to have one of these. Lost it years ago!"

"That's you and Jim's dad?" Ridder said, amazed.

"Will you tell us about it, Mr. Burns?" I asked. "I never knew my pa. I was only two when he died. But I know that he never fought again after he fought you. He died in March of that year. When was the fight? I mean there were only two months before he died. What happened?"

"You say your pa died that March?" Blood Burns bowed and shook his head. "Well, that explains it."

"What?" I asked, swallowing hard.

"I wondered why I never saw your pa again after he brought me the money. I wrote to your ma. Course she told me he died, but I didn't get the letter until late that year. Months had gone on by. I didn't know it happened so suddenly. What a shame, what a shame."

Blood Burns lived in his own thoughts for a few moments. Then he resumed.

"Jim, your pa and I fought against our wishes. We were friends. I don't know if Charlotte told you about that or not. We had knowed each other for many years during our A.A.U. days. That's the Amateur Athletic Union. It was just started a few years before, and your Pa was whuppin' everybody in sight in the middleweight class. We got to know each other in a big tournament in St. Louis. I was winnin' in the heavies, so I turned pro. Not your pa. Your pa was different. He was always havin' ideas in his head. There was always a right way and a wrong way to do anything, and your pa was a great one for always wantin' to do the right thing. He thought professional boxing was brutal with the small gloves and the fifteen rounds and what have you. The pros was usin' the Queensberry Rules, which softed things up a bit, but it was still pretty ugly."

I didn't want to interrupt. This was a story that Ma never told me and it was filling in some big gaps for me.

"Well then, after a while most everyone was wantin' Tim and me to get into the ring together. We was both undefeated. Course I was a lot bigger than your pa. I was a heavyweight and your pa was a middle. But he was a tough one, he was, your pa. He coulda been champion of the world, no doubt about it."

"Champion of the world?" said Ridder.

"Yep . . . Ridder, Jim's pa was the best fighter I ever saw. And you wanta know something else, Ridder? Timothy 'Bronco' McLaverty whupped your pa proper! This is just amazin'—here in real life is Tim's son. A course he talked about you, Jim, and your mother, Charlotte, too."

I knew that, so it didn't come as a shock to me. But Ridder figured his dad was the greatest fighter of all time. He just stared at his dad, speechless. He left the kitchen and sat down heavily on the sofa in the parlor.

"We fought in January of that year, Jim. Early January 1904. It was snowin' outside in the normal way of Chicago. . ."

"But why did you fight, if you both were friends? Why did Pa fight when he didn't believe in it?" I didn't want to interrupt and here I was doing exactly that.

A big pot of coffee was steaming on the woodstove. Blood Burns lifted his heavy frame out of the chair, grabbed some cups and set them on the table. He grabbed the huge gray enameled pot.

"I was gettin' to that, Jim. It's a long story and we can save most of it for some other time. But it was your pa, Jim. He was something special."

He poured three cups of coffee.

"Your pa was a coffee drinker, Jim. I spose you are, too?"

I nodded. Ridder came over to the table again.

"Ridder's ma was dying of the consumption. It didn't seem right that someone that beautiful could be coughing up blood all the time. It was a terrible thing to see. We needed to send her to Arizona somewheres. The air down there is high and dry, you know. The doctor knew about a special hospital, a sanitorium or somethin' or other. Well, I never let on to Jim about it. At least it never occurred to me to have the fight. But when this big promoter from downtown offered us $10,000 each to have an exhibition match, well, that's when Tim just up and said we'd do it."

"To pay the medical bills?" I asked.

"Yep. That's right. So Tim and me agreed to do this exhibition match. A promoter's dream, that's what it was, they said. I mean, all the papers in Chicago were billing this one as an amateur against a professional. But that wasn't true, a course. Tim had to turn pro to do this one fight. At first I didn't think much about it, but after Christmas, you know, the Christmas of 1903, Tim, he began to brood when he come up on the train from Missouri. He'd take the train in from St. Louis and just sit around our little apartment and think. Brood, I called it. He came up three, maybe four times before the fight and everytime he was gettin' worse about this broodin'."

"What do you mean, 'brood'?" Ridder asked.

"I mean he sort of went into himself, if you know what I mean. He wasn't the same Tim I knew. I never really thought too much about the fight. I thought I would just go out and dance around a little and clobber Tim with a couple of heavy rights and then, well . . . that would be it."

"Well, why didn't that happen?" I asked, knowing that Pa had won the battle, but not how.

"Because, Jim, your pa wouldn't have it that way. I mean to say, he thought he could whup me!"

Blood Burns took a big sip of coffee and brought the cup down hard. I looked at the clock on the wall. Obviously not working, it was stopped at three. But it was already beginning to get darker. It must have been drawing close to six in the evening. The Commander would be worried about me, even though Kenneth Joe Tracker would have told her where I was. Mr. Burns saw me look at the clock.

"Belonged to Ridder's ma. Don't work, but I ain't never going to get rid of that clock. She loved it. Come down from her family."

I spent over two more hours with Geoffrey "Blood" Burns and his son, Ridder, that evening. He told us the wonderful story of how Pa had defeated him before a huge crowd. Blood Burns really got into the story. We went into the parlor, sat around the woodstove, and listened.

The fight was well advertised. The Police Athletic League in Chicago had also encouraged the match because of Burns's reputation as a brawler. He generally knocked out his opponent in the first round. Some New York promoters were hoping to get a fight with the famous Jack Johnson. *The Tribune* picked up the fight when they first heard that Pa was an amateur from somewhere out in Missouri. Most of his fights had been in St. Louis and Kansas City. The poster had said that Blood Burns was from Chicago. It's true he had lived there for many years and it was now his home, but he had originally come from Amesbury, Massachusetts. He was thirty-one years old. Pa was twenty-eight. For years Blood had not fought professionally. That is, under the control of clubs and gymnasiums. But he had received payoffs on the side bets in many a Saturday night casino brawl. Burns's reputation continued to grow until he defeated Tommy Burns in an unofficial match. Tommy Burns, no relation, would go on to win the heavyweight championship of the world until he fought Jack Johnson in 1908, when he was badly hurt in a fourteen-round struggle. But Blood Burns continued on undefeated for three more years and fifteen bouts.

If it hadn't been for that fateful night in January 1904, Blood Burns would probably have gone on to the heavyweight championship of the world. Jack Johnson or Jim Jeffries could not have lasted against his right. They weren't quick enough. But Pa was.

Their styles were remarkably different. Pa was extremely quick on his feet, constantly circling his opponent and charging in and out with quick jabs, hooks, and straight right hands. When he had worn down his competitor—up to this point in the standard amateur three rounds—he advanced more directly, taking complete charge of the fight. At such times he always carried the attack, never stopping his punching in a wild, unflagging combination of lefts and rights. Amazingly, Tim McLaverty never seemed to tire, at least not in those three-round fights. A fifteen-rounder might be something different.

A true middleweight, Pa's biceps nevertheless measured 16 inches. In terms of pure strength, Blood Burns had met his equal. Burns would try to make for that balance with his weight and raw power, using his back and shoulders as he punched. But then, Burns wasn't taking the fight as seriously as Pa was. Burns figured he had the fight in the bag. He just didn't want to hurt Pa too much. Pa had other ideas.

Burns, too, was fast with his feet—it was with that quickness combined with his weight that he had knocked out his opponents. He never, however, moved in and out. He always pursued, stalking the other man. He was a brawler.

The ring was 24 feet square with muted white canvas stretched across the springy surface. The 2-inch ropes were wrapped in red cotton. The fight was held, as usual, late at night at the end of a series of preliminary bouts. By this time the cigar smoke hung low under the ring lights and created unearthly coils of haze that obscured all but the first few rows of seats.

The big money, obviously, was on Geoffrey "Blood" Burns. Larger bets were made, handfuls of paper money changing hands even as Burns climbed into his corner. Wagering continued from the time Burns towered over his shorter opponent during the ring announcer's introduction. And round by round, the bettors would assess their chances and continue their wagering.

But the smart money was on Tim McLaverty. At least what there was of it. Burns later said the smart money was Tim's because for some reason he gave $30,000 for his wife's hospitalization instead of the promoter's contracted $10,000. Burns never asked Pa where he got the other twenty, but he had a good idea. As Pa stepped into the ring that night, according to Burns, anyone could see that calm manner, the dark, determined eyes—they pierced Burns as they stood facing one another in the center of the ring and Burns had turned away. Pa did not waver.

The first round, Burns said, should have been the giveaway.

"I was too stupid," he told me on that evening above Donnenwirth's General Store, "to realize that I had a crafty animal on my hands!"

While the fans roared and laughed and clapped and smoked—cigars continued to send a blue haze toward the high ceiling in the arena—Burns stalked Pa around the ring, but landed only two solid punches. Both landed accurately, snapping Pa's head back, but Pa's agility kept the bigger man from doing serious damage. As Blood Burns told me this, I thought back to that very morning when Ridder had snapped my head back after I had quickly backed away from him. I guess Pa and I had that in common. While Burns charged, Pa counterpunched and jabbed, opening cuts under Burns's eyes.

By the fifth round, Burns was drawn into the trap. Angry and humiliated, he raged at Pa, lunging and chasing. He missed nearly all his punches, telegraphing his intentions. Pa, meanwhile, was pounding Burns's face into an unrecognizable mass of cuts. His face was swollen, puffy, splotched with red—and both eyes were nearly closed. Pa had taken several hard punches and had been knocked down twice, once in the third and once in the fifth. Burns was astonished to see Pa jump up each time, not even waiting for an extra count or two. Experience had always shown him that no one could get up after a direct right to his opponent's head. It began to take the heart out of Pa's friend. Pa seemed barely hurt and was still quick on his feet.

As the crowd began to rock and cheer in the tenth round, Pa

realized that Burns's right no longer hurt him. Pa changed his tactics. He charged into the staggering Burns, completely overwhelming him. He bore in on Burns's body and face recklessly. Pa received some terrible punches now in return as the desperate Burns backed up for the first time in his professional career. They fought punch for punch. A large bloody split opened across Pa's nose. Sometimes they stood toe-to-toe, Burns slumped now a bit, more sluggish. Pa refused to back away for the rest of the fight and was again knocked down. Relieved, thinking he was victorious at last, Burns turned away and raised his arms. When he spun back around Pa was already on him, prepared to continue the bout against his disheartened friend.

In the end, it was fatigue that took Burns apart. Pa never seemed to tire, while the heavyweight lost his punching speed and accuracy. Soon it appeared that Pa would permanently alter Burns's face, so bloody and pulpy it was. Left—right—left—right, Pa delivered an onslaught of blows to Burns's body and face that would surely kill him. The crowd cheered as Burns stood almost helpless now. Pa must have realized what he was doing to his friend, but he continued his relentless pounding. Burns would not quit, and that is what Pa wanted him to do. He knew that Burns had predicted an easy victory for himself, that he would easily defeat his smaller middleweight friend. Now he was finding out. Lost in the moment was the reason for the fight in the first place. Pa continued his pounding. Burns's eyes closed completely. He was a blind man flailing in the darkness. Pa retreated to Burns's body.

Everyone knew the fight's direction now. At the end of the twelfth round Burns sat on his chair, a bloody mess. The referee stopped the fight. Burns was helped from the ring by Pa and several attendants. Pa didn't even enter the ring again to raise his arm in victory. He never entered any other ring. He was afraid of what he had done. He had listened to the urging of the crowd as it hooted and roared in approval, egging him on, pushing him ever more strongly into aggressive slugging and brawling.

There were no more cheers, just polite accolades as Pa helped Geoffrey "Blood" Burns to the training room at the back of the arena. He stood back, crying, while doctors ministered to Burns. The gravity of the pounding Burns had taken was punctuated by the doctors' grave looks, the shaking of their heads, and a quick call for an ambulance.

Neither fighter would ever fight again. Burns lost part of his sight in his right eye and was partially paralyzed in his left arm. It was a miracle he could still think straight. I learned that Pa had been hurt, too. The doctors were puzzled by his burst appendix back in Moberly. Pa had lots of hurts inside, both physical and psychological after the Chicago fight. Ma never told me much about it. Pa was silent most of the time when she asked him about it, anyway. After Burns's story, I felt I knew more than I had a right to know. I guess now that Pa's life was shortened by the beating Burns had given him, although Blood Burns never knew about it. Pa only visited Burns one more time in Chicago before he died. That was in early March of 1904 when he gave Burns the $30,000 for his wife's medical treatment in Arizona.

Serena Burns lived for three more years in northern Arizona. I wished Pa could have known that. But Uncle Martin, who had traveled to Chicago to see the fight, kept in contact with the Burnses and did know that. He had made several offers to Blood Burns over the years to come to Endemeo. Blood Burns and Ridder had kicked around in Arizona, doing odd jobs here and there for several years. A few years later Ma, too, had tried to locate the Burnses, she said, but she never knew of Uncle Martin's offers. They had left with no forwarding address, becoming part of Ma's roster of those who fallen off the face of the earth.

Before I left for home that evening I hugged Blood Burns. I think he was surprised, but I held him for a moment, anyway. I grabbed Ridder's hand and shook it. He shook my hand in return, and managed a bare smile. I hugged him, too, and I could tell at first that he was embarrassed. Then he clung to me for a second and turned away, shaking and crying. John Thornton circled us as always when any hugging was going on. He must have thought it a strange sight indeed to see the boy who bloodied my nose hugging me like the best friend I ever had.

As I left, Ridder said, "I won't never hit you agin. I'm sorry I done it. You're a lucky guy, Jim, to have a girlfriend like Lucy."

I opened my eyes as wide as my swollen face would allow and said, "Ridder, I don't think . . ."

"I hope your face gets better fast . . . Like I said, I'm sorry I done it," he interrupted.

"You know, Ridder, I think . . . maybe it was supposed to happen," I said, and left, John Thornton brushing past me and down the steps. On the way home I saw Pa for the first time without a horse. He was boxing Geoffrey Burns, and I burned with a newfound strength as I saw him standing over the man who just helped me discover part of Pa's life.

Stay away from boxing, Jim. You aren't fit for it. No one is.

Chapter Twelve

THE DRIVE

We drove nearly 350 head of cattle over the Buck's Ranch Road beginning the last weekend in October. Uncle Martin lingered too long to begin the five-day drive, giving the first snows a chance to sprinkle the higher passes with snow. He couldn't make up his mind whether to send the cattle down to Oroville on the train as he had the bulls two weeks earlier. In the end, he couldn't break tradition, even though the Western Pacific train had been running up the canyon four years now.

The days were alternately warm and cold as the sun broke through vast cumulus cloud formations moving from the west, painting the sky a brilliant blue against these white monsters. We all wore heavy coats as proof against the gusty winds that blew on and off for the entire five days. Even at night around the glowing campfires we found slight relief from the wind.

"We need to get the cattle moving, Martin," Kenneth Joe Tracker had said.

But Uncle Martin was too busy with the mines and he wouldn't think of letting Kenneth Joe Tracker and the hands go without him. So the days moved by and everyone grew restless. It was The Commander, finally, who got things rolling. When she took charge all dillydallying came to an abrupt halt.

"Martin, those cattle have been out in the field now for two weeks!" she said one evening. "If you don't get the drive going, I'm going to lead it myself!" That did it. Uncle Martin directed Kenneth Joe Tracker to inform the cowhands and get moving the next day. The extensive preparations for the drive were in place. Chuck wagons full of food, bedrolls, spare tack and other supplies for all the hands followed the cattle.

Kenneth Joe Tracker took special interest in the menu for each day. Naturally he was used to the cooking of The Commander and Blue Song. They weren't going on the drive this year, so he had hired two cooks out of Reno who said they had cooked on various ranches up and down the West for years. That wasn't good enough for Kenneth Joe Tracker. He was worried about the "down." He had them cook two or three meals before he hired them, sitting in sole judgment of their performance. They must have passed muster because they were hired. I still remember Kenneth Joe Tracker holding forth on the various dishes they had served him down to the finest detail.

In previous years Dutch Coder would be helping us get the cattle down to Oroville. This year Dutch was busy with the Bacala cattle on the Humboldt Road drive, and we wouldn't see him for several days. York, not pleased that Dutch wouldn't be going, hauled along a leather bag full of art supplies to pass his spare time.

When we finally succeeded in prodding the huge herd forward, the morning opened gray and crisp. School Teacher, our faithful alarm clock, had made sure of that. He crowed well before the sun got up every morning. Frequent rains had dampened the trail leading out of Quincy through Tollgate and the cattle raised no dust at all. Maybe waiting this late wasn't so bad. At least York and I would be out of school for three or four days, but Mrs. Eldred would demand a complete accounting in the end. Altogether Kenneth Joe Tracker had gotten together twenty-two cowhands, some of them buckaroos from the Monitor Valley, east of Reno, to run the 350 head of cattle over the Buck's Road into Oroville.

Uncle Martin, at my urging, had employed Blood and Ridder on a permanent basis at Endemeo and had given them a small cabin 2 miles out of town near the western border of the ranch. Blood and Ridder were good workers, quickly learning the little odd jobs that kept the huge ranch going. Kenneth Joe Tracker was more than just sympathetic. He took on the training of Blood and Ridder with real enthusiasm. That is, when he could find Ridder. Ridder had never lived in this kind of luxury, around all these horses and cattle, surrounded by countless buildings. Ridder spent a lot of time just wandering, trying to locate more than idle points of interest. He was in the process of gaining his own bearings in life.

I explained to York what had happened. The whole episode didn't surprise him, but Ridder felt rather foolish the first time the three of us were together on the drive.

"Sorry I done all that . . . called you some bad things . . . ," Ridder stammered.

"Yeah, well you aren't so pretty yourself . . . I only make peace with enemies, Ridder Burns," York had said. "I knew you weren't my enemy—you were . . . just stupid."

Ridder showed just the trace of a grin. I'm not sure he understood what York was telling him. I was the only one who laughed, but everything worked out for the three of us after that. Mrs. Eldred didn't want Ridder to miss three days of school, so The Commander drove up and down the Buck's Ranch Road in the Imperial to pick up Ridder and to bring in extra supplies. Blue Song and The Commander were the only ones left to take over milking Priscilla and Cleopatra, but they were both down to one milking a day by this time anyway.

I was constantly surprised by Blood. He could do just about anything, in spite of his handicap. The one bad eye was not a problem, but his partially paralyzed left arm forced him to develop a large repertoire of tricks to do the lifting and pushing one takes for granted on a working cattle ranch. His most impressive effort was digging fence post holes through the tough rock and gravel and soil of Indian Valley. He guided the heavy steel rod up and down to loosen the soil while Ridder used the special shovel to remove the soil. Blood's shoulders had grown stronger from digging in his mine up by Genesee, not from waiting on customers at Donnenwirth's.

Kenneth Joe Tracker had given Blood and Ridder two good saddle horses for the five-day drive. I was riding Moon on the first long ride of my life. She was as gentle as ever, but my handling of her had improved, too. Astride a natural cutter, I found myself really just going along for the ride.

York towered over all of us on Meshuga. The Black's seventeen hands put him in clear sight above the herd even at a great distance, his dark ugly head held high over the plodding Herefords. Uncle

Martin was working Sudan, but I thought the Arabian was confused and unsettled. The stallion was not used to these common efforts, and we all plainly saw that Uncle Martin spent a lot of time just trying to settle down his prized Arabian.

We broke the herd into two groups when we reached the summit. Blind Charlie and York and I worked the rear of the second group. Hercules ambled along everywhere Blind Charlie was. By the end of the third day we had passed through Buck's Valley and were working our way down the last 50 miles to Buckeye, Berry Creek, and Oroville. We frustrated several motorists trying to negotiate their motorcars through 350 Herefords. At this point we weren't trying to stay far from the road. My rear felt like one large sore bone. Each step Moon took sent a searing pain up my back. But I would not have complained to save my life. The specter of Pa breaking in on my thoughts was too strong. I couldn't let him down. *Sit in your saddle a little easier, Jim.*

The camp that third night was quieter than usual. Kenneth Joe Tracker said the forward group had set up their camp 2 miles ahead of ours and one of the chuck wagons had gone on ahead. Kenneth Joe Tracker joined our group because he liked Harry's cooking better than Bill's, who had gone ahead with the forward chuck wagon. Kenneth Joe Tracker, as usual, didn't miss a beat when it came to cooking and eating.

York had stopped twice along the way to sketch. I watched as he captured the struggle between Uncle Martin and Sudan on the second day only to have Uncle Martin ride up to camp that evening and find York at work on a drawing again. York had quickly put the drawing away in his leather case, but Uncle Martin had become irritated for no logical reason, anyway. I looked down.

"A drive's for working cattle, York," he said.

York said nothing about the drawing but looked over at Sudan and offered to tether him next to Meshuga to settle him down.

"Yeah, well I think I can handle my horse, York," said Uncle Martin. He was getting more irritated and his words literally exploded from his mouth. "YeahwellIthinkIcanhandlemyhorseYork," it came out.

Uncle Martin continued muttering to himself as he hobbled Sudan away from the other horses. Sudan stomped and snorted most of the night. But you couldn't tell Uncle Martin anything—at least York couldn't. Hercules wasn't tethered. He roamed everywhere with his bright red headstall and either sat near us by the campfire or wandered among the trees and grass.

The clouds had covered the stars, but the temperature was milder because of the weather front moving in. The heavy overcast dampened the campfire. The smoke whirled around as though it had no place to go—except in our eyes. I thought we would all just get to sleep early after a dinner of thick steaks and potatoes baked in the hot coals of the campfire, but everyone in our group, about fifteen of us, gathered closer to the fire. Kenneth Joe Tracker had completed two full courses of Harry's chuckwagon menu in total silence and then explained to all of us what he had just eaten—down to every fiber of meat and grain of salt. He said the steaks could have been improved with some sauce Blue Song and The Commander made, but of which both Harry and Bill were entirely ignorant. He couldn't find a sympathetic audience, so he and two others took the first evening patrol of the grazing herd. Hamstring was always right at Kenneth Joe Tracker's heels, waiting for him to move. The kelpie lived to work, and somehow he knew they wouldn't be in for several hours. Ridder and Blood were with the forward group but Kenneth Joe Tracker had sent them back down to our group for the night, and I was glad that Ridder would hear Blind Charlie's tale. Uncle Martin went to bed.

Most of us sat around the fire and talked. Blood Burns told about his boxing days in Chicago. Since most of the cowhands were Tosi-Koyo Maidu from Taylorsville or Susanville and had never been farther east than Reno, it might just as well have been tales from Cairo. The boxing tales were a big success with them and even Blind Charlie deferred to Blood as he carried on for over an hour. He didn't talk about his fight with Pa, except to say he was paralyzed as a result of his last fight. Only Ridder and I knew that story.

Later the clouds lifted and parted a little, and we saw traces of moon and stars. The smoke began to wind almost vertically from the embers. I sat across Blind Charlie and saw him squint his eyes at the fire. He was lost in thought as Blood Burns ended his tale.

We all drifted off to bed, searched for our bedrolls, and moved closer to the fire before going to sleep. Kenneth Joe Tracker returned and passed out bright red woolen blankets from the wagon, while an exhausted Hamstring crawled underneath next to one of the wheels and immediately went to sleep. I wished I had brought John Thornton, but he never would have been able to keep up with the kelpie. We tucked the woolen blankets as extra bedding into our bedrolls. It would be a cold night. Ridder established his sleeping site practically in the fire. York sat up and worked on a sketch. Just before I lay back, I saw Harry throw several more large logs on the fire. It flared up into a bright blaze, but the fire soon grew silent except for an occasional crackle.

Chapter Thirteen

THE BET

I can still hear the voices. Voices of laughter and polite accusation, dares and deceits. Uncle Martin's unmoving upper lip spurting out words like, "Lead your aces, Kenneth," and "Trumps are diamonds, Hannah!," and "I thought you'd have more of trump considering your bid. We're going set."

If Uncle Martin had had his way we might have spent that entire winter playing pinochle in the evenings. We had returned home by rail to Endemeo after the drive ended at the McLaverty Ranch in Oroville. A few days later a huge Alaskan storm blew into northern California and blanketed Indian Valley with snow. Short dark days and deep snow kept Uncle Martin at home when nothing else would, and usually it was two decks of pinochle cards scattered across a table in front of the kitchen stove that lifted his mind from business worries at the mines.

They talked about other things, too. The Commander complained about her favorite MJB Coffee going all the way up to thirty-five cents a pound. Uncle Martin announced that he had received his first speeding ticket since the state had established a maximum speed on all roads of 30 miles an hour. In Taylorsville the limit was 10. Kenneth Joe Tracker said the ice crop was going to be a big one and that all the ice houses would be completely filled this year. The evenings seemed marked out by the chatter of shuffling card decks or explosive exclamations of "No!" or "Hah!" whenever the unexpected card fell with a slap on the table surface.

Blind Charlie would sometimes come over to Endemeo to watch these games, always drawing up a chair backwards and leaning over with his arms crossed. He never said much or wanted to play, often shaking his head and laughing, saying only "Truly!" As one with the heart of a poet he was intrigued more by the motion and color of the game than he was in tactics or strategy.

The routine of our evenings was interrupted twice more by bats before 1914 drew to an end, although the brown hairy spiders continued to harass my aunt every day. The Commander wouldn't let Uncle Martin bring out the double-barreled shotgun again, so Kenneth Joe Tracker had designed a long hoop with a bag of netting. This contraption reminded me of an advancement on a butterfly net. In truth, Kenneth Joe Tracker had used the device to catch frogs in ponds all over the valley. Unfortunately, the pole was so long that it was effective only in the cavernous parlor at Endemeo. But Kenneth Joe Tracker bagged his quarry both times, saving The Commander a lot of weeping over fallen plaster and shattered walls. Kenneth Joe Tracker went on and on about how successful the net was, talking about patents and production until Uncle Martin told him it had no economic future.

By January of 1915, over 4 feet of snow lay on the ground. Kenneth Joe Tracker and I waded waist-deep one morning through freshly fallen snow to milk Cleopatra and Priscilla. Soon, they would be dry until their new calves arrived in spring. John Thornton loved the snow and bounded through the deep drifts, his nose in the air.

Kenneth Joe Tracker said, "That dog looks like the seals I seen down in Monterey one time."

I had never seen a seal except for the drawings in books, and I thought Kenneth Joe Tracker must have been right—John Thornton was neck deep in the dry snow, sending waves of powder around and above his head. Back in Missouri the snow had been wet and the air heavily damp, the storms never dumping snow this deep. Here the snow was dry and powdery, the air crisp and thin.

When we returned to the kitchen I spent several minutes removing large snowballs of ice attached to John Thornton's tail and underside, while he eyed The Commander guiltily with sad, pleading eyes. The Commander was not about to allow the dog to melt pools of ice across her carpet in front of the fireplace, John Thornton's favorite resting place.

Because the days were shorter now, I had to hurry home after school to finish my chores. Ridder was always there to help me now in the afternoons. In the mornings he worked with Blood chopping wood and feeding the stock hay and grain. By five it was dark. Many a night in that winter I taught York and Ridder how to tie flies, using a small improvised vise. York picked up fly tying in his nimble artistic way, but Ridder's big fingers couldn't handle the delicate threads and feathers, especially on no. 16 hooks. Ridder's mop of hair hung down over his eyes and chubby face, frustrating his efforts even further. The Commander gave him a haircut every two weeks, but his hair grew like a jungle. Ridder's flies generally resembled the hatch I removed from fishes' stomachs. I tried to explain to ridder that fish usually like to eat live flies, not dead ones—so the idea was to reproduce the likeness of a healthy "live" fly—but he didn't find the joke particularly funny. When it came to rewinding my H.L. Leonard rods with their new dark green thread, I wouldn't let Ridder even get close, let alone work on one of Pa's treasured Tonkin rods. That winter the three of us tied over a hundred flies to use the next season. We had quite a collection of Adams, Cahills, Quill Gordons, and other patterns. The mosquito, I knew, would bring lots of strikes on Indian Creek, so we tied a slew of them.

Other nights I spent at Blind Charlie's cabin, listening to his never-ending flow of stories. Blind Charlie got around quite a bit for an old man. He always told York and me every detail. One day it might be about Coal Oil Charlie, who sat in front of his barn on the other side of the valley and drank from a small bottle all day. It always seemed full—which he said he filled from a drum of coal oil. He wasn't going to last much longer, Blind Charlie said, so he visited him every week or so. Then there was an old Maidu woman, Lizzie Mose, who shot and killed a Mexican mine worker at Tent City— near Uncle Martin's Engle Mine. Blind Charlie said that he heard it was self-defense, but he also knew "Old Lizzie" had shot up other folks in earlier days. The sheriff wasn't convinced either, because he hauled Lizzie screaming and scratching to jail. It seemed like when anything happened anywhere Blind Charlie knew about it well in advance of the weekly newspaper. Naturally, York and I considered him the very fountain of information. The town's merchants and other folks would run out of the stores and stop him in the street when he and Hercules happened by just to pump him for any news.

As I listened to these stories, I watched York carry his sketches toward completion—large pen and ink drawings or oils. Through all the stories York remained impassive, but I knew he was listening.

Moseley's Skating Rink in Quincy—where we spent many hours for only twenty-five cents a day—closed for the month of February, so one Saturday Lucy, York, Ridder, and I skied down Mt. Hough. We made the skis ourselves out of oak. They were monstrosities, long 8-foot skis that must have weighed 5 pounds each. Kenneth Joe Tracker helped us to steam the tips so they curved slightly upward. Then we tacked thin sheets of metal on the tip for extra strength. We made crude metal cradles for our boots about midway on top of each ski and attached straps from some of Uncle Martin's old tack. We had worked for three Saturdays on those skis and were very proud of them. We varnished each ski carefully and, when they dried, waxed them until they were shining. Carrying them up the mountain via the old Grade Road was no easy task, considering how deep the snow was. York only made it about a quarter mile and had to stop. He couldn't breathe and this incident helped to remind us that York was not getting any better. He said he would wait for us, for us to go on to the peak. He knew it would take us nearly four hours to reach the top, but said he would be here when we came down. Disappointed, the three of us left York and trudged eagerly up the narrow road to the summit. We only made it halfway up. Although the snow was crusty and hard about a foot below the newly fallen snow, we simply couldn't go fast enough to reach the summit.

But from our perch we could see most of Indian Valley, thousands of acres of flat white carpet, intersected by the wavy gray line of Indian Creek and its rows of bare cottonwoods and alders. To the north we saw smoke rising from the distant Lassen Peak. Some geologist had said in the newspaper only last week that Lassen was really going to rip this summer. Already ashes were noticeable just north of Greenville. Putting the fear of lava and exploding volcanoes out of our minds, we shot down from Mt. Hough in just a few minutes, dodging trees, crashing over banks, and snagging our skis in drifts and branches. But once we aimed these monsters in a downhill direction, we gained speed rapidly, usually out of control, innocently unaware of our own inertia and the increased weight of our bodies as we hurtled downward, locked in the unyielding bindings. We couldn't turn the heavy skis very easily, but they tended to track in our footsteps we had made coming up. How we kept from shattering our legs or permanently relocating our knees is one of the mysteries swallowed up forever in those days of youth.

True to his word, York was waiting for us when we came down. He had been there almost five hours. He hadn't been idle. He had spent the time sketching a drawing of his brother, Walker—peering from a trench in France. By this time we knew Walker was in the heat of battle somewhere "over there." While we had dwelled on the explosive Lassen Peak, York was brooding over explosions of a different kind—Ypres. I sensed a sadness in York that I had never seen before. I think the others saw it, too. In the months I had known him, York had been proud, undefeated. He had a powerful, obstinate way of doing things that overcame his weakness. But on that day in February something had changed. I knew he was tired. I tried to put these feelings out of my mind as we laughed and talked while we removed the cumbersome skis and trudged home together, wet and eager to sit by The Commander's kitchen stove.

As I look back on that winter I am impressed by the solitude of the long nights, not when I was with Ridder or Lucy or York, but when I was alone. Electric lights, a single telephone, and gravity-flow running water filling an elevated tower behind the ranch were the only modern conveniences I can remember back in 1914 at Endemeo—radio wouldn't come to the valley for ten more years. There is no quietness like a winter night in the Sierra when the snow has blanketed the ground and the trees, and a heavy overcast muffles everything like a gigantic tent for miles around. On such nights I sat by the fire in the parlor reading books from The Commander's library. I sat in Uncle Martin's huge green overstuffed chair next to my reflection in the paned window, while John Thornton sprawled in front of the hearth a few feet away. Alexander Dumas was on the shelf. I picked out a huge black clothbound book containing nearly 1,500 pages, *The Count of Monte Cristo*. I knew the title, and I launched into the reading of it immediately. By the time Edmond Dantes has been cast into the infamous Chateau d'If, an island prison fortress near Marseilles, I was angry and read for nearly two weeks to see how he would escape and take his revenge. When I finished, I decided I would read every book by Dumas The Commander had on her shelves. Thus, the hours and days and weeks went by—alternately by reading, repairing fly-fishing equipment, or tying flies—and daily through Mrs. Eldred's demands on our scholarship.

When Uncle Martin wasn't ruthlessly imposing a game of pinochle on the others, The Commander was again at the piano. She began always—as she had when I first arrived at Endemeo—with church hymns. Then she would work through pieces by Chopin and Mozart, her two favorite classical composers. Ma had played the piano, too, but not on a piano so grand as The Commander's Beckwith. I, myself, never learned to play the piano. My musical skills were limited to serenading trout with Fanny Crosby songs along Indian Creek. The Commander saw that fly-fishing was not compatible with the hours she might have demanded of me, perhaps. But as The Commander spent those confined evening hours playing his compositions hour after hour, I learned to recognize at once all the ballades, "tudes," nocturnes, and other pieces of Chopin's legacy. Mozart was more difficult for me to analyze because of the range and diversity of his work, but it was because of Mozart that I became an opera enthusiast years later. Mozart was more energetic, louder, and always put me in the mood to do something. Chopin was better for reading, Mozart for winding thread and feathers on a hook, even doing a load of dishes in the kitchen.

By April the once heavy snow was reduced to shady patches of dirty white, and the spring grasses swelled new green on the valley floor and leaped gracefully up the hillside behind Endemeo. Most of the snow was replaced with endless pools, muddy tracks, the freshness of new things growing. The Commander's lilacs were beginning to show a bit of purple, and her daffodils lined the drive with yellow. Thousands of Canadian geese honked for hours in mornings and evenings all across the valley. Both Sudan and Meshuga were racing about their corrals one of these April mornings, snorting and jumping and calling. The sun was breaking through the kitchen windows onto our breakfast table when we were having breakfast. Uncle Martin, Kenneth Joe Tracker, and I listened.

"Sounds like the horses need a run," said Uncle Martin. "I'm thinking about entering Sudan in that big 100-mile endurance race down near Portola in June."

I looked up, surprised. I had seen the posters in town advertising the race to publicize the opening of the Feather River Inn, a new resort on the Middle Fork of the Feather River. From what I could gather the race would attract horses from all over the country, mostly prized Arabians from rich owners. Several were even coming from Europe and England to participate. The $10,000 winner's purse had been put up by a wealthy steel producer from Pittsburgh and two Englishmen. Everyone was excited, and several California horses were expected to enter. I wondered about Meshuga. This race was made for Meshuga, but how could York ever manage the $25 entry fee?

"The pastures are clear of snow down front all the way to the creek," said Kenneth Joe Tracker. "Maybe we should let them run. I seen them posters. I bet Sudan would take the race!"

"Jim, you take care of that today, will you? Give the horses a run in the big field," suggested Uncle Martin. "I suppose you better ask York before you turn out the Black."

For Uncle Martin, this was a major concession to York. I was secretly pleased that he would even think about York.

"Meshuga would win!" I blurted.

"Meshuga could not even stand against Sudan, Jim," Uncle Martin erupted. "I heard some of the country's best horses are going to compete. These horses have run in many of these long-distance events."

"Well—Meshuga would win! I know it—don't ask me how . . . I just know it!" I repeated.

Uncle Martin stared at me. He was irritated at first, but then the beginning of a rare smile transformed his annoyance into a taunt.

"How's York gonna come up with $25?" he said.

Kenneth Joe Tracker remained quiet, his head down.

"Don't I have $25 in the bank from Ma?" I knew that I had

thousands of dollars in my name under Uncle Martin and The Commander's guardianship. I wasn't very bold customarily, and now I wondered if I had upset my uncle with this rude outburst.

"Jim, your aunt Hannah and I can't allow you to waste your money on this folly."

I thought about Pa—and once again, the guilt and intimidation. *What are you waiting for, Jim?* I took a deep breath, gathered my courage, and continued. I desperately wanted to point out to Uncle Martin that he was willing to spend $25 on Sudan. Why couldn't I spend $25 on Meshuga? But I thought that approach might infuriate my uncle, who had a violent temper anyway.

"Uncle Martin, you're right . . . it may be foolish. But York and Meshuga saved my life. I would like your permission to pay York's entry fee for Meshuga."

"I just can't do that, Jim . . ."

"All right, Uncle Martin," I interrupted, "I have an idea . . . let's match race Meshuga and Sudan. Everyone's been wanting that for months now . . . let's say, a 4-mile race. If Meshuga wins, we get to enter Meshuga. If he loses . . . we forget about the money." I was just twelve years old, and I was shattering the quiet morning with my enthusiasm. The Commander came down the stairs and into the kitchen.

"Lord, Jim, I could hear you all the way upstairs! What in the world is going on down here?" She asked.

Uncle Martin was thinking. "I'll consider it," he said, "but Meshuga is no match for Sudan. It'll just make York feel worse than he's feeling already. Everyone knows he's getting worse."

"Martin, nothing could make him feel more like living than this here race," said Kenneth Joe Tracker. Kenneth Joe Tracker got up from his chair and went outside. He felt he had overstepped his friendship with Uncle Martin and had to escape. But Uncle Martin was deep in thought, and he was feeling boxed in.

"Will somebody tell me what is going on here?" The Commander asked again.

"Damn!" said Uncle Martin, and left the room.

Alone, I explained our discussion to The Commander. She sat down at the table and took my hand.

"Does York know about this?" she asked.

"No, he doesn't . . . we just started talking . . . the horses outside . . . I mean they need exercise, and one thing led to another . . . I don't know, Aunt Hannah, I shouldn't have talked to Uncle Martin that way."

"I think you should tell York. He'll be here soon with Mr. Charlie—and I'll take care of Martin!"

"I will, Aunt Hannah—I mean, thanks—and I will talk to York."

"Jim . . . I suppose you know that York's health is failing . . . "

"Yeah . . . I've noticed," I said, not knowing what else to say.

Aunt Hannah's eyes were red.

Later that morning when I told York what I had said to Uncle Martin he was his old self again. The spark returned, his eyes shone, and he couldn't think of anything he would rather do. He, too, had seen the posters and wanted desperately to enter Meshuga in the 100-mile race.

Strangely, York was unmoved about the $25 I was willing to put up for Meshuga. I marked it up to an artist's temperament. He didn't think much about money, anyway. Perhaps he knew that $25 was nothing to me, considering the huge amount of money I had salted away in my name from the sale of the Missouri farm. I was grateful that I didn't have to waste a lot of time convincing York to accept the money. I mean, I had the money, but I had barely gotten out of the Headlight overalls. Money hadn't helped me to escape the dreaded oversight of The Commander. Why should I have thought money would help me in anything? As I look back on it, this was the first time in my life that I realized the power of money—that I had gained a measure of respect from Uncle Martin for even mentioning it. Like the true businessman he was, he recognized that tiny bit of me growing up, and maybe he sensed a little of his brother Timothy.

A few nights later I was sleeping fitfully, dreaming scenes so real and terrifying I woke up sweaty. My heart was thumping in my chest. I woke from dreams of rattlesnakes dancing on Ma and Pa's graves and Mrs. Dovey was beating on them with a rod—with Ezekiel's snapping bones multiplying into images of human skulls with bloody teeth eating arms and legs and sailing through a dark void and falling, falling . . . off Ma's face of the earth. Then I saw the skulls eating their own bodies and I almost got sick. A black horse was flying silently, chasing these disembodied skulls. One broke away, screaming like the wind, and thundered into the side of our barn, Cleopatra's barn . . . where Sudan and Meshuga were stabled. Splinters of wood ripped my dream down the center . . . .

The crash was so real. I lay on my pillow, breathing heavily in the dark. Outside the wind was howling through my barely open window, whistling through the narrow gap with each strong gust. The panes rattled. I couldn't get the crash out of my mind—it was heavier than the dream. Had something fallen outside? I heard footsteps in the hallway outside my room. I jumped up from bed and dressed. John Thornton lay still, uninterested in my movements at three a.m. I pulled on my long rubber boots, ran down the stairs and out the back door.

I was surprised to find that a late spring snow was falling and nearly a foot of new dry powder lay on the ground. In the darkness and through a thick screen of falling flakes, I could see a yellow light. It seemed to be coming from the barn, so I ran through the powder toward Sudan's enclosure. The crash! Had it come from the barn?

As I drew near I was sickened to see Uncle Martin's snow-covered jacket leaning through a maze of branches and pulling them back from the dark form of Sudan. His stallion seemed to be pinned against a huge oak branch, nearly a foot through and 30 feet long. In the dim light I could see that the fallen branch and broken two of the stout rails encircling the pen and was resting on the bottom rail. Sudan was trapped between the branch and the corner of the corral. The snow was much deeper where Sudan stood because the barn's roof had dumped several loads where the oak branch lay.

"Is he all right?" I yelled, wiping the wet flakes from my face, squinting in the snow.

"Yes . . . I think so . . . can't tell for sure . . . yet . . . get another lantern out of the barn, will you?"

I came back with the lantern and Uncle Martin lit it. With two lanterns now glowing I could see the problem. The oak was resting so close to the fence Sudan could not turn. The oak seemed to pin

Sudan's hindquarters against the broken top rail, but the full weight of the oak was partially carried by the bottom rail now. Otherwise the tree might have destroyed Uncle Martin's prize stallion.

"Can we pull him out . . . or saw down the fence?" I asked.

"Nope. Not enough room!"

Then I saw what might work. I ran to the tack room, grabbed a long coil of Kenneth Joe Tracker's rope. I threw one end over the fork of the standing oak's trunk, above the fallen branch. I tied the other end around the fallen branch next to Sudan. Uncle Martin nodded. He could see what I had in mind. I carried the remaining end of the rope over to Meshuga, whose dark head lay over Sudan's side of the rail. Racing inside, I lifted one of the saddles from the racks and set it down next to Meshuga. Meshuga backed up.

"Easy. Easy, Meshuga."

The majestic Black seemed to understand the urgency of Sudan's situation. He stood. I threw the saddle across his back and cinched it tightly. I didn't even think twice. I just mounted Meshuga like I had done it all my life. Kenneth Joe Tracker arrived at just about that moment, took in the whole situation, and grabbed the loose end of the rope, handing it to me. Winding the rope around the saddle horn several times, I yelled to Uncle Martin.

"I'm backing now . . . let's hope it works!"

Meshuga hadn't been saddled since The Commander's famous ride, but he handled beautifully backing for me with York's halter. As he continued backing in the deep powder, tensing against the heavy tree and the taut rope, the branch slowly lifted off the rail and back from Sudan, pulled upward through the fork acting like a crude block and tackle. When the stallion was well clear of the branch, he suddenly ran free. I could barely see Sudan's outline in the darkness, now that he was well away from the lantern.

Uncle Martin yelled, "Let it go, he's all right!"

I released the rope from the saddle horn and the oak branch crashed back down to the bottom rail, smashing through this final obstacle.

While Kenneth Joe Tracker and I unsaddled Meshuga, Uncle Martin ran his hand over every square inch of Sudan, searching for anything broken or cut. When Kenneth Joe Tracker and I came up with our lantern, the gray looked as fit as ever.

"Thank God," said Uncle Martin.

"I heard the crash . . . I thought it was in my dream at first," I said.

"I didn't hear nothing," said Kenneth Joe Tracker, "but Blue Song, she said something was going on out here at the barn and I had better go see what it was. You done a good job, Jim."

Uncle Martin was trying to catch his breath. He looked at me in the dim light of the lantern. He was wearing his long johns under a heavy slicker and boots. His bald head was wet with falling snow.

"Thanks, Jim. If Sudan can race, she will. That Meshuga's one special horse . . . and . . . well, I mean that. You tell York what that Black did tonight."

I nodded, smiling inside—warm even in the spring snow. It was strange having this conversation with my uncle, a man I barely understood, in the middle of the night against a howling wind.

"Your dad'd be proud, Jim," he said.

I felt good as Uncle Martin and I trudged back to the house and up to bed.

"We'll race Sudan and Meshuga as a tune up in two weeks," he said in the darkness at the bottom of the stairs, "and Meshuga and York race in the 100-miler, win or lose against Sudan, Jim . . . and . . . I pay the fee. "

Uncle Martin spoke as rapidly as ever, but I caught all the words. I sifted their meaning for York as I climbed the stairs.

Chapter Fourteen

YORK

I watched the season's last thin blanket of snow melt over the next few days in the bright spring sunlight, finally announcing a dazzling panorama of green and blue.

On race day Meshuga splashed from one end of his muddy corral to the other while Uncle Martin saddled the quieter Sudan and led him away. Meshuga stopped pitching and dancing when York entered the corral holding his silver-studded bridle.

"Easy, easy, Black!" he said quietly.

Obediently, the Black marched over to his master and lowered his head. We led him over to the dry ground under the barn's overhang and we both brushed him and rubbed him down until he shone. In the crisp morning air Meshuga's flared nostrils expelled trails of fog along with York's heavy wheezing and coughing.

"He looks like he wants to run, York," I said, alarmed more by York's condition than I was expectant of Meshuga's victory.

"Oh he'll run, all right . . . and win, too," he replied.

York, as usual, would ride the 4-mile race bareback, so it wasn't necessary to select a colorful saddle blanket from the tack room, as Uncle Martin had done.

News of the race had spread. Now in mid-May Dutch Coder and Blind Charlie had set out a course for Uncle Martin along the Genesee Road starting near the old millrace, about a mile out of town. The narrow road up there was still ankle-deep in mud, but the gravel bed through town was firm and damp. At first, Uncle Martin had designed a simple race down the Old Taylorsville Road, but all that changed when Taylorsville merchants convinced him to run it through town. The course would follow the road through Taylorsville to a point 1 and a half miles north near Endemeo. There the horses would circle a wagon manned by Kenneth Joe Tracker and return to the finish in front of Donnenwirth's General Store—a crude racecourse, but a good 4-mile run. The horses would pass the spectators twice—a mile after the start and again at the finish. Already on this Saturday, motorcars and horse-drawn wagons gathered along the main street.

Uncle Martin was rounder and heavier than York, who appeared light and small atop Meshuga. The smaller Sudan, like most Arabs, looked overloaded with Uncle Martin in the saddle. As the horses walked by the spectators on the road to the start, Meshuga and the smaller York towered over the gray-white Sudan and Uncle Martin. Meshuga's head was not pretty to look at, not at all like the aristocratic dished head of Sudan, but Meshuga's size was impressive, easily seventeen to eighteen hands. Always blinded by Meshuga's reputation, I never had noticed his bowed hind legs and awkward, jerky walk until now. As he strode by with York, I saw that the beauty and conformity horse fanciers appreciated weren't part of Meshuga's bearing. His black coat was shining, and York's red shirt was brilliant, but my confidence waned. York's simple style—no saddle, and he was barefooted!—contrasted preposterously with Uncle Martin's smart brown boots and gabardines. Hatless, Uncle Martin was smiling and gesturing, while York was contained and grim. Sitting on the long bench in front of Donnenwirth's, Blind Charlie wouldn't look up as Meshuga and York paraded past. He was sitting quietly next to The Commander and Blue Song, who both waved.

Blind Charlie was suffering inside. He knew York had spent the morning coughing and wheezing again, signaling a decline in his usual ability to hide pain. His brow was pale, even purplish, and was protruding darkly over his eyes. This was not the York that Lucy, Ridder, and I knew even two days ago. Earlier that morning they had looked back and forth from York to me, silently commanding me to do something. York and I had just finished his brushing and the three of us were leading him up to the house next to where Uncle Martin had left Sudan. York's wheezing was shallow and short now. We all knew that York was slipping away from us.

"York . . . do you feel all right?" I finally managed to stutter.

York didn't answer, kept on fiddling with Meshuga's straps.

"Can you ride, York?" I persisted.

"Meshuga's what matters, Jim . . ." he said.

"I know, York, but . . ."

"I just feel tired. I can ride. This is Meshuga's day."

Uncle Martin came out of the house, and we didn't say anything more.

We walked behind York and Uncle Martin as they passed Donnenwirth's. Some of the crowd, seeing York for the first time, were hushed by his face. Used to this, he kept his eyes straight ahead. Before we left him, York looked down at me and smiled. I still remember how shocked I was to look into those dull, blank eyes, the fire gone. The whites of his eyes were moist and red and glistened now. Then he leaned over to Ridder, curiously, and said something I couldn't hear. Ridder nodded, looked up, and watched York quickly catch up with Uncle Martin. We continued to watch Meshuga and the others—several riders were accompanying York and Uncle Martin to the starting post—up the Genesee Road where Dutch Coder was waiting with his pistol to start the race. They were just red, black, and blue specks in the distance when we climbed up on the roof of the porch to get a better view.

The day had started bright and clear, but by mid-morning fast-moving gray clouds closed off part of the blue sky, and it looked like rain and gusty spring winds might spoil things. The race would begin in another thirty minutes, around twelve noon.

Dutch Coder's Colt .45 would be loud enough to hear. We all waited for its report. The Volunteer Fire Department had cordoned off the main part of town with ropes and wooden barricades, and Deputy Lewis kept the children back out of the street. But as soon as he turned away, the children darted back and forth from side to side. The Women's Auxiliary of the Methodist Church had coffee and cookies for sale on the west side of the street, so we had to cross the street, anyway. The ladies all had umbrellas in case of rain, but the tiny patches of blue sky that still remained gave the others hope that the horses would beat the storm.

The crack of Dutch Coder's pistol echoed off the mountains behind the cemetery. The crowd clapped and stirred, followed by an expectant silence. It would be a minute or so before we could see the horses approach, but we all looked intently down the empty silent street, anyway, expecting both riders to materialize instantly out of nowhere. I began inventing the race in my mind, and now I imagined that Meshuga was pulling away from Sudan, while Uncle Martin urged his stallion on, slipping ever farther behind York.

This momentary fantasy was broken finally by little Bart Fosse, who had climbed a tree at the south end of town. He was screaming his seven-year-old head off, yelling the same thing over and over.

"I see 'em! I see 'em! I see 'em! I see 'em! I see 'em! I see 'em!"

"Lord, why doesn't he shut up!" said The Commander down below.

Soon, Bart was joined by others.

"Here they come!"

"The Black's in the lead!"

"No he ain't! The gray's up!"

"I can't see! Looks like their runnin' together to me!"

Two dots, at first a dim blur in the locus between two towering sugar pines, grew larger. The damp spring road offered no dust to obscure the rapidly approaching riders. It was easy to spot Meshuga by his color and size from our station on top of the overhang. We could see and hear the horses now—a steady beat of the hoofs and other noises of slapping leather and expelled air.

Lucy yelled first. "Meshuga's leading, Jim! Meshuga's ahead of the Arabian!"

"I see, Lucy . . . right! He is leading! C'mon York, c'mon York!"

"Go Meshuga, go Meshuga!" yelled Ridder.

A low rumble from the crowd increased to a uniform roar as the horses came within 100 yards from Donnenwirth's General Store. The horses were running full out now, saving nothing for the next 3 miles, their tails straight and their heads low and straining forward. Uncle Martin was shouting at Sudan, but the beautiful gray stallion struggled a head behind the Black.

"Go Meshuga, win Meshuga!" someone in the crowd screamed.

"Meshuga, Meshuga, you've got it!"

"Look at that mustang beatin' the Arab!"

"Ha-ha, that's a home-grown mustang for ya . . . go Meshuga!"

No one rooted for Uncle Martin as they approached. He was in a classic racer's position, leaning low, legs held loosely against the saddle, reins brought up snugly. He looked like he knew what he was doing, but his fat, red face was twisted into a rage.

But I was watching York. Something was not right. He was leaning down, almost lying on Meshuga's back—he wasn't even holding the reins! They were looped uselessly over Meshuga's neck, wrapped around York's arms, but not in his hands. His untucked red shirt was flapping like a warning flag.

A gasp broke from the crowd. A woman screamed. It was The Commander.

"Someone help him! Stop the horse! Stop everything! Do something!"

"Get a doctor! Is Doc Rutledge here?"

"York ain't ridin' the horse! The Black's just carryin' 'im!"

"Look, he's holdin' on to Meshuga's mane!"

"His eyes are closed!"

"He don't even know where he's goin'!"

Nevertheless, Meshuga increased his lead by half a length as the two horses raced through town and down the Old Taylorsville Road where Kenneth Joe Tracker was waiting at the turnaround. Blind Charlie hurried out into the street, looking after the retreating figure of York. Old as he was, Blind Charlie was running and stumbling now after York. I sprinted after him.

"He'll be all right. The horse'll be comin' back this way, anyways!" someone shouted.

"Yeah—that's right, the race'll be over soon!"

Blind Charlie stood in the middle of the road and waited.

We watched nervously as the two horses disappeared around the last curve north of town. Soon they would be passing around Kenneth Joe Tracker . . . and then . . . we would see. Meshuga still held the lead when they disappeared from view. I was sick inside, a growing fear that worried me almost to a fever, but in my denial I thought maybe this was just York's tactic. You could never tell about York. Then just as quickly, I knew that I was wrong. York never rode Meshuga like that.

The minutes ticked agonizingly by. One minute, two minutes, three, four, five, six . . . .

Moments later, the yelling started up again.

"Here they come back!"

"Meshuga's way in back!"

"Three . . . maybe four lengths!"

"Here comes Sudan!"

"Sudan's going to win!"

The Arabian was finishing fast, now that the white chalk finish line was less than a few furlongs away. Meshuga had slowed his pace to an awkward, jerky gallop and was several lengths behind. York was still in the same position, lying on his horse's back, his legs dangling uselessly at the mustang's side, the reins wrapped tightly around his arms. Then as Sudan thundered toward the finish from the north end of Main Street, Meshuga seemed to explode. No one who was there that day will ever forget it. Behind by over ten lengths, the Black drew from his infinite supply of energy, the energy from the Smoke Creek Desert, and closed the gap on Sudan as they both neared the finish line. Uncle Martin was sweating and kicking—his arms and legs all in a flurry—as he bolted across the white chalk line in the dirt. He had won by barely a length, and as his horse cavorted and danced he turned to see his opponent, who was running erratically now down the street past him. The crowd was silent. Uncle Martin, worried now, sat waiting.

Blind Charlie and I had run along the side of the road back to the finish and the crowd. In all the confusion I lost Blind Charlie for a moment.

Then there he was, grabbing Meshuga's reins and pulling him to a stop. Uncle Martin dismounted and raced to York's side, pulling him off the big Black and laying him gently on his back. Blind Charlie sat down and rested York's head in his lap. The crowd seemed paralyzed, almost a tableau. Where seconds earlier they had screamed for their favorite, now they were muted. Several offered to help, but Dutch Coder—who had arrived to see the finish—yelled for everyone to "st-st-stay back." Dutch looked stricken at his young friend lying unconscious in the middle of the road, unaware that he had lost. I wished the race had never been run. It was my stupid idea. Shocked, all I could do was stand there helplessly and let the sickening events unfold.

York died there in Blind Charlie's arms. There was none of the heaving or choking he usually suffered. Just a peaceful leaving. Blind Charlie took off his black hat and pulled it hard down over York's head and eyes. He bent over him and held him tightly.

"My . . . river boy, he be gone, Ben . . ." Blind Charlie faltered, talking to his old long gone friend, Benjamin Kurtz. "At last, poor Yor-eek, I knew him . . . Ho-ray-sho . . . Ben . . . ."

"I'm s-s-sorry, Mr. Ch-Charlie," whispered Dutch.

York's race was a mystery. None of us knew how he had managed to hold on to Meshuga for those 4 miles—that was a story that only Blind Charlie could explain. I closed my eyes and imprinted the memory of my friend lying in his red shirt in the middle of Taylorsville. Meshuga was a few feet behind, held by Uncle Martin. The scene was frozen for me then, and it is cut like stone into my memory even today. The Commander, bigger than any of us, cried more than most of us, too. She got down on the ground next to Blind Charlie. She had on a beautiful white dress with tiny blue flowers all over it, and she just kneeled right down in the gravel and put her arm around Blind Charlie. The big straw hat she was wearing got in her way, so she just tossed it aside. I watched the wind catch it and roll it down the street, spinning and flipping with little Bart Fosse in pursuit. I looked back to Blind Charlie, and he looked over to where I was standing.

"Ooooh, truly, Jim . . . Little Jim . . . York, he love you."

I nodded and the well broke loose, just standing in the street and crying, heaving convulsively, muffling my grief. I walked over to them.

"Ooooh, it be awright, Jim . . . oh York, he gone be not hurting all inside no more, truly."

Blind Charlie lifted his adopted grandson off the dirt and carried him over to Kenneth Joe Tracker's wagon. The crowd slowly dispersed, and Reverend Wenk came over to Blind Charlie and asked to help, even say a prayer to calm the hurt feelings. He didn't know what else to do.

"Truly, Mr. Wink, ooooh York, he be liking your prayer. He read the pis-alms three-nine all the time this winter." Even in his grieving, Blind Charlie was chattering away.

"Psalm 39?"

"Truly."

That was news to me. By The Commander's decree I had to keep up a fairly regular diet of Bible reading, and even now I couldn't tell you what was in Psalm 39 and what would attract York to it. I never saw York read scripture much, but then a lot of things about York surprised me. York's death did not define that May afternoon in 1915 for me. York's passing would strike a deeper chord as the days and weeks went by. What defined that incredible race day was that I learned what true gentility was. No one was as gentle and graceful and honest as that old man, an old Maidu Indian named Blind Charlie, on the day he lost what he loved most.

When The Commander and Blue Song brought up the Imperial a few minutes later, Blind Charlie lifted York out of the wagon and placed him on the back seat. He got in and closed the door, cradling York's head under the black hat and the tail feathers of the red-tailed hawk.

I shouted through the closed window, "I'm sorry, Mr. Charlie . . . it was my fault."

Blind Charlie opened the door and looked at me in the same way I had seen him months before on the train, a vacant stare, like a blind man. His aged red eyes looked through me and beyond me, and once again I saw the little red tributaries running in all directions and disappearing behind his weathered face. He was an eagle, soaring alone above my fly rod on Indian Creek, seeing everything.

"No, Jim . . . truly, it be not your fault . . . you know, Jim, it gone be a good story . . . you know? Everything be a story. York be a story. You be a story. Ole Meshuga, he be a story. Some story be all done. Sudan's story be all finishing . . . Some story not be finished yet. You know what gone to be next, Jim? Yes? Ooooh, truly, this story is not gone be finishing yet, you jes wait. York, he be a great Maidu, you know . . . what old Ben be calling the hero. You gone be the hero, too, Jim." Blind Charlie's sad face broke into deep smile. "Truly, you know?"

I nodded, and Blind Charlie closed the door on his eloquence.

The Commander and Blue Song drove them away toward Greenville. Kenneth Joe Tracker tied Meshuga and Sudan to the back of the wagon and climbed in the driver's seat. Uncle Martin and I sat in back, silent, our legs dangling off the end.

"Someone's waving, Jim."

I looked up. As the wagon rolled out of town I was looking back between Sudan and Meshuga. I saw Mrs. Eldred in a long horrible gray dress standing next to Ridder and Lucy. They waved and I waved back. Then everyone began running in different directions as the rain began. The street was completely empty before we made the first turn at the south end of town. Looking up through the beating rain, I saw the black and threatening sky. My wet shirt felt good, and for some crazy reason I wanted to get back to John Thornton and go fly-fishing. But as I looked at Meshuga walking along behind us, I knew a bigger challenge than catching a 4-pound rainbow was ahead. I think it was on that day that I first began to understand that York's giant mustang was the horse of my troubled dreams.

Meshuga lost the race and York, but I thought that my Uncle Martin, sitting silently next to me, must know by now that Sudan was no match for the tall black horse following behind.

Chapter Fifteen

THE ROLLING SKULL

Blind Charlie and Uncle Martin brought back York's body the next day in a plain wooden box and they placed it across two sawhorses in the parlor at Endemeo. Blind Charlie wouldn't have a fancy metal casket, even though The Commander put up a raging fit.

"It gone be a simple, truly" is all he said, after listening patiently. It was the first time I ever saw The Commander meet her match.

It was Sunday afternoon and we all were sitting around the house. I couldn't even remember Reverend's Wenk's sermon that morning—my mind wandered back over the months I had known York, mostly on the day Palawäiko bit me. It seemed like years ago. The graveside ceremony would be held the next day at Endemeo. York would be buried up a short draw behind the main ranch house, where some of Blind Charlie's Indian Valley ancestors lay under piles of smooth round river stone. Blind Charlie liked Reverend Wenk, so he agreed to have the "White Medicine Man" do the ceremony. Blind Charlie said he didn't think any story he could tell was as good as The Commander's "Jee-zoose on the cross" and he knew Reverend Wenk was "gone be telling us bout that story, truly." Blind Charlie said that he had memorized John's Gospel when York read it to him once, and I believed him—he could remember anything. But The Commander didn't think it would be a good idea for Blind Charlie to do his special rendition of John with Reverend Wenk and his daughter in attendance. The Gospel according to Blind Charlie might raise eyebrows among even the most tolerant of Taylorsville households. The Commander wasn't about to risk hearing it in the company of the Wenks.

Friends from all over the valley came and went. Nearly all the Tosi-Koyo and Ta-Si-Dum mingled now in circles throughout the house and out back on the porch. Ridder came in with Blood and they both sat down in the parlor. I had never seen Blood Burns in a suit, but now he was uncomfortably tight in a black coat that he must have had years ago in Chicago. Blood sat down self-consciously by Willis, York's older brother, who was staying the weekend from the Bureau school in Greenville. I sat next to Ridder and we talked while the others in the room listened to The Commander play the piano. I think she wanted to distract visitors paying their respects from paying more attention than was absolutely necessary to York's plain pine casket.

"You know who John C. Bender is, Jim?" Ridder said.

"Who?"

"John C. Bender."

"You mean Chief Bender's brother? Why?" But I was already thinking about John C. Bender now and the seed of revelation was planted.

"Well, you remember that day that York struck me out . . . you know, last summer? I was givin' him the devil, you know, making funna his ugly face and all. Well, he stared back at me with that face of his and said somethin' about John C. Bender . . . said he was an Indian who stabbed his manager."

"Yes, I know that story . . . Yes, I remember him talking to you about something, but I was on second base. I wondered what was going on."

"I never been scared before, Jim, but that . . . well, that scared me."

"I'm sorry York did that . . . "

"No, it ain't nothing to be sorry about. I'm gonna miss York. I didn't know him that well . . . but I'm gonna miss him . . . I just thought you might know who John C. Bender was, that's all."

"Why are you asking me about that now?" I asked, curious.

"Yesterday . . . as York was coming through town before the race, you remember?"

"Yes . . . "

"Well, you know that York leaned down and said somethin' to me, you know . . . "

"Right, I remember that. What did he say to you?"

"I can't figure it out . . . he said, 'Don't ever forget John C. Bender, Ridder.'"

The revelation was in full bloom.

"Well, Chief Bender, the Athletics pitcher, was York's favorite player. York told me the story a couple of times about his brother, John . . . ," I faltered.

"Someday I'm goin' to find out, Jim. I'm goin' to be a good baseball player, too, on account of York. He made me a better player. Him and John C. Bender, whoever he is . . ."

"Ridder . . . I know the important thing about John C. Bender . . . I mean really important . . . I know why he said that to you."

"Yeah . . . what?"

"John C. Bender's glory!"

"His what? I don't get it."

"Ridder! York knew he was going to die yesterday at the race, and he told you! John C. Bender died doing what he liked to do best, too—pitching! He died of a heart attack on the pitcher's mound in some Canadian league. York told me that story at least twice. I can't believe I forgot it."

"Well, why'd he tell me for? I ain't never been special to him!" Ridder said.

"I guess it was York's way of saying he was sorry. The story he told you the day he struck you out had a better ending . . . he just wanted you to know that."

Ridder just shook his head over and over and bent down. He didn't say anything more. This was a lot for Ridder to digest in one sitting. He wasn't Mrs. Eldred's brightest student, and unraveling the irony might have taken him all afternoon. I would tell Blind Charlie about this later. He would make this nugget the centerpiece of another story.

We buried York under clearing skies. Reverend Wenk said a few things about York's life, but he hardly knew him. He talked about Jesus and salvation and life after death, all the things Blind Charlie hoped he would say. He spoke, as usual, as though he were preaching before thousands, his deep voice carrying all the way to town. Blind Charlie smiled and nodded through the short ceremony. Blind

Charlie looked peculiar without his black hat, his black hair matted, beginning to show gray. York had taken his grandfather's storied possession with him.

Reverend Wenk had asked me to read Psalm 39. Blind Charlie had that memorized, too, but The Commander feared his democratic interpretation, so I read it as loud as I could under a canopy of rustling trees. My voice seemed puny in the openness of the draw, but the words carried across to the fifty or so in attendance. I read David's psalm from Ma's big leather Bible, slowly, haltingly:

Psalm 39

I said, I will take heed to my ways,
That I sin not with my tongue:
I will keep my mouth with a bridle,
While the wicked is before me.
I was dumb with silence, I held my peace, even from good;
And my sorrow was stirred.
My heart was hot within me,
While I was musing the fire burned:
Then spake I with my tongue,
LORD, make me to know mine end,
And the measure of my days, what it is;
That I may know how frail I am.
Behold, thou hast made my days as an handbreadth;
And mine age is as nothing before thee:
Verily every man at his best state is altogether vanity.
Surely every man walketh in a vain shew:
Surely they are disquieted in vain:
He heapeth up riches, and knoweth not who shall gather them.
And now, LORD, what wait I for?
My hope is in thee.
Deliver me from all my transgressions:
Make me not the reproach of the foolish.
I was dumb, I opened not my mouth;
Because thou didst it.
Remove thy stroke away from me:
I am consumed by the blow of thine hand.

When thou with rebukes dost correct man for iniquity,
Thou makest his beauty to consume away like a moth:
Surely every man is vanity.
Hear my prayer, O LORD, and give ear unto my cry:
Hold not thy peace at my tears:
For I am a stranger with thee,
And a sojourner, as all my fathers were.
O spare me, that I may recover strength,
Before I go hence, and be no more.

Everyone drifted off after the reading, leaving Blind Charlie alone
with York. Blind Charlie, always stiff, sore, and partially bent over,
was going to fill the grave himself. I started to leave with the others,
but Blind Charlie asked to me to stay. Together, we shoveled the dirt
on top of York's casket, as Hercules stood curiously by and watched.
We didn't talk until we had finished an hour later.

Tired, we sat down next to York's mound. Blue Song appeared
with two large mugs of coffee.

"You two might like this," she said, and returned to the house.

"Jim, you know the story of ole Rolling Skull?" he said.

"No, I don't, Mr. Charlie. I don't think I ever heard you mention
that story."

"Truly, Jim, ooooh truly, ole York, he is a rolling skull. I gone
to tell you that story now, O.K.?" He sipped his coffee and leaned
against an oak. I moved over next to a fallen log and got comfortable,
while John Thornton came running from the house, released by The
Commander. His huge black frame nearly flattened Mr. Charlie as he
ran his tongue over his grizzled face. I laughed and he lay at my side.

"York is Rolling Skull?" I asked.

"Truly, Jim, York is the Rolling Skull."

"What does that mean, Mr. Charlie?"

"Ooooh, truly, Jim, you be listening now, and ole Charlie, he
be telling you.

"York, he be hunting deer one day long, long time ago . . . who
be knowing how long ago? The ole Maidu, they not be counting
these things.

"He be hunting up and down all the land, and everybody, they be calling him the rolling-skull man, Ono-toi-kom Maidu, the Skull of the Maidu.

"He be traveling a long, long way from the valley, they say, and he be finding a good place to sleep down for the night. Ole York, he be finding a good place, cuz it is holy place for the Maidu, the big fall on the creek where the water all flowing . . . truly . . . all flowing down over the rocks and bubble all be forming.

"York, truly, he be looking into the dark pool . . . all deep and clear and all like silver. The water, it be cold as ice and York, he be shivering. York, he gone eat is supper and he look up and be listening to the water come over the rocks and be falling into the pool. It is being like music, you know, truly, like the music.

"Truly, York is Skull . . . and now skull, he be building a small fire in the rocks, and truly . . . the lights, they be reflecturing off those big rocks going way, way up to the sky, you know . . . and the moss, it is being green and all sticking to everything on the rocks, and the rocks, they going up and up.

"Ooooh, Jim, it is being a very dark night when the fire, it is going down. So ole York, the Skull, he look into the fire and be thinking it need to be bigger fire, so he is throwing all the wood into the big fire. It roar like the mountain lion into a big leaping of fire.

"Way, way up in the tree, ole owl, Muk-a-law-sem, Muk-a-law-sem, he be looking down on poor ole York, the Skull. Ole owl with the bead eyes is Muk-a-law-sem.

"Muk-a-law-sem, he is hooting and hooting at Skull and he be watching Skull from the big tree . . . truly, Skull is hearing the Muk-a-law-sem and be looking up to the dark and he cannot be seeing Muk-a-law-sem.

"Ole Skull, he is raising his arms and be answering Muk-a-law-sem. He is singing the same song as ole Muk-a-law-sem. Truly, you know what the ole Maidu, they say, Jim? They be saying Skull lost his heart then. Ole York's heart, it fly right out of his body and up into the tree and sky. It gone be flying into the dark and up into the canyons. Now, truly, York, the Skull, his voice it be raising up and down like Muk-a-law-sem's voice . . . and with his heart all gone, his voice it is being loud.

"Truly, York, he is being mad Maidu now. . . his hooting, it be reflecturing off the canyon and back all over. York is being made, crazy, Meshuga, ole Ben he be saying.

"York, truly now, he be dancing by the fire and he is a Maidu and shadow all together. But pretty soon the shadow, it gone be bigger than York, and York, he gone be little Maidu. The shadow, truly, is dark on the rock and pools. Ole York, he be dancing all night and soon the sun, it be coming up over the mountain.

"York, the Skull, he dancing for two days . . . yes, for two days he be dancing by that fire.

"Then, truly, after three days gone, York, he ate his hand. He is eating and chewing the hand, and the arm is all that is being left. Up and down he be swinging his arm with only one hand. He, truly, is lifting his knees high and dancing . . . and then ole York, he is tearing like a lion into his shoulder."

"York he is chewing on his arm now and eating it until it be gone . . . and it is taking him a full day. Up high ole Muk-a-law-sem is looking down on York-Skull and he is smiling.

"All the while he being dancing and soon . . . chop . . . chop . . . he is eating his left arm . . . poor ole Maidu, now he have no arms, just holes where his arms once be.

"He, truly, cannot be swinging his arms no more, so he beginning to eat his legs . . . first he be eating his left leg and then he starting on his right, and the blood, it is running down into little pools on the rocks. Ole York, he is a monster now, in the dark he is being a monster, all the while ole Muk-a-law-sem is watching.

"Truly, ooooh truly, York is a small shadow now. He is being like a rolling ball with no leg and arm. Poor York-Skull . . . no leg, no arm, and now he be thrashing and jumping and bouncing . . . and all while ole Muk-a-law-sem, he be watching.

"The winds, they be howling like the coyote now and all the Maidu in the valley, they look up and thing why the storm is being come so quick. So they gone asking Kadayampa why, but they be getting no answer.

"Ole York-Skull, he is stretching his neck now and he is bending his back and his teeth they are snapping and biting and tearing . . .

"All gone, all gone . . . soon the body, ole York's body . . . is it all gone. And York-Skull now a head, rolling, rolling across the rock and there be red, red blood all round, and it be rolling and dancing to music the wind be making."

I was terrified out of my wits. Even on this bright afternoon, with the honkers trumpeting in their nesting fields barely 100 yards away, I was scared by Mr. Charlie's story. Blind Charlie told me now that the Great Rattlesnake, Palawäiko, came down from the Indian Falls ridge toward York's head. Attracted by the increasing wind, the ceaseless moaning, Palawäiko had sought the source of the storm. Palawäiko laughed when he saw York for he recognized the one who had crushed him with a giant rock. And he laughed when he saw York's eyeballs fallen upon the ground from the jarring movement of the head in its violent dance. The skin and the nose were skipping off the bones now, the ears, the hair, tangled, shredded, peeling of flesh, lips, and sinew. Laughing, Palawäiko slipped into the rolling skull, through eye sockets he wound, and he ate the brain.

Nothing was left then, Blind Charlie had said. No eyes to see, no mouth to sing, no ears to listen with, no heart for feeling. Only a rolling skull, moving to the tensing of Palawäiko's muscles.

Blind Charlie went on to say that when the Great Snake had eaten all the contents of York's skull, he found to his dismay that escape was temporarily impossible. He writhed and jerked and pushed within his cranial prison, but he was too fat from all that eating and he could not get out. The motion became more strenuous and finally so passionate that his exertions sent York rolling into the canyon, over rocks, across sand beds, and up dirt roads toward the valley ahead.

Palawäiko struggled, and York, the Skull, rolled, Blind Charlie said.

York and his prisoner returned to the village. The families ran in horror, the children and women up into the safety of Mt. Hough on one side of the valley, and up Keddie Ridge on the other. The women and children stayed in their high perches for several days before they ventured to come down again. The men, too, ran. In a day or so they returned, lured by the strange songs the stories say came from the moaning skull.

When they finally got close enough to see Skull clearly, the rattlesnake was gone. Now they didn't see the terrible mottled skin, the rattles, and the forked tongue shifting and shimmering inside the white skull. The moaning was gone, replaced by a soft hoo-hoo-hoo. The Rolling Skull is recovering, the legends say. The men looked down upon the quivering, rolling skull, recognized their brother, and told him he was foolish. The Rolling Skull stared from his black sockets and moaned his terrible tale. He was impulsive, hasty, and angry . . . and they understood why. But the men said he was crazy for eating himself like that. Why had he done such a thing? Crazy, they said. Rolling Skull had no heart now, and with no heart, he was mad. "York-Skull, truly, he be waiting . . . and high up ole Muk-a-law-sem is be watching. And now he be flying away and going in one big circle . . . round and round this big circle."

Blind Charlie moved his hand in a slow descending circle.

"Closer and closer and closer is being come Muk-a-law-sem and soon he land on top of ole York. All the Maidu, they be scared and be backing away, while Muk-a-law-sem, truly, he picking up the skull and be flying away.

"Now ole York, he be crying and crying so that all the Maidu, they be running after ole Muk-a-law-sem and throwing rocks at him. All the village, they be following the Great Owl until it is coming to the falls. And, truly, when all the Maidu reaching the falls, ole Muk-a-law-sem, he drop York into the dark pool. So, truly, they all be looking down in there, down into the bottom of the dark pool . . . and Jim, what do they be seeing?"

"The Rolling Skull," I said.

"You be right, truly, but he is not being there today, you know, and all you kids, you be swimming and diving where ole Rolling Skull was sleeping long, long ago . . . down there. It is deep there, you know, and no one can be diving deep to be touching the Rolling Skull, but gone on the down the river, he gone on down, rolling, rolling down the river.

"He, truly, gone on down to the Great Valley all flat and big where ole Ben and me, we be finding the Rolling Skull being born a little Maidu."

I looked up and saw that Blind Charlie's tired, dark face was marked by two narrow traces, tears coming hard from a man who told his tales largely unadorned by sentiment. He was looking far away, I don't know where, maybe back thirteen years ago when he and Benjamin Kurtz found York abandoned and alone.

"Where did York come from, Mr. Charlie?" I asked.

"I thing bout that and I thing bout that, Jim . . . and I don't be knowing how that be. Truly, that ole Sacramento doctor, he be saying that York is being white and he is being Maidu. But I be thinging, you know, truly. Maybe Ben, he is being right when he be saying that ole Shaky-Spear know all bout York. This ole Indian, he don't ever gone to be knowing."

When Mr. Charlie finished, I didn't want to say anything. We both sat there for a long time. Our coffee was still in the cups, cold now. Soon the sun would sink behind Mt. Hough. We both got up then and drifted away, he to return to his cabin, alone, while I struggled with my afternoon chores, trying to make a connection with Blind Charlie's story of the Rolling Skull and the York who had been my friend.

Chapter Sixteen

YORK'S RIDE

The Mohawk Valley Race would be held on June 25, 1915, nearly a full year after Ma died. Two Englishmen and the manager of the Feather River Inn wanted to celebrate with other enthusiastic guests for the Inn's grand opening that year. I had seen small block ads in several of Uncle Martin's magazines—ranching journals and horse quarterlies—but I really hadn't given the race much thought until I saw the poster in Taylorsville. The all-comers endurance horse race over a distance of 100 miles might not have attracted people to travel to remote Plumas County—but the $10,000 first-prize money made it one of the richest purses of any horse race in the world, and certainly the biggest plum for long-distance racing, a sport which had been popular in the West for several years now.

Just a few years earlier, long-distance horse racing had gotten a bad name, but with the notorious Chadron to Chicago 1,000-mile race, humane societies had forced race handlers to station veterinarians along the route and to disqualify mistreated animals. The Mohawk Valley Race would be one of the fairest, safest, and most rugged endurance races of its kind, an improvement over the earlier races that still rankled a vigilant public.

The $10,000 prize had been guaranteed by several wealthy easterners who would become regular visitors to the Inn over the next several years. The Pittsburgh steel manufacturer had called it a "diversion." A year earlier, he and others had dreamed up the idea while playing whist on a resort's huge covered deck overlooking Lake Champlain in upstate New York. As I heard the story years later, it had been an idle summer evening. Jason Thompson and Walter Ruggles-Spencer, the two Englishmen, had worked themselves into a heated argument over the relative merits of the Arabians they owned. Creighton Luke, from Pittsburgh, had intervened and suggested a long-distance race between the two. Luke was also the principal owner of the Feather River Inn in faraway California. One thing led to another. The next day they made plans to hold more than just a match race between the two Arabians. It would be an international race and would be staged at the opening of Luke's new California resort, which the *Plumas National Bulletin* described as "a magnificent nineteenth century French baronial structure, among rugged mountains, fast running creeks, and picturesque mountain valleys."

The "splendid idea" grew. Before that summer in New York had ended and the packing of their several leather portmanteaux was finished, the three men had produced careful instructions to an agent in San Francisco to establish the race for anyone who could lay down the $25 entry fee. The agent would work with local officials of the United States Forest Service to map out a suitable course through the rugged mountains and valleys between Portola and Genesee. Arrangements were made with the railroad to transport horses to Blairsden from all points east.

Over the next several months the advertising had stimulated international interest. By May, over 175 horse owners, determined cowboys, and gamblers backing long shots had coughed up the entry fee. They would be coming from all over the United States, England, and a few from France. Two entrants would come from Argentina, both owners of large cattle ranches. A German nobleman, Baron Ernst Richartz, would come, despite the furor over the sinking of *Lusitania*—128 Americans were among the 1,195 lost at sea as result of a U-boat attack. A strong anti-German sentiment was sweeping America.

Although most would arrive for the horse race only, the Feather River Inn was the perfect place to hold such an event: spacious green lawns, a splendid main structure of French Colonial design, a lush golfing course, a tennis court, manicured equestrian trails, a large swimming pool, the beautiful Middle Fork of the Feather River, and the scenic mountains all around.

By the end of May, the Inn's stables were bulging with costly, blooded horses. The Inn wouldn't open for another week or so, but Creighton Luke had made special arrangements for the horses that would be arriving by train at the Blairsden depot. Stallions, mares, and a few geldings swelled the corrals and paddocks on the Inn's spacious grounds. Trainers, seconds, and grooms had accompanied most of the animals weeks in advance of the owners' arrival. Some of the horses wouldn't arrive until two or three days before the race, while some of the locals would come just a day early. By mid-June the place was beginning to resemble a cavalry remount station, but to the trained eye these horses were too fine a collection of blooded stock to bear close comparison to military equipage.

In early June, a few weeks after York's death, John Thornton and I were sitting by the fallen log where Palawäiko and York and Meshuga had come into my life almost a year ago. I had this empty feeling in my stomach, and I felt very alone. Uncle Martin had paid the entry fees for the upcoming race. No one had mentioned who would ride Meshuga. I thought for sure that Uncle Martin would give Meshuga back to Dutch and that would end the matter. Instead, Uncle Martin ignored the subject of Meshuga and told me one night at dinner that he would ride Sudan and an Arabian mare he had just purchased from the same ranch in Stockton. I didn't say anything. The Commander didn't say anything. It was an awkward silence. I spent several evenings with Blind Charlie, but he didn't talk about Meshuga either, except to ask once or twice, "What that crazy horse be doin'?" Blind Charlie, at least on the surface, was not crushed as I was by York's death. He had seen so much more of death than I, even though I figured that for a boy who had just turned thirteen, I was moving along that path more quickly than most. Mr. Charlie's cheerfulness and stories, at times, made us both feel like York was alive in the room with us.

Kenneth Joe Tracker had ridden Meshuga almost daily, keeping him in shape, but found the big Black too wild to take out of the large south pasture. He just rode in large circles around the pasture's perimeter. I had watched him almost every day with a growing fear of Meshuga, a fear brought on by Pa's voice: *You're going to ride him, Jim.*

So I was out on the stream with my rod and flies. But I couldn't fish. I just sat there, thinking. I took a folded piece of paper out of my pocket, York's entry receipt and rules. I carefully unfolded it and read:

All entrants shall begin the race at the Mohawk Valley bridge at 6:00 a.m. on Saturday, June 25, 1915. Riders will proceed at any pace over the distance, arriving at each checkpoint at several stations along the course. At each checkpoint the rider's number will be marked by officials as the entrants proceed toward the finish at the Feather River Inn entrance gate. A rider may enter two horses, stationing the second mount at any checkpoint along the racecourse route. The first rider who crosses the finish line, having first been acknowledged by each checkpoint official, shall be declared the winner and recipient of the entire prize of $10,000. A rider is not required to use established roads and trails along the route. <u>Any shortcut or cross-country route is permissible so long as the rider passes through each checkpoint</u>. A rider must stop for thirty minutes at two of the checkpoints where a veterinarian will check each horse's pulse. It must decrease to a rate of 70 within the thirty minutes or the horse and rider are disqualified.

The rules were simple enough. The pulse rate rule was a good one for the safety of the horses. I folded the paper and stuffed it back into my pocket.

Pa's voice wouldn't go away.

You're going to ride him, Jim. It's your time. The only way you'll ever know you're up to it, is to do it . . . it's time, Jim . . . you've only got three weeks . . . what are you waiting for?

"What am I going to do, John Thornton? I can't ride Meshuga. I'm nothing but a coward . . . I'm not as good as Pa . . . don't know that I'll ever be."

John Thornton jumped up and ran his nose into my face, licking me all over. I grabbed him by his ears and wrestled him to the ground. School was out next week, and I had a whole summer of fishing and John Thornton and . . .

C'mon, Jim, you can always go fishing.

I watched from the front porch as Uncle Martin and Kenneth Joe Tracker loaded Sudan and his new mare, al Khansa, into the back of the truck for the 50-mile drive down to Blairsden. Kenneth Joe Tracker loaded Moon into the truck for himself, so he could ride over to the Flournoy checkpoint with Sudan. Tomorrow morning the race would begin. In his pen, Meshuga couldn't understand why he wasn't being loaded, too. He ran back and forth, frantically at times, before Uncle Martin and Kenneth Joe Tracker drove out of sight. I watched them go until I couldn't see them anymore. Just before they vanished beyond the last point, Kenneth Joe Tracker turned around and waved. I waved back. My stomach was jumping and churning as crazily as Meshuga was jumping in his corral.

Maybe you . . . don't . . . have what it takes, Jim.

The sun was warm on my back. I shoved my hands in my pockets stiffly and trudged wearily down the road in the opposite direction toward Blind Charlie's cabin. My thoughts were always filled with Pa now. It was like he was living inside my head and I couldn't get away. Maybe I could talk to Mr. Charlie. The Commander and Blue Song were inside the house, but I needed to talk to Blind Charlie, not my aunt. As I neared the old log cabin, I wasn't even sure he was home. Blind Charlie was nearly always gone in summertime, wandering around the country with Hercules. I hadn't seen Mr. Charlie since last week. He had just come by for a cup of coffee. Before he left he had looked at me in that distant way of his and said, "How be that crazy horse a York's, Jim?" And then he was off, not really wanting an answer.

Blind Charlie was sitting on the porch sleeping. I tried to be quiet as I tiptoed onto the wooden boards across to his side.

"What's ole Jim gone be doing today?" he said, not opening his eyes.

"I thought you were asleep, Mr. Charlie," I said, sitting down on the old wood bench. next to his chair.

"Truly, I bin sleeping until ole Jim come stomp all over my porch and be waking up ole Charlie from the bestest story ever was."

"I'd like to hear a story, Mr. Charlie, but . . . I can't just now . . . my head's all messed up inside . . . Pa keeps talking to me. He wants me to ride Meshuga in the race. I think everyone wants me to ride

Meshuga . . . but I can't . . . well, I can't do it. I'm . . . afraid of him
. . . and Pa wouldn't have been."

"Truly, I knowing all bout that . . . ole Moon Man, he always
be talking to old Charlie long, long ago when I be a little Indian.
But, truly, Jim, you be right . . . that black is crazy, crazy horse. Old
Charlie, he don't want you be riding that crazy horse, truly. Old Jim
Pa, he be crazy like Moon Man be." Mr. Charlie's eyes were still
closed and his hands were crossed in his lap.

"No . . . Mr. Charlie, my pa's dead. Moon Man was alive when
he was talking to you. My pa's dead. How can he talk to me?"

"Ooooh, Jim, truly, cuz he being *inside* your head."

"What do you mean, Mr. Charlie?" I asked.

"Truly, this old Indian ain't gone be saying no more bout
that . . . that story ain't be happening yet . . . it be in the pickser,
truly." Charlie lifted his head off the back of the chair and looked
at me with his red eyes, far away as always, but close as ever.

"What picture, Mr. Charlie?"

"York, his big pickser . . . ole York, truly . . . he be knowing the
story afore ole Charlie, he be knowing it."

"What picture are you talking about, Mr. Charlie?"

"Truly, Jim, maybe you don't be ready to see that pickser . . .
and maybe, old Charlie, he be thinging Jim do be ready to see that
pickser . . . this old Indian, he jes don't be knowing . . ."

Go ahead, ask to see the picture, Jim.

"Mr. Charlie, I think I've seen all of York's pictures."

"Truly, maybe you seen all ole York's picksers, but there be one
you ain't be seeing yet."

Ask to see the picture, Jim.

I sensed something very important was happening. My heart
was beating away in my chest, so hard and loud that I thought Mr.
Charlie must hear it. I took a long deep breath.

"How'd you know I would come to see you today, Mr. Charlie?"

"Truly, I be having the idea you be coming."

"Where is the picture, Mr. Charlie?"

"Ooooh, truly, I thing Blue Song, she be hanking it in old Kenneth's tack room this morning. It be hanking in there with the old
saddles and straps and thinks."

"In the tack room next to Meshuga's paddock?"

"Truly." Blind Charlie closed his eyes and laid his head back. I saw just the twinge of a smile.

Get running, Jim.

I turned and ran all the way back to Endemeo. I didn't stop at the house. I ran on past the back porch, past the milk rooms and creamery and on down to Meshuga's pen. Meshuga was as black and elegant as ever. He looked brushed. His coat shone like silver in the sun.

I walked on past him and into the tack room. The sun was shining dusty drafts through the two windows facing west. I looked across at the distant wall and there was York's last painting. It was hanging above a black saddle on one of peeled poles, simple and unadorned, but of skilled workmanship. The saddle was new, but it had been carefully and lovingly worked with a cream, so the leather was soft and supple. I moved closer until I stood in front of the saddle and looked up.

The oil painting bore a title, something York did occasionally with his work. He had called it *York's Ride*. The painting had been completed in the colors of the mountains, blues and greens and browns, dominated by the great black horse sprinting across the finish line in the great Mohawk Valley Race. Like all of York's work, the painting had captured the excitement and emotion of the moment, the movement and rush of the horse and . . . rider!

The shocks of recognition and understanding seemed almost to knock me down. This is what Blind Charlie had wanted me to see. For it was not York who was riding the Black . . . it was I, Jim McLaverty! I hadn't noticed this at first. I had taken in the picture as a whole and then began breaking the scene into parts as I looked first at Meshuga . . . and then . . . .

"York's Ride!" I said aloud. York had known he wouldn't be here for the big race!

"York's Ride! *York's Ride!*" I screamed, and then I understood something about the wisdom of old Blind Charlie and the brilliance of York. Then it hit me. The simple truth of Blind Charlie, no self-glorification in his prophecies, none of the pride that Ma always warned me about. It came to me in a flash. Honesty and love.

It was clear now. York's ride was my ride. His story was my story. Did I have the courage to be part of a greater story than I had lived up till now?

Well, what are you going to do, Jim?

Do? Of course, I knew what I was going to do. My fear was falling away from me as quickly as I walked toward Meshuga's paddock with York's silver studded bridle. Pa's voice was no longer Timothy "Bronco" McLaverty. Pa's voice was just Pa. Laughing and crying and full of a joy I hadn't ever known before, I called Meshuga to me.

"G-G-Get up, J-Jim." Dutch was shaking me. It was four-thirty in the morning, and already riders were busy saddling horses, making breakfast, and getting ready for the six a.m. starting time. All around me were sounds of movement, horses stomping and snorting, voices of men getting up, laughter, curses, the sounds of a cavalry camp coming alive just before dawn. New campfires were flickering everywhere, bursting into new flames, unlike the orange-red embers of the night before.

I had ridden down to Blairsden, a 50-mile ride just the day before, not arriving until just before midnight, surprising Dutch and Kenneth Joe Tracker as I rode the makeshift camp near the starting line. Uncle Martin had gone to bed, but the others were playing cards around a campfire late.

I had traveled quickly on Meshuga, sitting comfortably in the handsome black saddle and green blanket—covering the 50 miles in eight hours, alternately walking and trotting the big Black. I had not been afraid, and Meshuga had responded as gently as Moon. But I knew I had an explosive animal under my saddle, and I had to use the tough spade bit often to keep Meshuga from running. I wanted to save his strength for the next day's race. Kenneth Joe Tracker and Dutch jumped up when they saw me ride in.

"E-E-Everybody m-m-might jes as well quit r-r-right now, cuz here c-c-comes the winner!" he shouted. The others laughed at first, but when they looked up and saw it was the famous Meshuga, the horse that whipped Sudan a month ago, they showed a sudden interest.

"Who's ridin' him?"

"How come heez comin' in so late . . . izzhe crazy?"

"I thought that Indian kid died . . . never thought nobody'd ride that Black agin."

Now Dutch and Kenneth Joe Tracker were smiling and trying to get me up and ready before the start. Kenneth Joe Tracker, as usual, was more concerned with my diet than anything else.

"You ain't gonna be any good at all less you eat a big breakfast, Jim," he said, as I jumped into my jeans and shirt. The gray sky was just hinting of a blue sky in the east, still a black ceiling with a million stars. "Dutch and I gonna make you a first-rate breakfast a eggs and ham and some a The Commander's biscuits I'm gonna heat up in the pan."

"L-L-Lord amighty, J-J-Jim, you know how m-m-m-many miles you gotta ride t-t-today?" asked Dutch, knowing full well that I did, but amazed I had waited until the day before the race to get any practice in on Meshuga.

"I'm going to win this race, Dutch," I said without hesitation.

"I-I-I don't d-d-don't d-doubt it, Jim . . . yur ridin' him the whole d-d-distance, ain't cha?" Dutch smiled and shook his head.

"As far as I heard, no one else is doin' that, Jim—you're the only rider with a single horse in the race . . . all the rest have two . . . that bother you any?" asked Kenneth Joe Tracker.

I shook my head, "Nope. This is York's Ride."

They seemed to understand what I meant.

"Now you lissen to me, Jim," said Kenneth Joe Tracker, as he cracked some eggs into the skillet, "I'm goin' to be near the sixth checkpoint. You know about the part in the rule which says you go anywheres you want to so long as you goes through the checkpoints?"

I nodded.

"If you ain't ahead then—at the sixth checkpoint—I got an idea about how you can *get* ahead . . . only Meshuga could do it . . . you'll jes take 'im right up over the top of the ridge—I'll show you on the map after breakfast—and on down to the next checkpoint, checkpoint seven. 'Tween six and seven there's a shortcut, only Meshuga's the only horse in the whirl which can do it," said Kenneth Joe Tracker.

"What if I'm ahead?" I asked.

"Yeah, well, you probably will be . . . but jes in case . . . guess you know there's some a the bess horses you'll ever see here for this here race. You wait till you see those two Englishmen and their 'rabians. They've got two mounts and they're takin' 'em over to checkpoint four for the second half. You're goin' up 'ginst fresh horses in the last 50 mile, Jim."

By the end of the race, toward evening, over four hundred people would line the sides of the Portola to Quincy highway, a gravel road running along the Middle Fork. Now at the start, just a few quiet, half-sleepy spectators gathered at six a.m. The race began 2 miles from the Inn where the bridge crosses the Middle Fork. The course then followed a tree-lined road northwest along the old highway through Sloat and Long Valley to Greenhorn Creek. There the trail veered under heavy timber northeast and climbed nearly 3,000 feet over rocky Grizzly Ridge at an elevation of 8,500 feet. The course continued on down into Genesee Valley, past Argentine Rock, by Hosselkus Ranch, where several hundred head of Uncle Martin's cattle were grazing. Here was a principal checkpoint, the Hosselkus Store. The trail turned into a road there and followed Indian Creek to the Flournoy Ranch, an old stage-line depot that ran to Beckwourth years earlier. Following this stage-line route, the course continued on over Squaw Valley to Portola. The last 10-mile leg was a wide gravel road from Portola to the gates of the Inn, the finish line. The course was roughly 100 miles, but Kenneth Joe Tracker said it was probably a bit longer than that.

Nearly 175 horsemen—two were women—amassed at the starting line in uneven rows going back nearly a hundred yards from the bridge. The sun was not yet up on the tangle of horses and riders, but in the gray morning light I could mark dark horses and light, steady animals and high-strung. Anxiously, I held Meshuga near the rear. Meshuga seemed much more subdued than I. He wasn't affected, apparently, by the prerace jitters. I wanted all the horses to clear out, for the early pandemonium to cease, before I really let my Black go.

I had seen the two Englishmen up front earlier as I paced Meshuga along the side of the road. They both had come alongside me in the semidarkness of morning and appraised the Black.

"McLaverty?" asked one of them.

"Yes, sir," I answered surprised, looking down on their shorter mounts. They were obviously English, and somehow they knew my name.

"This is Meshuga, the Red Indian's horse?" the other asked.

"Yes. He was York Toby's horse."

"All we've heard since our arrival is how bloody great this Meshuga is! He looks big enough—does he have stamina? I heard he was soundly beaten in a race a few weeks ago!"

"He's a mustang! And he won't ever lose again!" I said, feeling like King Saul, standing head and shoulders above his people. But I didn't want to be a Saul and look all glittery and great on the outside. I wanted to be a King David and slay Goliath.

"You don't say, now?" laughed the other. "I'm Thompson, and this is Ruggles-Spencer. We're riding Arabians which are quite good, too, McLaverty. I'm on Loki Dute II for the first leg and pick up Legion at the Flournoy crossing for the final go. Perhaps you've heard of Legion?"

You had to have lived in a cave all your life not to have known Legion. Legion was known everywhere, had run in the United States many times and never lost.

"Yes, sir . . . everyone knows Legion." The two Englishmen were taunting me. I should have been upset and intimidated, but I felt strangely secure on Meshuga.

"When did you get in, McLaverty? We've been looking for you all week. Some said you wouldn't be here . . ." said Ruggles-Spencer.

"Got in last night . . . rode 50 miles and got here late."

"What? The devil, you say! Fifty miles the night before the race! You're round the bend, man!"

"Just a workout," I said.

"Hah! Good luck, McLaverty!" Thompson said, and they both rode off back toward the start. I was sure I heard muffled laughter, but with all the other horses and general prerace mayhem, I stifled a prideful urge to ride after them and continue our exchange.

The betting favorite was with the Thompson entries. His two dark Arabians were 2-1 to place first. Ruggles-Spencer's two horses, Moira and Matchem, were 3-1. Meshuga was not mentioned by anyone. Apparently, the Plumas County crowd, who knew and glorified Meshuga's legend, were not equipped to bet heavily on their favorite. They just talked a lot, and the story of Meshuga and York had spread during the week prior to the race.

When I led Meshuga from his quarters following breakfast that morning, I was not wearing the colorful clothing of my competitors, but simple dungarees with a tan moleskin shirt. The richer entrants were wearing jodhpurs, high shiny boots, comfortable cotton shirts, with jackets rolled behind the cantles of polished saddles.

I held Meshuga still as the race was about to begin. The sun was higher behind the mountains to the east now. Through the haze of bluish-gray dust, I could the see 175 riders becoming quieter now. There was tug on my leg. I looked down to see Ridder in the middle of the road.

"Ridder! What in . . . how'd you get here?"

"The Commander, she drove me down with Blind Charlie and Blue Song."

He told me they were up ahead off to the left among the trees with some other folks from Taylorsville. He had a red cap in his hand.

"Jim, this here's a St. Louis Cardinals cap. They're my favorite team and I just want you to have it. The Commander, she sewed it up in back so it would fit yuh . . . will you wear it?"

I reached down and grabbed the bright red cap. The Commander had altered the size somewhat and it fit snugly down over my head.

"Thanks, Ridder . . ."

"*Get ready*!" a voice echoed from a platform at the starting line. The starter was speaking through a huge megaphone. Everyone became completely silent. I moved away from Ridder and got ready.

A bugle sounded and suddenly the earth trembled under me as the horses began moving, walking at first, and then trotting as the space between the competing animals widened. Soon, many of the riders were galloping their horses, hoping to impress spectators and bettors at the beginning, but I walked Meshuga slowly, holding his reins securely in my right hand, until the herd had disappeared out of sight. Meshuga was ready to explode, and I held him in check with the spade bit pressed against the roof of his mouth. Meshuga tossed his head up and down, wanting to go after the others.

"What you waiting for, Jim?" It was Kenneth Joe Tracker. Dutch was standing there, too.

"I want everything spread out. Everyone's too bunched together!" I shouted.

I knew the time had come. Dutch Coder laughed. "I thing y-y-you got p-p-p-plenty of space now, Jim—you b-b-better git going!"

"Win for York, Jim!" someone shouted. It was The Commander, sitting in the Imperial among the trees with Blue Song and Blind Charlie, now donning another black hat. I was glad to see John Thornton stick his black head above the back seat, his tongue hanging out in its usual undignified way. I sucked in my breath.

"Where's Uncle Martin?" I yelled.

"He's up in front on al Khansa!" she yelled back. "Go get him!"

"Go, Meshuga!" I said, and released the hold on the reins.

Meshuga burst forth in a full gallop. It was like the rattlesnake run all over again, this time without the confident York's help. I knew my responsibility would be to pace Meshuga and run the race wisely, not to overextend him and be disqualified if his pulse did not reduce to the required 70 within thirty minutes. The small crowd who had arisen early to watch the start must have wondered at the sight of the biggest horse, black Meshuga, spinning and waiting, while the thundering herd of racers had roared forward.

By the time the horses passed through the first checkpoint I had passed all the others, including Uncle Martin. My uncle warned me to slow down and pace the big Black.

"Jim, you're going ahead too fast. Slow down and save Meshuga's energy. He's a crazy horse . . . you've got to take control of him. If you don't you kill him!"

"I'll see you at the finish line, Uncle Martin," is all I said.

"You're like your father, Jim," he said as I looked back. "He was just as crazy as that horse . . . Jim?"

I looked back.

"Meshuga's a better horse than Sudan!" He waved me on. It was good to hear Uncle Martin say that to me. It was the kindest thing he ever said in his life, and we both knew it was true.

I waved my St. Louis Cardinals cap in front of Thompson as I galloped past Loki Dute II, who was in the lead.

"You'll not last long at that pace, McLaverty!" he shouted as I passed.

This early pace had not been my plan. Meshuga just took control of things at the start, and I went along for the ride. Meshuga was not fatigued as I rounded the last bend in the road before looking for the trail marker indicating the route east up the ridge toward Argentine Rock.

I had left the others well behind now—out of sight—as I looked for the turnoff. Looming ahead were two officials wearing green vests, the uniforms of each checkpoint. I pulled back on Meshuga's reins to slow him down. Meshuga didn't respond, running faster if anything.

"Hold up there, this is the turnoff . . . you're the first one through . . . hold up!" he yelled, putting out his hand.

I didn't expect the disaster. My handling of Meshuga the afternoon and night before had gone smoothly and without incident. I gained the confidence I needed to go with him the hundred miles. Now, excited by the race's beginning, Meshuga wouldn't turn and he wouldn't stop. We galloped past the point as both men watched us. In tears of frustration, I tried to control Meshuga, but he seemed bent on going in this direction. This was the way home. Maybe he was going there. I yanked back on the spade bit, alarmed that I might hurt York's horse. Meshuga responded by turning abruptly and running through the trees at the side of the road.

I tried to duck when I saw the branch was too low, succeeding only in scraping the shirt and tearing skin off my back. My stirrup caught on something, perhaps a lower protruding branch, yanking the saddle sideways. I fell off, hitting the ground with my shoulder. Meshuga ran on until I couldn't see him any longer, my beautiful black saddle rolling underneath the Black's belly sending the stirrups dangling, dragging.

Now what are you going to do, Jim McLaverty? Are you just going to sit there? Find the horse, Jim, find the horse. Get up, Jim.

Pa's voice again. I didn't want to think about Pa or to contend with him. My back was bleeding. I could feel streams of warm blood running down the small of my back. My tan moleskin shirt hung in shreds down the side of my dungarees. My left shoulder was numb, but when I touched it, the pain was not severe enough to make me think it was broken.

I had never fallen from a horse. I knew that falling from a horse as tall as Meshuga, and running as he was, could be serious. But fortunately, I was all right. I got up and brushed myself off and tried to gain my bearings. Looking back, I saw the tree where I had snagged the saddle and scraped my back. My St. Louis Cardinals baseball cap was lying in the dirt. I walked back, picked up the cap, and unbuttoned my shirt. I removed the shirt and tried my best to dampen the bloody abrasions on my back. The bleeding seemed to have stopped, but the burning pain grew worse.

I was hurting inside, too. A sense of hopelessness followed by anger at Meshuga for destroying York's opportunity. But, as I sat down hard in a carpet of pine needles, I was really angry at myself for not living up to the responsibility I had set for myself. Gritting my teeth, the heaving started deep down inside—I couldn't control the tears. They just oozed out against my will and fell off my dirty cheeks.

I wished I could have fallen off the face of the earth.

Chapter Seventeen

THE FINISH

Something soft and wet was nudging my face. Smells of horse and grass and leather. I don't know how long I slept. I awoke with the sun shining down in shafts through the tall pines and firs—through four black legs and a suspended tangle of stirrups and straps . . . standing next to me. It was quiet, peaceful. For a moment I was back on the creek in Missouri, fly-fishing with John Thornton without a care or responsibility. I thought how nice it would be to just go back to sleep. But this wasn't right. The horse should have been rearing, snorting, ready to brain me. . .

Meshuga!

"You crazy horse, where've you been?"

Meshuga was standing next to me, running his nose and mouth across my face.

Let's get going, cowboy!

I jumped up, not very stylish in my ripped, bloodstained shirt. Not too eager, either with my sore shoulder and burning back. Meshuga stood while I pulled the saddle up and over his back. I loosened the cinch and pulled the saddle off. The green blanket was gone. I checked the saddle to see it was not damaged. Aside from a few battle scars and a heavy film of dirt, the saddle was in perfect condition. Hurrying now, I saddled Meshuga without the blanket and dragged my hurting body up, pulling hard on the horn. Once I was seated comfortably in the saddle, I ran the seriousness of my setback through my mind.

How many minutes, hours, had passed? I walked Meshuga carefully back through the trees to the road.

"We've got a lot of ground to make up, Meshuga? You up for it?" I spoke aloud in the middle of an empty road, but I didn't feel alone. "Go, Meshuga!"

Arriving at the checkpoint a few minutes later, I learned that I had lost over an hour. But this part of the course ran steadily uphill, a steep climb of over 3,000 feet in just 5 or 6 miles. I knew Meshuga was at his best in these conditions. I pushed him hard.

Arriving at the Argentine Rock checkpoint, I had gained enough ground to reach the rear group of riders. A veterinarian would check Meshuga's pulse now. We were one-third finished.

Meshuga's pulse quickly dropped down to an acceptable 70 beats per minute, and I was on my way. Meshuga's conditioning would help me make up time, although several of the horses were disqualified at the Argentine Rock stop.

Going over the top of Grizzly Ridge, I could see the long trail of horses strung out in varied colors below me. Far in the distance, I saw the leaders, nearing the base of the ridge and moving into Genesee Valley. If Thompson didn't know what had happened to me, he would be pushing Loki Dute II harder than ever, trying to make up time before he changed horses at the Flournoy crossing. Then with Legion, he would only pass through one veterinary station before the finish. I had to gain a lot of ground to catch Thompson. But he would know I had passed the checkpoint on a runaway horse. He probably got a good laugh with Ruggles-Spencer about that. He would be basking in self-satisfaction that no one could beat him and Legion. That Meshuga rumor was just a lot of local color and imagination. I wasn't even an afterthought in Thompson's plans. Never had been, really.

I passed rider after rider tirelessly over the next two hours, passing through checkpoints two and three. Meshuga was thriving on the run, now. I was in a comfortable lope, alternating with a quick trot and fast walk. Unlike most horses, Meshuga had an easy, graceful trot. It was rhythmical, flowing—not hard or jarring. The gait was an easy one for Meshuga, and I used it often to restore his strength. We stopped for long drinks of water twice in Genesee Valley before we reached the Flournoy crossing.

Flournoy, the fourth checkpoint, was filled with tired horses and complaining riders. I dismounted, and an attendant immediately took Meshuga and walked him over to the veterinarian for an initial pulse count, while I walked over to the old stage depot. Uncle Martin was there, sitting on a bench. He watched me now as I limped over to him.

"Well, Jim, what in heaven's name are you doing here? I thought you'd be miles ahead by now."

"Meshuga ran on by the first checkpoint in Long Valley. Couldn't stop him."

"What's happened? You look a little roughed up. What's wrong with your shirt?"

I turned around and showed him my back.

"How bad is it?"

"Pretty bad, Jim. You better go see if the vet can help you. I don't think Meshuga needs any help from the smart way he just rode in."

"He's riding beautifully, Uncle Martin. I think I could have won the race, if he hadn't gone crazy on me back there."

"Well, I always told you—he's a crazy horse. I can tell you, you're lucky not to be hurt worse."

I watched as the attendant removed Meshuga's saddle. Angry, I got up and ran toward the group checking the animals' condition.

"Hey, don't take that saddle off. I'm riding him on from here!"

"Don't you have a second horse?" said the incredulous vet.

"No, no—Meshuga's going the whole way!"

"I heard there was one horse doing that," he said, smiling, "but I didn't believe it . . . not against the others using two horses."

In a few minutes Uncle Martin and I moved out together. For a few minutes, I enjoyed riding along with Sudan again, but after crossing Indian Creek and moving along Red Clover Creek, Uncle Martin started to lag behind.

"Be right behind you, Jim," he said as I loped on ahead.

In the next hour I passed the last few riders stretching between me and the leaders as I pulled my way steadily up the ridge to Squaw Valley and last loop of the race. Sudan stayed close behind me, not more than several hundred yards away. I estimated that about 25 miles remained to the finish. Somewhere ahead was Thompson and Ruggles-Spencer.

Kenneth Joe Tracker surprised me. He was waiting on Moon about halfway up the ridge. I pulled Meshuga to a stop. York's Black was as manageable as a pup now.

"Well, Jim, what did old Kenneth tell you? What happened to you? Your shirt looks bloody and ripped. York's horse throw ya?"

"Yes—but I'm all right . . . is this the place?"

"Yes . . . jes as I said. You're goin' have to do some handsome ridin' here on out to win, guess you know . . ."

"The rule . . ."

"That's right . . . the rules says you kin go anywheres you want so long as you passes through the checkpoints. The next checkpoint is down by Portola. You ain't goin' to catch Legion or that other horse—Matchem—unless you go over the top to cut 'em off."

"I don't know the way . . ."

Uncle Martin came riding up with Sudan. He looked weary and beaten, slumped in the saddle, but Sudan was eager.

"Having a conference, boys? There's a race on, you know."

"I'm tellin' Jim here about goin' over the ridge, only he don't know the way. It's the only way he can win as I sees it," said Kenneth Joe Tracker.

Uncle Martin stopped. He stared at both of us for a while in silence.

"I'm finished, Kenneth," he said. "I don't think I can go another mile. Why don't you ride Sudan on over with Jim . . . show him the way."

"No, Uncle Martin," I said. "That's not fair, you're one of the leaders."

"No, Jim . . . I can't go another foot. I'm tired. I'll just take Moon on back from here. Kenneth, you take Sudan. Only Sudan can get Meshuga over that mountain."

Sudan and Meshuga reached the divide by the middle of the afternoon. I was lost until we reached the summit, and then I understood why Kenneth was called Joe Tracker. He had an uncanny sense of direction and purpose when traveling over difficult and unfamiliar terrain. He knew these mountains like they were his own. And they were his own, his and the mother Maidu who had made these mountains and high valleys their home for countless centuries.

We had traveled cross-country. The pace seemed painfully slow, but we were traversing steep grades, sometimes so difficult we had to dismount and pull the horses up.

The road into Portola was obscured by the trees, but we knew that we had gained miles on Thompson and Ruggles-Spencer. We now had only to rush down the south side of the ridge and into Sierra Valley.

We passed Ruggles-Spencer just before reaching the fifth checkpoint, just outside Portola. The winded horse, Matchem, had slowed to a walk. Ruggles-Spencer didn't even look up as we passed. The race had taken a toll on him, too.

When we reached the last checkpoint on the Portola-Blairsden leg of the race, the final 10 miles, it was five in the afternoon. The official said that Legion was about five minutes ahead. Our trek across the ridge had been more than a shortcut—we had gained almost an hour on the leader!

"I'm goin' to slow up now, Jim. You go on ahead with Meshuga. You can win it if you keep 'im movin'."

I wanted to thank Kenneth Joe Tracker, but how could I thank him?

I waved, pulled down my St. Louis Cardinals cap hard on my dusty hair, and rode off.

Now is the time, Jim. Now is the time.

"Run, Meshuga, run! Let's win this one for York!"

A scattering of people walking along the streets watched as Meshuga thundered down the hard gravel highway, in some places covered by long, flat boards, a trail of dust behind us. They looked up as we galloped past. They didn't know the drama of the race or how the story was unfolding.

Outside Portola, about 8 miles from the finish, a motorcar moved alongside the leader, Legion. I could see it now, a dark maroon touring sedan, filled with people. They seemed to be pacing Thompson.

They hadn't seen me yet. I pushed Meshuga into a full run. We gained steadily on the group until I saw the men and women in the car, dressed fancily in hats under the glaring sun. I saw one of them point in my direction. There was a scream, and then everyone turned to look. Some of them had field glasses and now trained them on Meshuga and me.

The Arabian, who was casually trotting, broke into a run. I was still several hundred yards behind. In a few moments I was behind the car, and the people were waving and laughing. It was all just a diversion for them. One of them, a girl about seventeen or eighteen, waved a white handkerchief at me.

"Hello. I'm Katy-Lulu, Jason Thompson's granddaughter. Who are you? Are you going to catch Grandpapa?"

"Look, he's all bloody!" said another.

"My, yes, he's hurt! Do you need help, young man?" said an elderly lady from the front seat.

I didn't answer, but the motorcar pulled alongside me and she continued. "What is your name, young man? I say, what is your name?"

"Jim . . . Jim McLaverty and my horse is Meshuga. He's a crazy horse, so I would keep that car away from him if I were you . . . he might *jump* inside!" I yelled over the noise of his hoofbeats and the car's engine.

The car slowed and I was left alone, gaining rapidly on Legion, my shirt flapping out like a flag in the wind. The valiant Arab was moving at great speed, but he was nearing the end of his 50-mile leg. He was tiring.

Meshuga, on the other hand, was crazy again. He increased his speed.

The crowd lined both sides of the highway for the quarter mile of the race. Well over four hundred people waited at the finish line as Legion and Meshuga bore down in the last mile. Legion and Meshuga were running side by side, head to head. I looked over at Thompson. He looked tired and sweaty. He had taken off his smart riding jacket and was riding in a white dress shirt, now smeared with dirt and sweat. His smart hat had long since blown off, his thinning hair twisted and blown in the heat of the race.

As we neared the finish line I wasn't sure Meshuga had the pure speed to beat an Arabian of Legion's quality. I was just holding on, hoping that Meshuga would win. The crowd was roaring, but I couldn't see anything except a jumble of blurred images ahead and to my side. I was low in the saddle and talking to Meshuga.

"Win, win, win, win, Meshuga . . . win, win, win, win . . ."

As we made the long slow turn toward the gate at the finish, about 200 yards away, Legion had the inside. He pulled ahead half a length. This seemed to infuriate my Black. Deep from inside him, as deep as the memory of the Smoke Creek Desert and the ranging mustang stallion, Steel Dust, who sired him, Meshuga gathered his final burst. I took off my red cap and slapped Meshuga on the flank.

Meshuga won going away, by four lengths.

Past the gate, a surging crowd surrounded the victorious Black, pawing and grabbing me, cheering, screaming. Meshuga merely bobbed his head and scratched the green turf of the Inn as though he might run another 100 miles. He had negotiated the course in eleven hours and fifty-four minutes, beating Legion in the process.

A few minutes later The Commander drove up with Blue Song and Blind Charlie. Another hug was coming, so I braced myself for it. She wrapped my sore body in her big arms and lifted me off the horse. My back hurt like fire, but I was laughing anyway.

"You . . . you . . . Jim McLaverty, you did it!" she said, whirling me around like a doll.

When I was left reeling on my own two feet, Blind Charlie was standing in front of me. I didn't see the crowd then, the reporters, the celebrities, the cameras. I just saw my old friend.

"This, O' truly, gone be good story, Jim," he said, and we both laughed, his old brown face a map of wrinkles, while John Thornton raced up between us.

EPILOGUE

Nineteen fifteen was a good year. I banked $10,000. I would give it to Blood Burns and Ridder in time, but not just yet. It wasn't money I would ever need . . . the ranch at Endemeo seemed bigger that summer and I smaller. I was a year older, thirteen, but I couldn't help remembering the Psalm I had read for York, " . . . Behold thou has made my days as an handbreadth . . . and mine age is as nothing before thee . . ."

Meshuga and Sudan spent the summer grazing in the pasture down by the river. Those two horses always got along, but I think Meshuga knew somehow he owed Sudan. We didn't ride them much. Still, the big Black was much easier to ride these days, and Lucy and I rode the two of them down to Genesee and back one afternoon.

Uncle Martin spent more time at his mining operations than ever. He wasn't the rider he was, he said, and he was hurting inside, I think—the way people hurt sometimes when they can't ever have something they want very badly. That was a part of Uncle Martin I never understood, but I think it was the force that drove him through life.

"You and Kenneth Joe Tracker can manage things around here without me hanging around all the time, Jim," he said one day in August.

Walker wrote home almost every month, telling us how bad it was in France. But we couldn't understand, never did understand until he came home a few years later, scarred on the inside as well as on the outside. Blind Charlie said he was working on that story, but Walker . . . he didn't like to talk much anymore.

Ridder and I milked Priscilla and Cleopatra together all summer long. Ridder was a faster milker than I was, so he let me get away by myself once in a while to go after Esau. That rainbow had to be in the creek somewhere. Wednesdays and Saturdays Ridder and I played baseball. Ridder was going to be a great player if that summer meant anything. He hit .343 and was the best catcher we ever had.

Uncle Martin gathered us all together one evening to tell us about an art gallery in San Francisco. York's paintings and drawings were being shown during August. He was taking all of us down by train to see the big city and to celebrate the opening of York's work. Even Blind Charlie, who didn't like to leave his blessed valley much these days, agreed to make the trip.

The gallery owner greeted us for a special showing before he opened his doors on Post Street. Mr. Hyde shook my hand and congratulated me on the great race. It never occurred to me that people outside of Plumas County knew much about the Mohawk Valley Race.

I had seen him before, but I couldn't place where.

"Was your mustang as fast as Ghost Horse?" he asked, smiling.

"Faster, Mr. Hyde!" I said and recognized him as the man who had sat next to me on the train out from Denver over a year ago, the man who had read Thomas Hardy. How long ago it seemed.

"So I hear, so I hear," he said, and turned away to the others.

I had seen all of York's pictures, but I had never known the public's reaction to them. York's Ride was just another picture among many. Comments and reactions to it were not much different from other pieces of work York had produced. I'm glad York's Ride wasn't for sale. It would hang in the parlor at Endemeo, then. If York's work had been for sale, Blind Charlie and Kenneth Joe Tracker and Blue Song could have made a bundle of money. But when you live in Taylorsville in 1915, what do you need money for?

Lassen Peak exploded in the summer of 1915, finally really let everything go. Lava flowed down several sides and crowds of folks went up there to see a live volcano ripping. I couldn't imagine what all the fuss was about. Great story, everyone said.

I didn't go. Blind Charlie and Hercules walked up there to the Big Valley, the original lands of the Mountain Maidu. I spent all my spare time down on Indian Creek trying to catch Esau. Toward *the end of August when the mosquitoes really get bad, I was at Rattlesnake Pool, so named for a tiny bit of history I can claim on the creek. John Thornton by my side, I had walked down the path from Endemeo to the creek just outside Taylorsville. I realized that I was learning to see, not merely watching, but noticing nature around me in all its colorful variations, things bold and obvious, and things hidden and secretive. I was learning the way of the Maidu, learning the lessons of York, Blind Charlie, and Kenneth Joe Tracker. The sudden distraction of a red-tailed hawk sweeping down didn't blind me from the sudden rigid movements of an American bittern, thrusting its dark neck and long beak vertically, camouflaged against the tall marsh reeds and cat tails. I was part of this magnificent world of Indian Valley, a glorious tableau, merely following my path from Taylorsville to Genesee.*

Preferring dry flies, I was casting a small no. 16 Gray-Hackle-Yellow where old Agag rose last year. John Thornton lay asleep in the cool grass by the side of the creek not 10 feet from Palawäiko's spot underneath the fallen tree. I felt the breeze blowing softly, the lush and tangled meadow grass bent and sloped toward the pebbles glistening in the wet sand. I closed my eyes and could see Ratty ascending the farther bank, and, now smiling, I saw the shadows of Badger and Mole waving to me farther down above the reflective current. Ma was reading to me about Toad, and then suddenly Ratty pulled a little blue boat out of the weeds. Mole joined him and they rowed away from me, Ratty exclaiming something about the joy of messing with boats. Toad disappeared and I slapped at a mosquito and tugged my St. Louis Cardinals cap down tight over my ears, opening my eyes. As I lofted the fly carefully down on the far side of the pool, I watched the tan braided waxed line pull the silky gut leader and tippet slowly downstream to the rocky brink where the water cascades over a line of boulders. He took it with an explosion more colorful to me than a volcano. I pulled back quickly on my H.L. Leonard, setting the hook—Pa's Hardy sang, smoothly vibrating over the bamboo's 8-foot arc.

It was the best song I heard all summer. After ten minutes I pulled in a 4-pound rainbow I promptly named Esau. I don't really know that it was my elusive Esau, but I named him that anyway.

I noticed then that John Thornton was not sleeping by my side as I netted Esau and placed him in my creel. I looked upstream and saw that he was resting his head . . . on . . . on. . . . Lucy's lap! She nodded and smiled. I waved and wondered how long she had been watching. Then, shocked, I saw Meshuga reined and saddled several feet above the bank, watching us as if he were our shepherd. She dropped a green clothbound book by her side, no doubt one of her volumes of Jane Austen, but a few moments later I realized it was York's sketchbook, and she was waving his Cumbrian graphite pencil, a sense of joy and mystery filling my heart, which I realized was beating a bit faster.

Esau was momentarily forgotten.

The great black horse of my dreams was gone and never returned.

Well . . . this gone be good story, Jim . . . as my adopted grand-papa, Blind Charlie, would say.

Oh truly, ever thing gone be good story, ever thing.

ACKNOWLEDGMENTS

I could not have written this book without the help of the research facilities at the Plumas County Museum, Quincy, where I spent countless hours in the archives of the Plumas Historical Society and the many Plumas County newspapers published as early as 1856. The University of California and its cultural anthropology and ethnic studies libraries, the Phoebe A. Hearst Library of Anthropology, founded by Alfred Louis Kroeber, provided invaluable research assistance. Kroeber's *The Handbook of the Indians of California* is a rich trove of California tribal history. The Merriam Library at Chico State University provided a treasure of information and resources for this book.

I would particularly like to thank the late Warren A. Gorbet, a great leader among the Maidu, who cofounded the Round House Council, was a tutor for Indian Children Programs, and was Chairman of the Maidu Culture and Development Group. He was a good friend, a devout Catholic. My friendship with the late John "Johnny" Smith and his wife, Gladys, provided me with an understanding of the daily ranching life of the Maidu in Indian Valley. It is worth noting that both Warren and John were ex-military, Warren a marine in its Force Recon special forces in Korea, and John, a paratrooper in the 82nd Airborne Division—under the great General James M. Gavin in World War II. Ironically, Warren took care of a small Mongolian horse called Sergeant Reckless, although Warren never knew Meshuga in this story. Through many conversations with Warren and John while I lived and taught Maidu children in Greenville for seventeen years I learned the history and lore of their culture. Today, hanging in my den, is a magnificent color mixed-media drawing of the Maidu Bear Dance, done by one of my former Maidu students, Sanders "Buck" Bone. Buck's drawing inspired me to tell this story as a legend behind a work of art, *York's Ride*. Today, the Maidu traditions, art, and historical events are enriched by the ongoing work of the Maidu Summit Consortium, located in Chester, California, by the shore of Lake Almanor.

My maternal grandparents, Darrell and Leona Hudson, owned a 300-acre farm just outside of Huntsville, Missouri, where as a city boy visiting from Los Angeles, I first learned a bit about farm life. But later, as an owner of a 40-acre ranch 6 miles from Taylorsville for thirty-eight years, my wife, Joannie, and I—inspired by the writings of Wendell Berry, John Muir, David Brower, Wallace Stegner, and Edward Abbey—first understood the power and beauty of committing one's life to ranching and farming. It was there in the magnificent Indian Valley of Plumas County that I encountered the late Harvey Dolphin, a storied cowboy who lived in Taylorsville, surrounded by his many horses and stables. Harvey helped me to train and ride a black horse, part mustang and part Percheron, a horse of great stamina, that I, just barely, learned to ride over the perilous steep trails of Mt. Hough.

A powerful influence on my writing came from the legendary nature photographer, Philip Hyde, who with his wife, Ardis, lived for fifty years along Indian Creek, a short walk from Taylorsville—in a home he and Ardis built by themselves, an architectural master-piece, blending with the environment in such a way that you would think it had always belonged there. Philip traveled and hiked widely throughout the American West, leaving behind thousands of pho-tographs, and many books, some in collaboration with Stegner and Abbey, that describe nature in every season. Philip and Ardis were treasured friends with whom we spent countless hours around their fireplace discussing wilderness, organic agriculture—after sailing in our vintage mahogany *International 14* on Lake Almanor below Lassen Peak. Interspersed on their many bookshelves were a few beautiful baskets of Lily Baker, woven from redbud bark and wil-lows she had gathered—depicting scenes of local wildlife. Lily was the last of the great Maidu basket makers and was an inspiration for my Blue Song.

It was my privilege to teach hundreds of children at Greenville Elementary School and students at Feather River College. Many of those students were Maidu. They taught me as much as I taught them, being responsive to my own approaches to literature, while their family traditions in the stories and myths of an ancient culture never ceased to enlarge my understanding of the Maidu, particularly in the early twentieth century.

M.D.C.

Author's Note

This is a work of historical fiction. Although the geographic references are physically accurate, the ranch names and the inhabitants are in some cases imaginary, inspired by actual individuals who lived and worked in Plumas County, California, in 1914 and 1915. This is entirely a work of author's imagination, but if one searched through the archives of the *Plumas Independent*, the county's weekly newspaper from 1899 to 1945, and the libraries at the University of California, Berkeley, or the collections located at California State University, Chico, you would find many of the actual names of the people associated with the time, places, and the events in this story.

This story takes place primarily in the beautiful Indian Valley of Plumas County, in the northeast of California. On August 5, 2021, the Dixie Fire, one of the most destructive in the state's history, incinerated the historic Gold Rush towns of Greenville and Indian Falls, threatening the village of Taylorsville, where most of this story takes place. Crescent Mills, a small town between Greenville and Taylorsville avoided destruction; however, the historic home of the Maidu in Humbug Valley, the Tásmam Koyóm, was mostly lost— sadly, because these lands had recently been returned to the Maidu by the Pacific Gas and Electric Company. The fire destroyed many homes and outbuildings throughout the 26,000 acres where cattle have grazed for over a century. Countless homes and tribal buildings where the Maidu have lived for hundreds of years burned to the ground, including artifacts, documents, services dating back to the early days of the Bureau of Indian Affairs. Tragically, one person was lost, and fortunately no others were hurt, although the surrounding forest and the natural landscape was scorched and blackened right to the edge of Wolf Creek where it joins the larger Indian Creek that empties into the north fork of the Feather River. Although such fires consume materials and memorabilia, heartbreaking in scope, the Dixie Fire cannot take away the power of memory or intimidate the strength and resolve of the people who live there. The people of Greenville, Taylorsville, Crescent Mills, and Indian Falls—the Maidu, the ranchers, the loggers, the miners, the merchants, and the U.S.F.S. rangers of the Plumas National Forest districts are even now working to rebuild these communities up from the ashen remains. Such bravery and such spiritedness is almost incomprehensible. This book, this story from over a century ago, is dedicated to these courageous people.

About the Author

Michael Dennis Cassity recieved the 1988 California Educator Award, and was also the recipient of the 2001 Charles Hayward Award for Community Colleges. He is the author of *What Happens Next: Celebrating Stories with Children.* Cassity taught a full range of community college English courses, specializing in creative writing, children's literature, and environmental literature.